ACCLAIM FOR JEFF SMITH'S

Named an all time top ten graphic novel by **Time** *magazine.*

"As sweeping as the 'Lord of the Rings' cycle, but much funnier." —*Andrew Arnold,* **Time.com**

★*"This is first-class kid lit: exciting, funny, scary, and resonant enough that it will stick with readers for a long time."* —**Publishers Weekly,** *starred review*

"One of the best kids' comics ever." —**Vibe** *magazine*

"BONE *is storytelling at its best, full of endearing, flawed characters whose adventures run the gamut from hilarious whimsy . . . to thrilling drama."* —**Entertainment Weekly**

"[This] sprawling, mythic comic is spectacular." —**SPIN** *magazine*

"Jeff Smith's cartoons are irresistible. Every gorgeous sweep of his brush speaks volumes."
—Frank Miller, creator of Sin City

"Jeff Smith can pace a joke better than almost anyone in comics." —Neil Gaiman, author of Coraline

"I love BONE! BONE is great!"
—Matt Groening, creator of The Simpsons

"Every one of the zillion characters has a unique set of personality traits and flaws and dreams that are developed amid the pandemonium."
—Kyle Baker, Plastic Man cartoonist

"BONE moves from brash humor to gripping adventure in a single panel." —ALA Booklist

"BONE is a comic-book sensation. . . . [It] is a classic of writer-artist craftsmanship not to be missed."
—Comics Buyer's Guide

ROCK JAW
Master of the Eastern Border

OTHER **BONE** BOOKS

Out from Boneville

The Great Cow Race

Eyes of the Storm

The Dragonslayer

BONE

ROCK JAW
Master of the Eastern Border

BY JEFF SMITH
WITH COLOR BY STEVE HAMAKER

graphix

An Imprint of

SCHOLASTIC

Library of Congress Catalog Card Number 95068403.
ISBN 978-0-439-70627-8 (hardcover)
ISBN 978-0-439-70636-0 (paperback)

ACKNOWLEDGMENTS
Harvestar Family Crest designed by Charles Vess
Map of *The Valley* by Mark Crilley
Color by Steve Hamaker

30 29 28 27 26 25   19 20
First Scholastic edition, February 2007
Book design by David Saylor
Printed in Malaysia 108

This book is for Krishna and Avaday Iyer

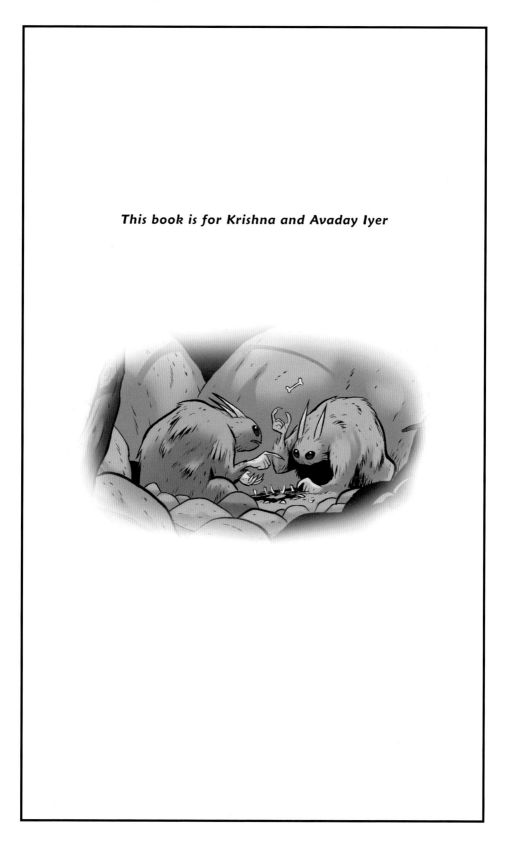

CONTENTS

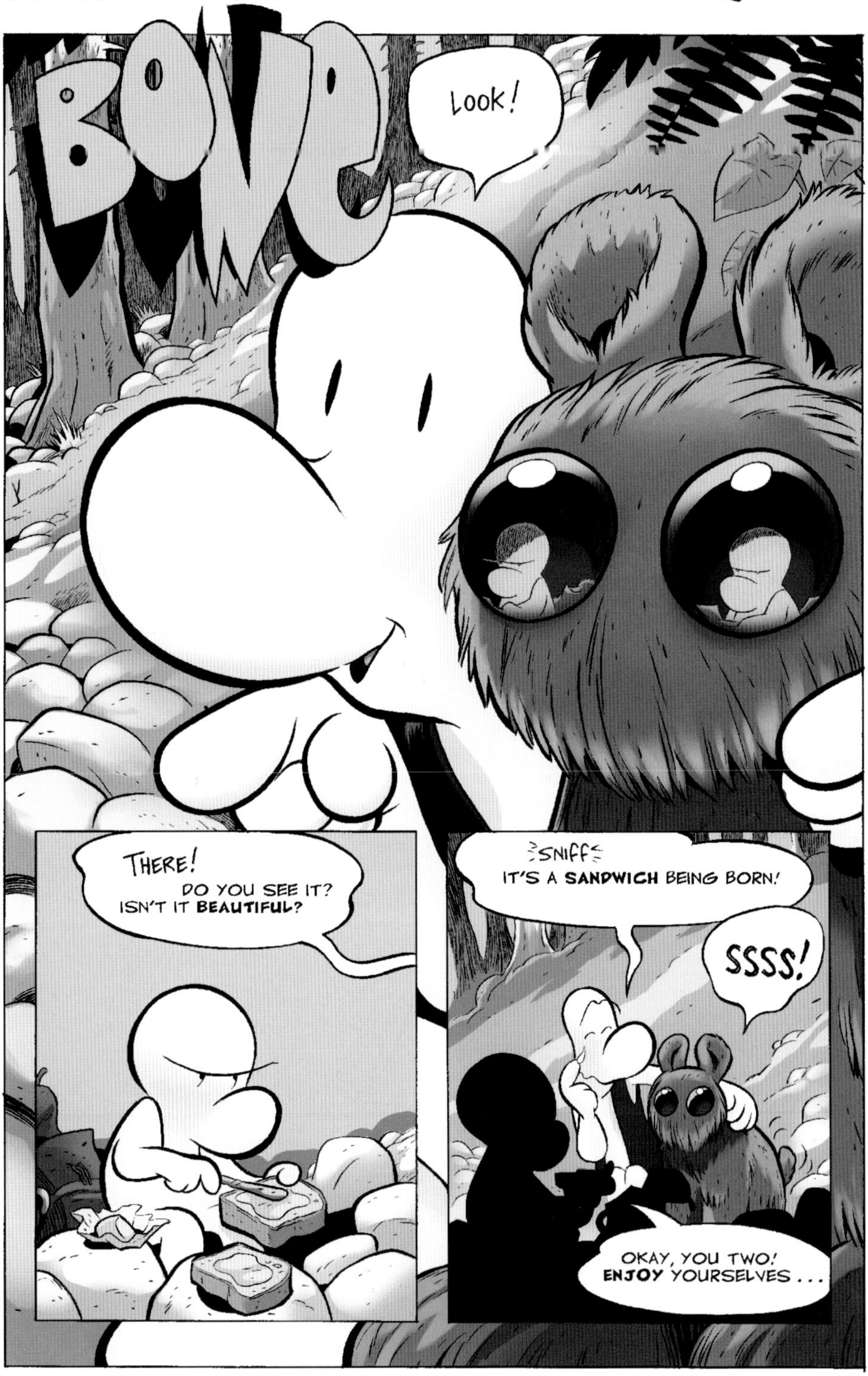
BONE
LOOK!
THERE!
DO YOU SEE IT?
ISN'T IT BEAUTIFUL?
SNIFF
IT'S A SANDWICH BEING BORN!
SSSS!
OKAY, YOU TWO!
ENJOY YOURSELVES . . .

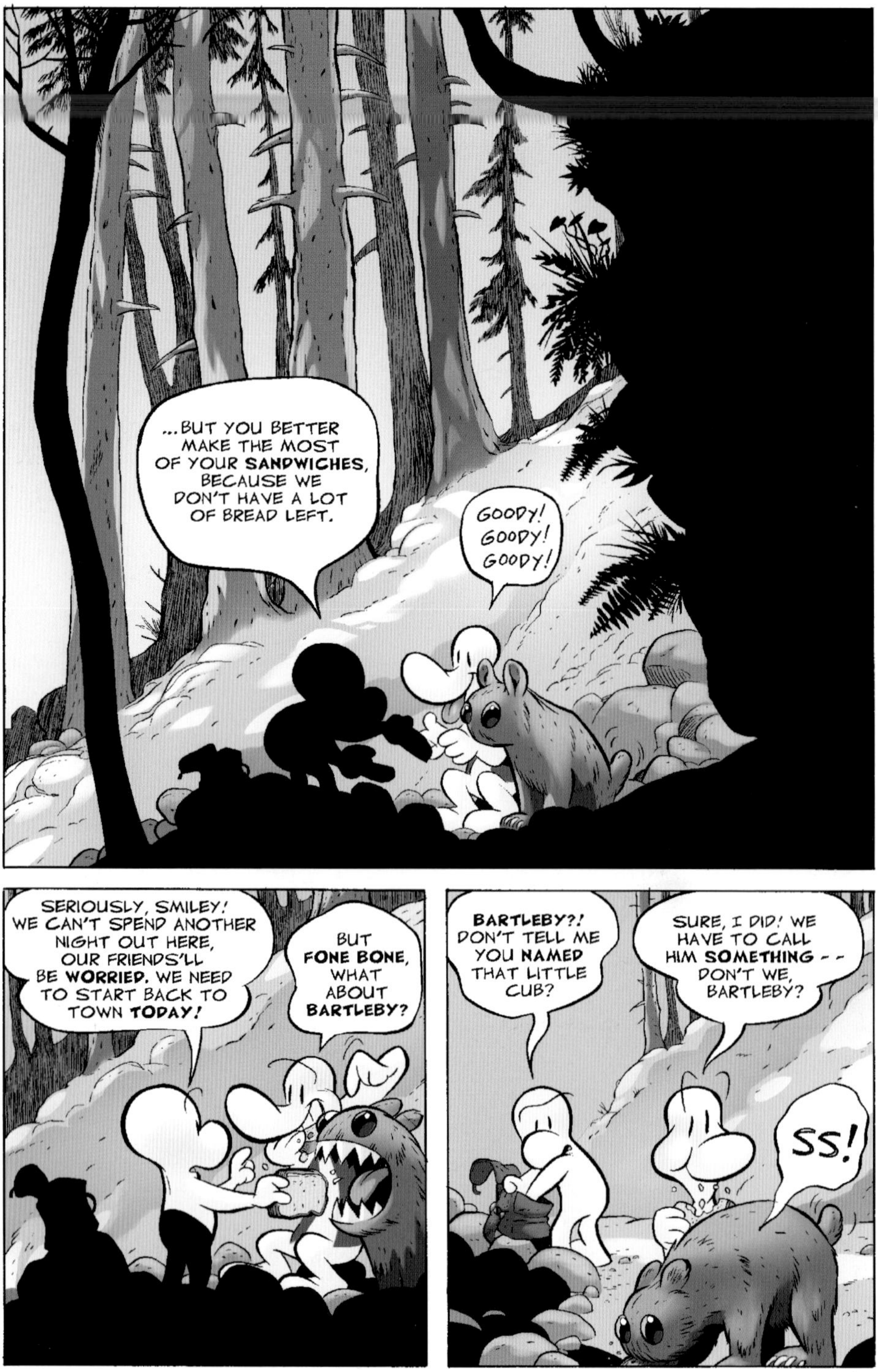
...BUT YOU BETTER MAKE THE MOST OF YOUR SANDWICHES, BECAUSE WE DON'T HAVE A LOT OF BREAD LEFT.
GOODY! GOODY! GOODY!
SERIOUSLY, SMILEY! WE CAN'T SPEND ANOTHER NIGHT OUT HERE, OUR FRIENDS'LL BE WORRIED. WE NEED TO START BACK TO TOWN TODAY!
BUT FONE BONE, WHAT ABOUT BARTLEBY?
BARTLEBY?! DON'T TELL ME YOU NAMED THAT LITTLE CUB?
SURE, I DID! WE HAVE TO CALL HIM SOMETHING -- DON'T WE, BARTLEBY?
SS!

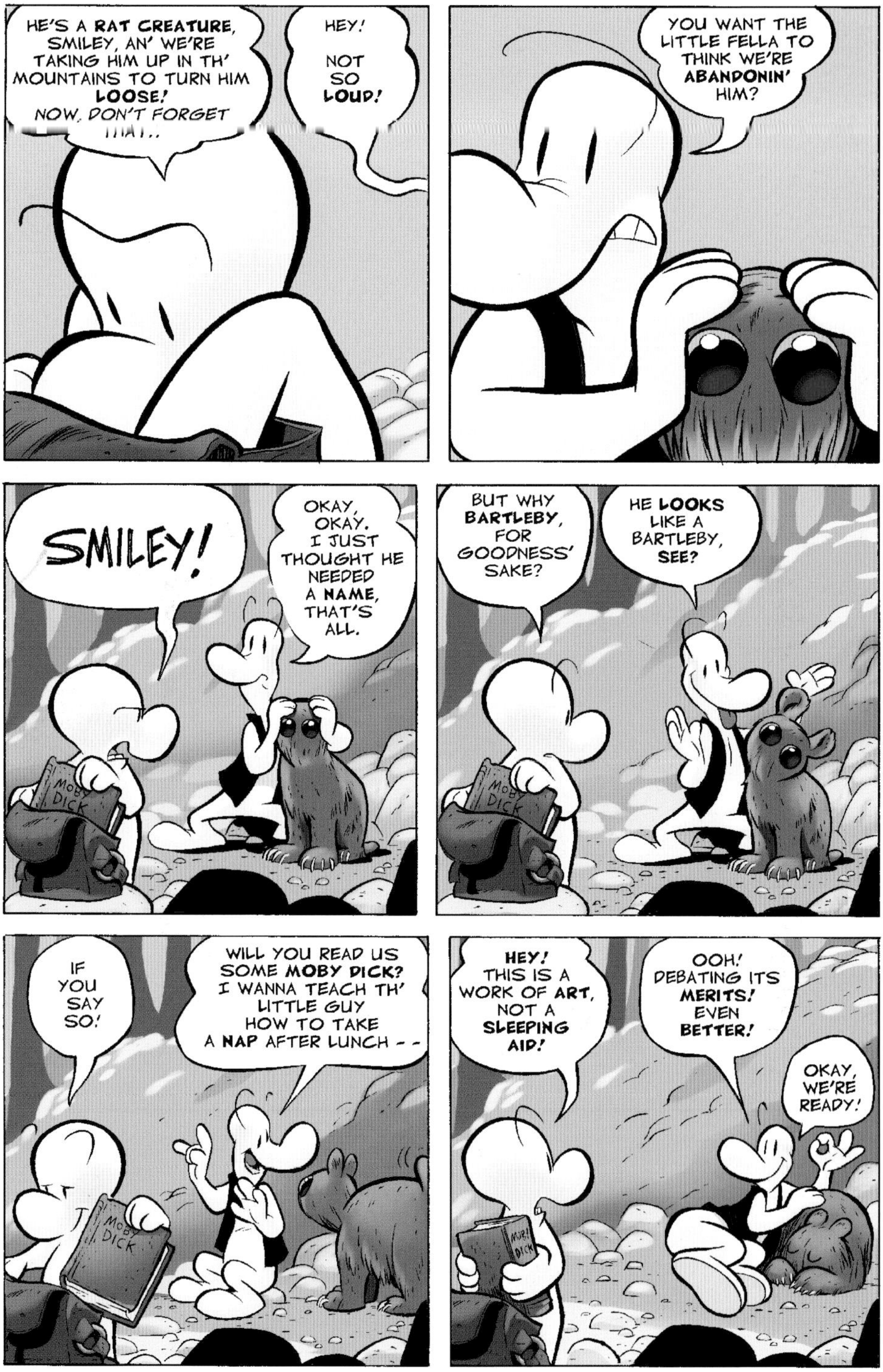
HE'S A RAT CREATURE, SMILEY, AN' WE'RE TAKING HIM UP IN TH' MOUNTAINS TO TURN HIM LOOSE! NOW, DON'T FORGET THAT..
HEY! NOT SO LOUD!
YOU WANT THE LITTLE FELLA TO THINK WE'RE ABANDONIN' HIM?
SMILEY!
OKAY, OKAY. I JUST THOUGHT HE NEEDED A NAME, THAT'S ALL.
MOBY DICK
BUT WHY BARTLEBY, FOR GOODNESS' SAKE?
HE LOOKS LIKE A BARTLEBY, SEE?
MOBY DICK
IF YOU SAY SO!
WILL YOU READ US SOME MOBY DICK? I WANNA TEACH TH' LITTLE GUY HOW TO TAKE A NAP AFTER LUNCH --
MOBY DICK
HEY! THIS IS A WORK OF ART, NOT A SLEEPING AID!
OOH! DEBATING ITS MERITS! EVEN BETTER!
OKAY, WE'RE READY!
MOBY DICK

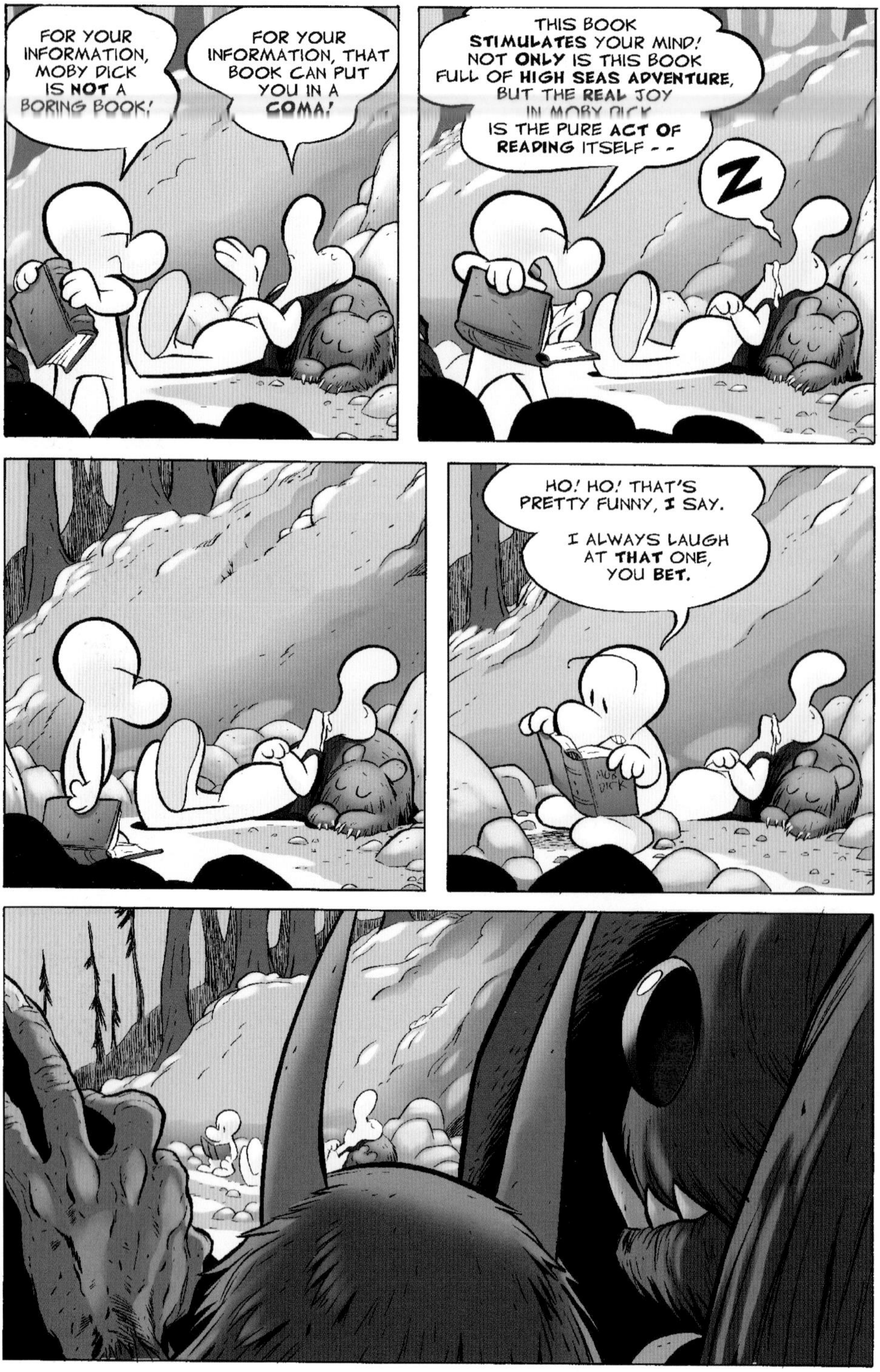
FOR YOUR INFORMATION, MOBY DICK IS **NOT** A BORING BOOK!
FOR YOUR INFORMATION, THAT BOOK CAN PUT YOU IN A **COMA!**
THIS BOOK **STIMULATES** YOUR MIND! NOT **ONLY** IS THIS BOOK FULL OF **HIGH SEAS ADVENTURE**, BUT THE **REAL** JOY IN MOBY DICK IS THE PURE **ACT OF READING** ITSELF - -
Z
HO! HO! THAT'S PRETTY FUNNY, **I** SAY.
I ALWAYS LAUGH AT **THAT** ONE, YOU **BET.**

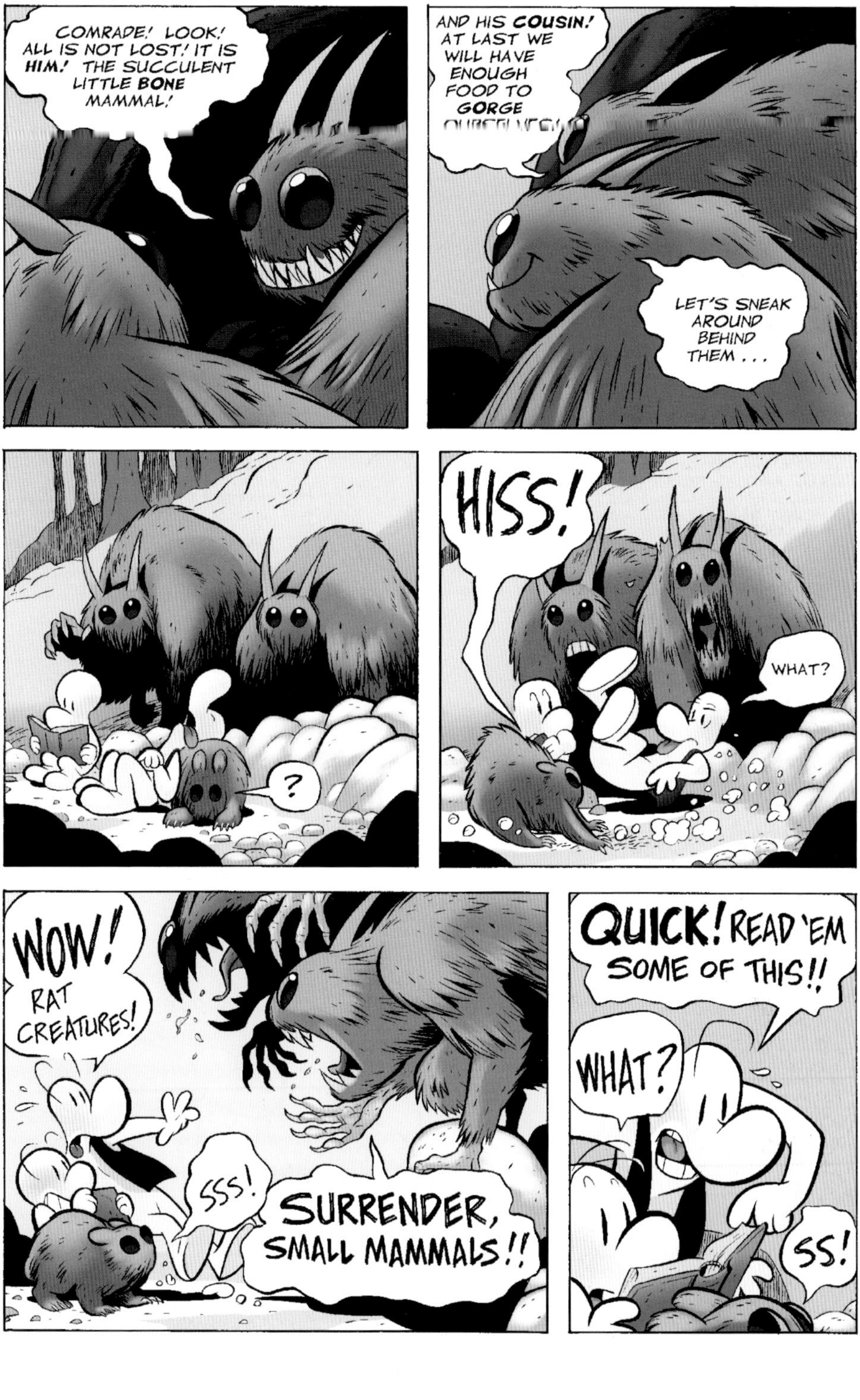
COMRADE! LOOK! ALL IS NOT LOST! IT IS HIM! THE SUCCULENT LITTLE BONE MAMMAL!
AND HIS COUSIN! AT LAST WE WILL HAVE ENOUGH FOOD TO GORGE
LET'S SNEAK AROUND BEHIND THEM . . .
?
HISS!
WHAT?
WOW! RAT CREATURES!
SSS!
SURRENDER, SMALL MAMMALS!!
QUICK! READ 'EM SOME OF THIS!!
WHAT?
SS!

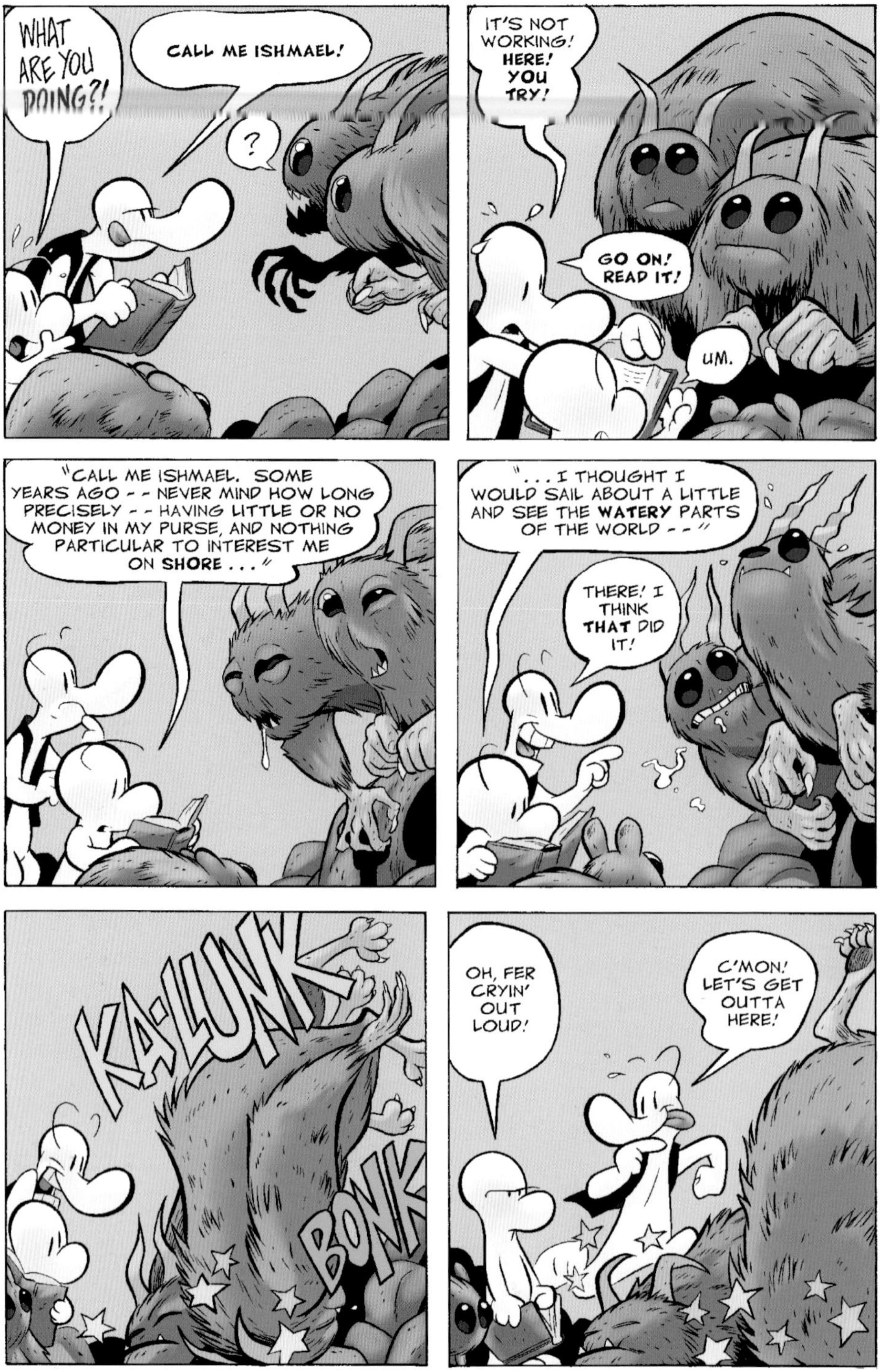
WHAT ARE YOU DOING?!
CALL ME ISHMAEL!
?
IT'S NOT WORKING! HERE! YOU TRY!
GO ON! READ IT!
UM.
"CALL ME ISHMAEL. SOME YEARS AGO -- NEVER MIND HOW LONG PRECISELY -- HAVING LITTLE OR NO MONEY IN MY PURSE, AND NOTHING PARTICULAR TO INTEREST ME ON SHORE . . ."
". . . I THOUGHT I WOULD SAIL ABOUT A LITTLE AND SEE THE WATERY PARTS OF THE WORLD --"
THERE! I THINK THAT DID IT!
KA-LUNK
BONK
OH, FER CRYIN' OUT LOUD!
C'MON! LET'S GET OUTTA HERE!

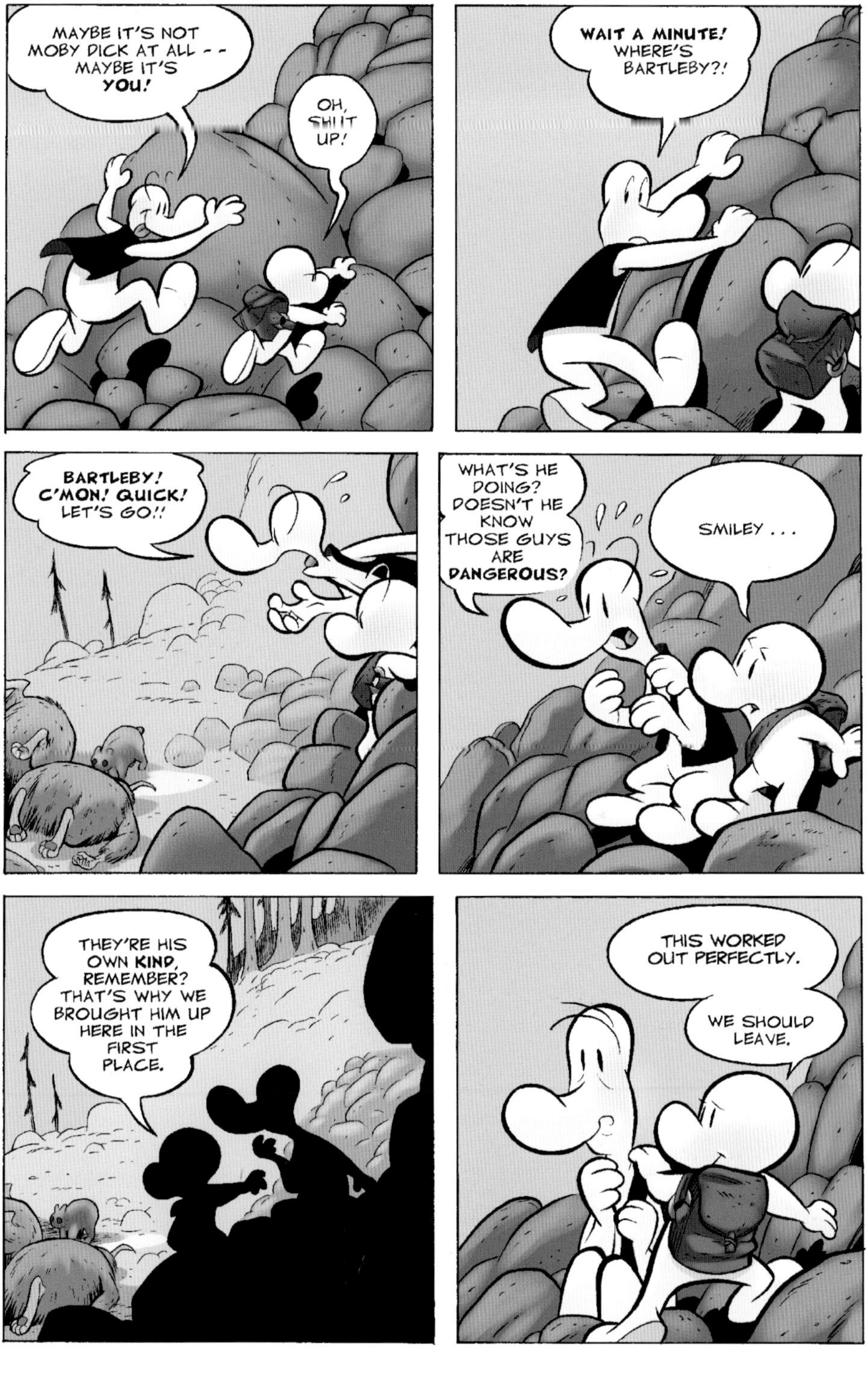
MAYBE IT'S NOT MOBY DICK AT ALL - - MAYBE IT'S **YOU!**
OH, SHUT UP!
WAIT A MINUTE! WHERE'S BARTLEBY?!
BARTLEBY! C'MON! QUICK! LET'S GO!!
WHAT'S HE DOING? DOESN'T HE KNOW THOSE GUYS ARE **DANGEROUS?**
SMILEY . . .
THEY'RE HIS OWN **KIND**, REMEMBER? THAT'S WHY WE BROUGHT HIM UP HERE IN THE FIRST PLACE.
THIS WORKED OUT PERFECTLY.
WE SHOULD LEAVE.

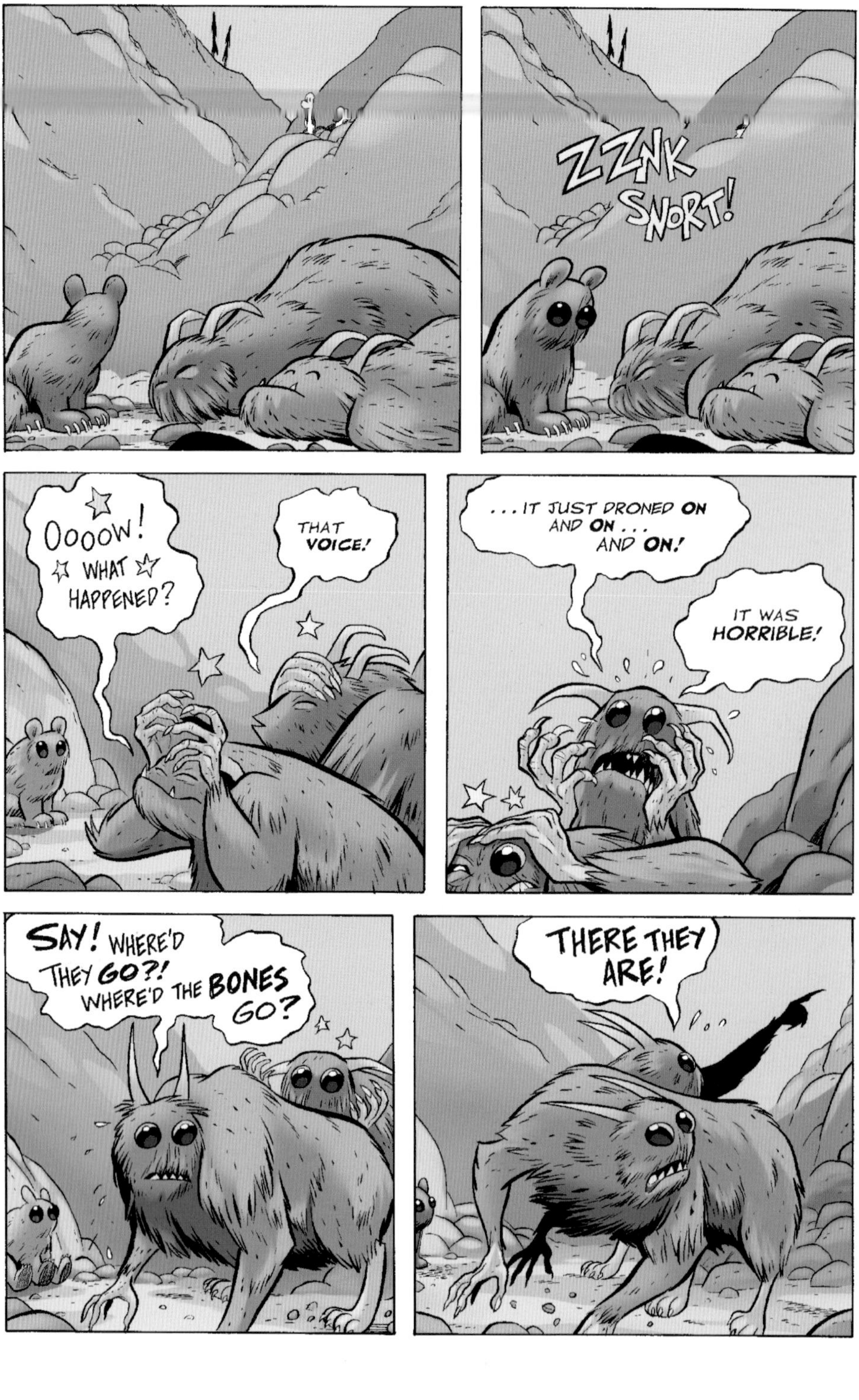
ZZNK
SNORT!
Ooooow! WHAT HAPPENED?
THAT VOICE!
. . . IT JUST DRONED ON AND ON . . . AND ON!
IT WAS HORRIBLE!
SAY! WHERE'D THEY GO?! WHERE'D THE BONES GO?
THERE THEY ARE!

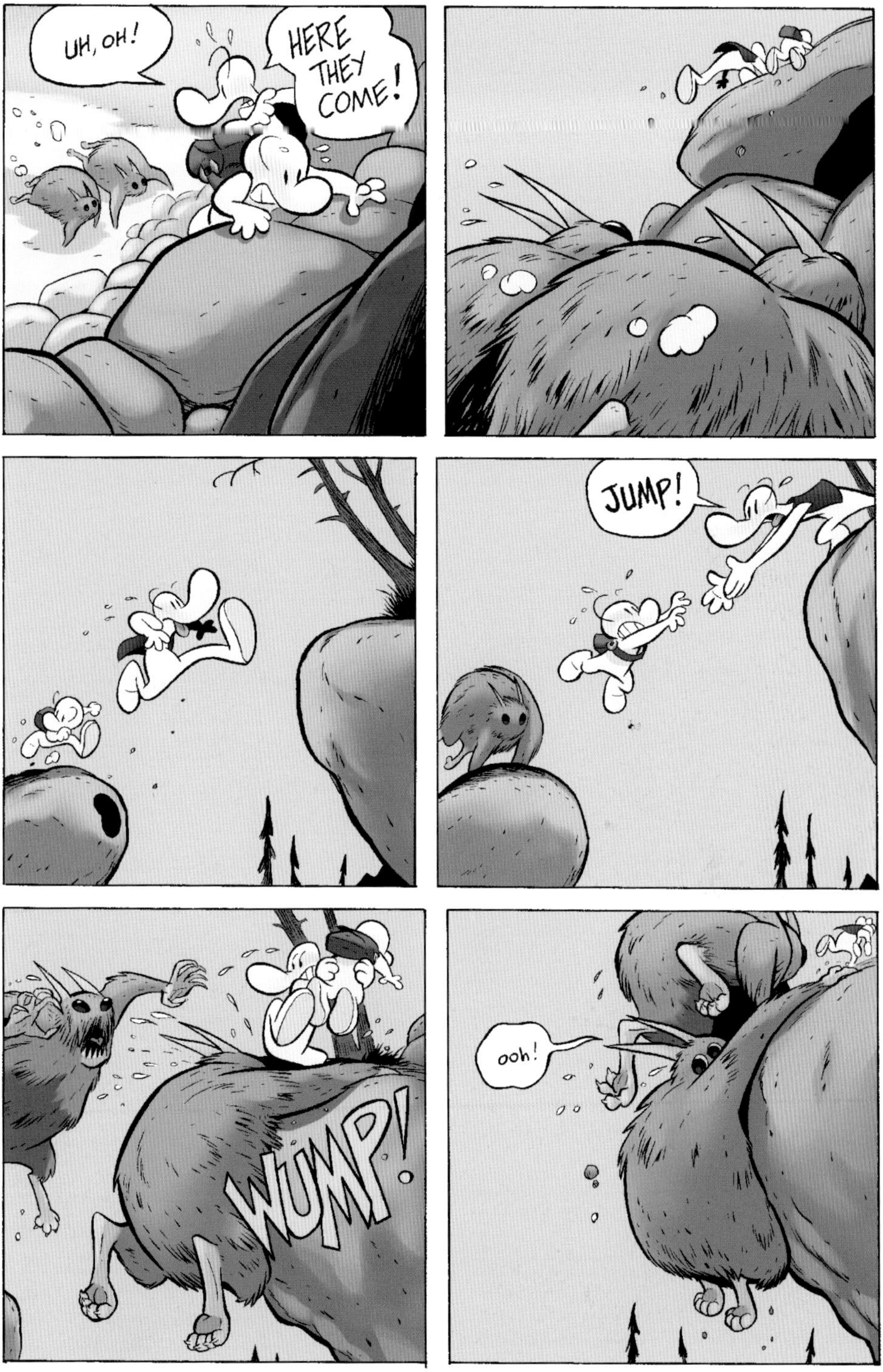
UH, OH!
HERE THEY COME!
JUMP!
WUMP!
ooh!

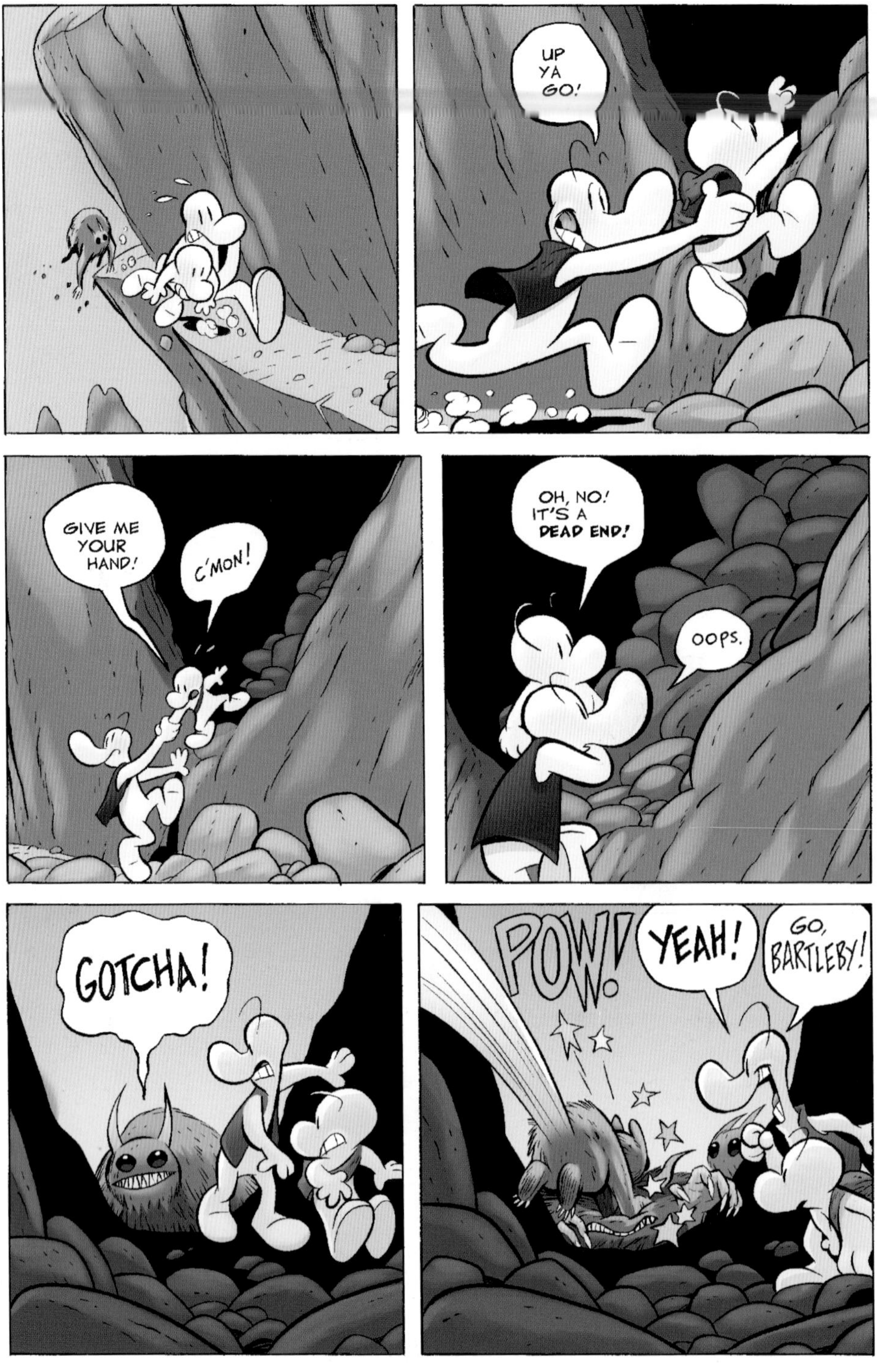
UP YA GO!
GIVE ME YOUR HAND!
C'MON!
OH, NO! IT'S A DEAD END!
OOPS.
GOTCHA!
POW!
YEAH!
GO, BARTLEBY!

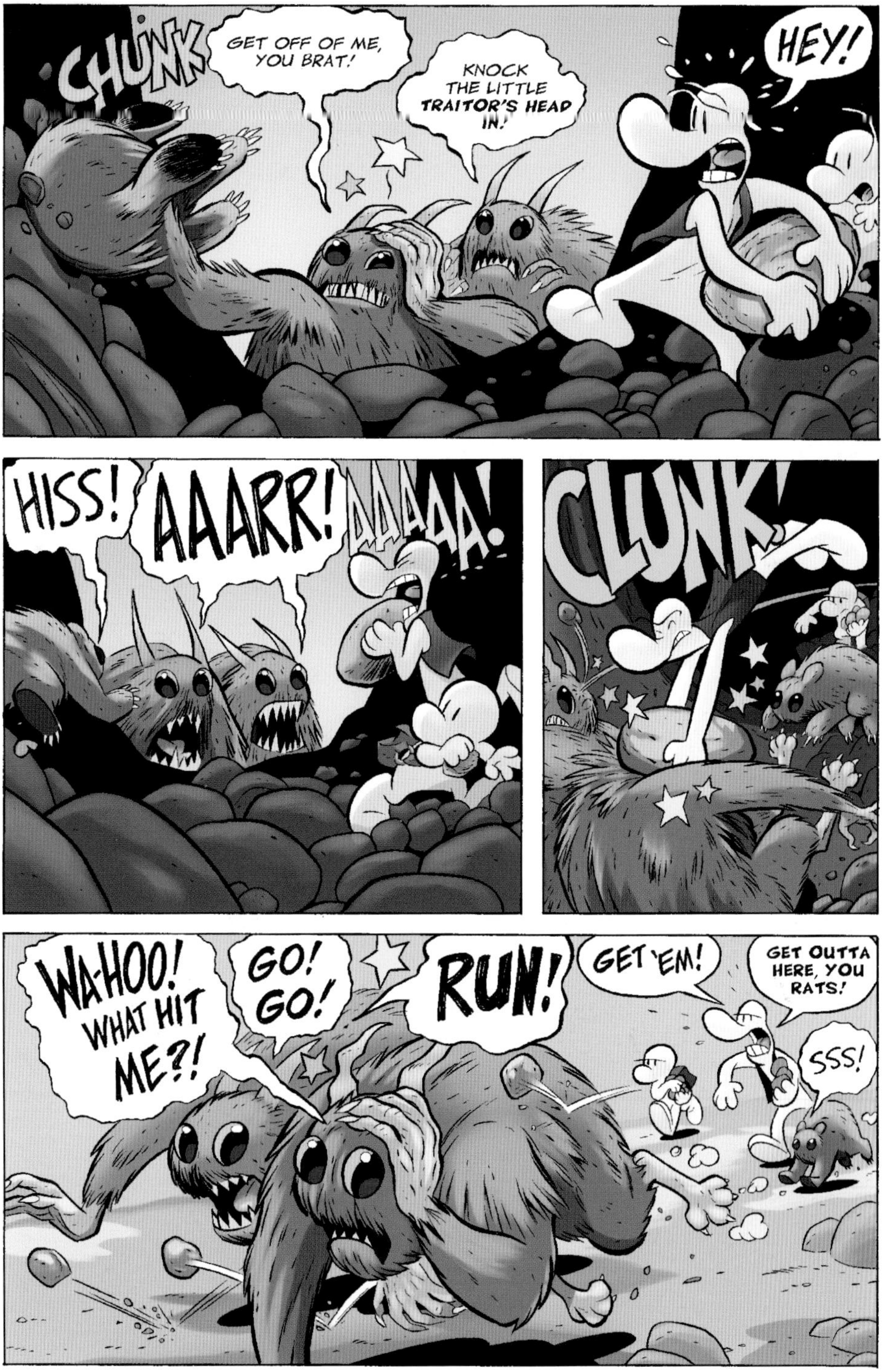
CHUNK
GET OFF OF ME, YOU BRAT!
KNOCK THE LITTLE TRAITOR'S HEAD IN!
HEY!
HISS!
AAARR!
AAAAA!
CLUNK!
WA-HOO! WHAT HIT ME?!
GO! GO!
RUN!
GET 'EM!
GET OUTTA HERE, YOU RATS!
SSS!

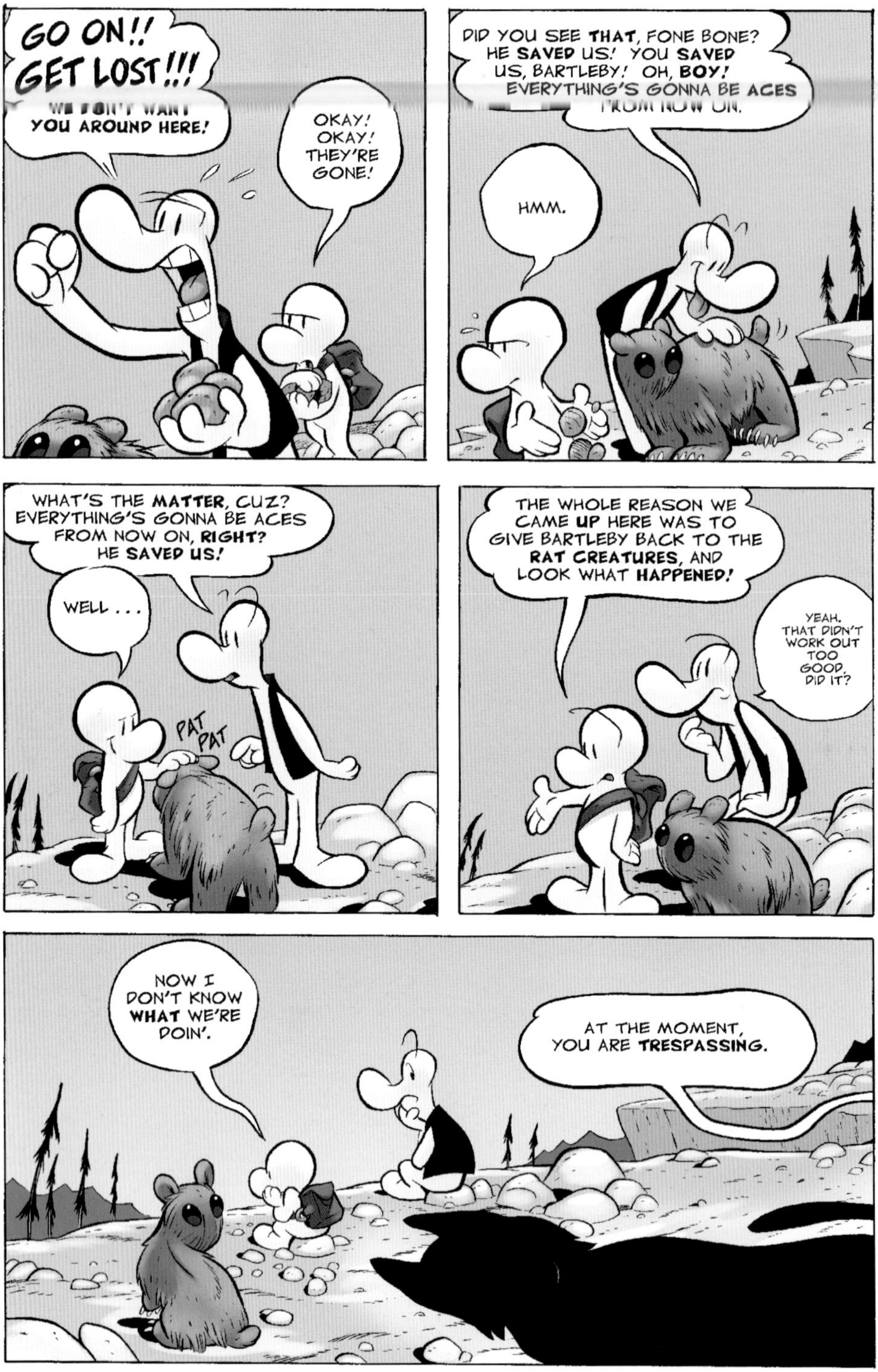
GO ON!! GET LOST!!!
YOU AROUND HERE!
OKAY! OKAY! THEY'RE GONE!
DID YOU SEE THAT, FONE BONE? HE SAVED US! YOU SAVED US, BARTLEBY! OH, BOY! EVERYTHING'S GONNA BE ACES
HMM.
WHAT'S THE MATTER, CUZ? EVERYTHING'S GONNA BE ACES FROM NOW ON, RIGHT? HE SAVED US!
WELL . . .
PAT PAT
THE WHOLE REASON WE CAME UP HERE WAS TO GIVE BARTLEBY BACK TO THE RAT CREATURES, AND LOOK WHAT HAPPENED!
YEAH. THAT DIDN'T WORK OUT TOO GOOD, DID IT?
NOW I DON'T KNOW WHAT WE'RE DOIN'.
AT THE MOMENT, YOU ARE TRESPASSING.

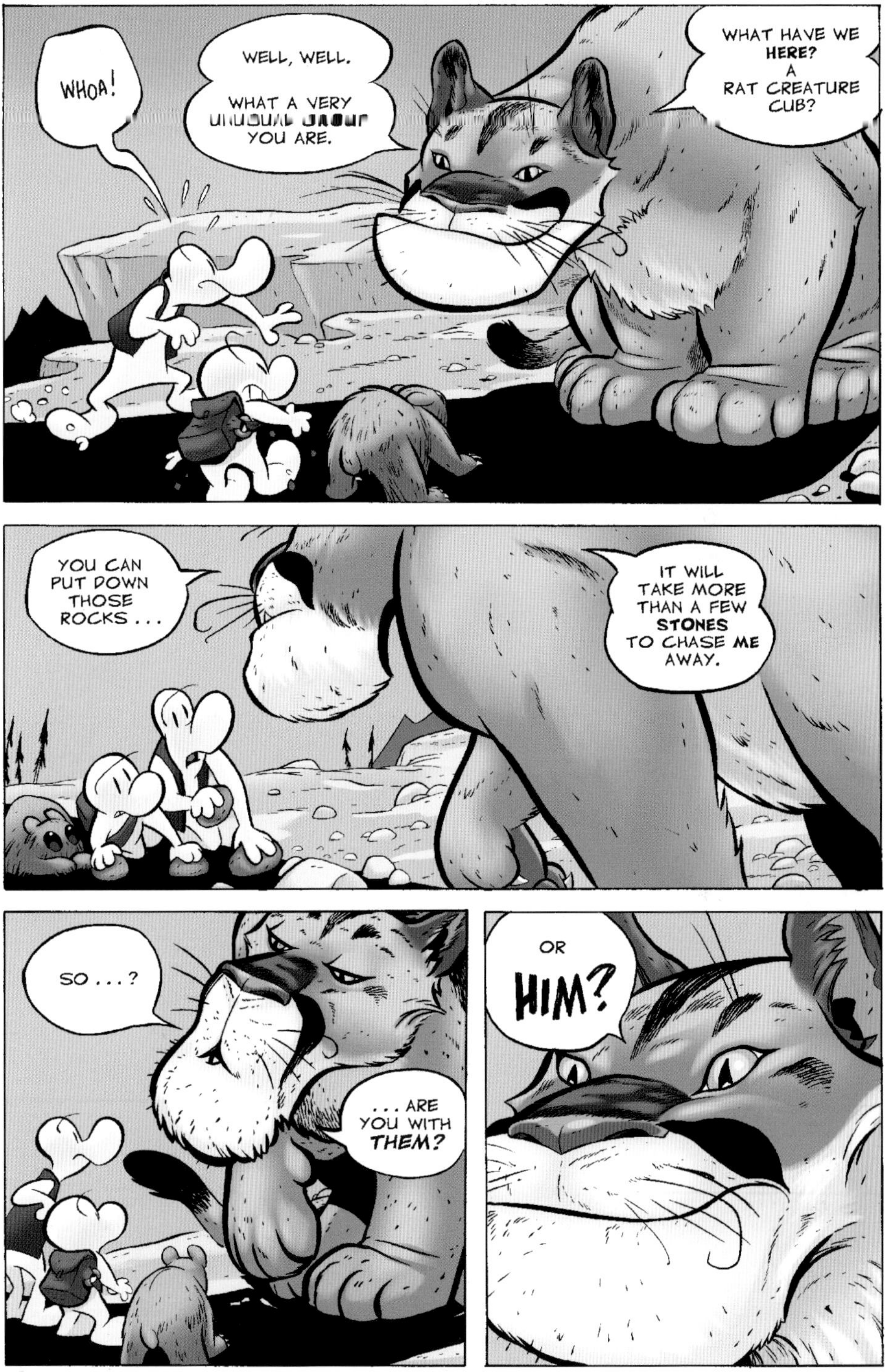
WHOA!
WELL, WELL.
WHAT A VERY UNUSUAL GROUP YOU ARE.
WHAT HAVE WE HERE? A RAT CREATURE CUB?
YOU CAN PUT DOWN THOSE ROCKS . . .
IT WILL TAKE MORE THAN A FEW STONES TO CHASE ME AWAY.
SO . . . ?
. . . ARE YOU WITH THEM?
OR HIM?

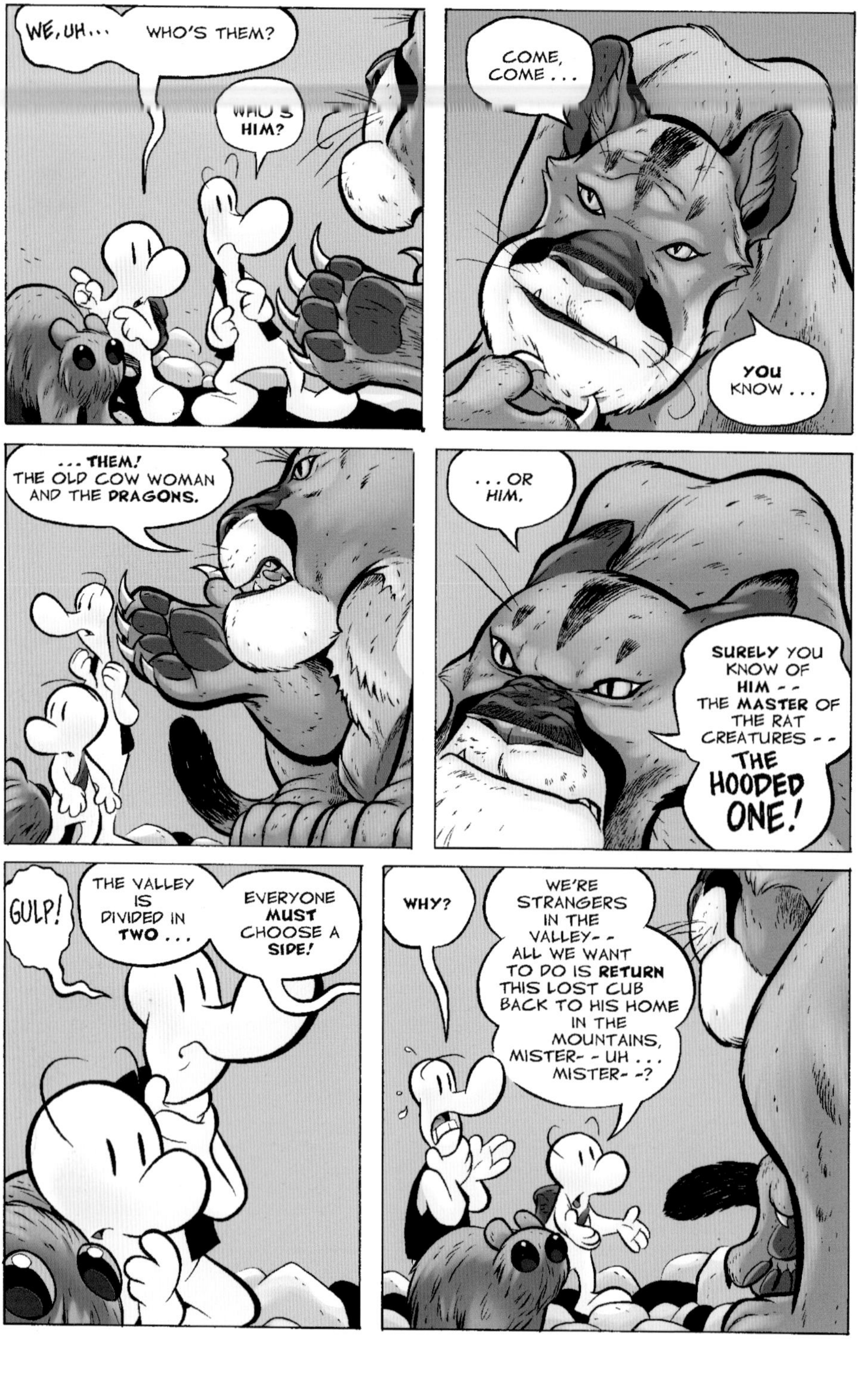
WE, UH...
WHO'S THEM?
WHO'S HIM?
COME, COME...
YOU KNOW...
...THEM! THE OLD COW WOMAN AND THE DRAGONS.
...OR HIM.
SURELY YOU KNOW OF HIM -- THE MASTER OF THE RAT CREATURES -- THE HOODED ONE!
GULP!
THE VALLEY IS DIVIDED IN TWO...
EVERYONE MUST CHOOSE A SIDE!
WHY?
WE'RE STRANGERS IN THE VALLEY-- ALL WE WANT TO DO IS RETURN THIS LOST CUB BACK TO HIS HOME IN THE MOUNTAINS, MISTER--UH... MISTER--?

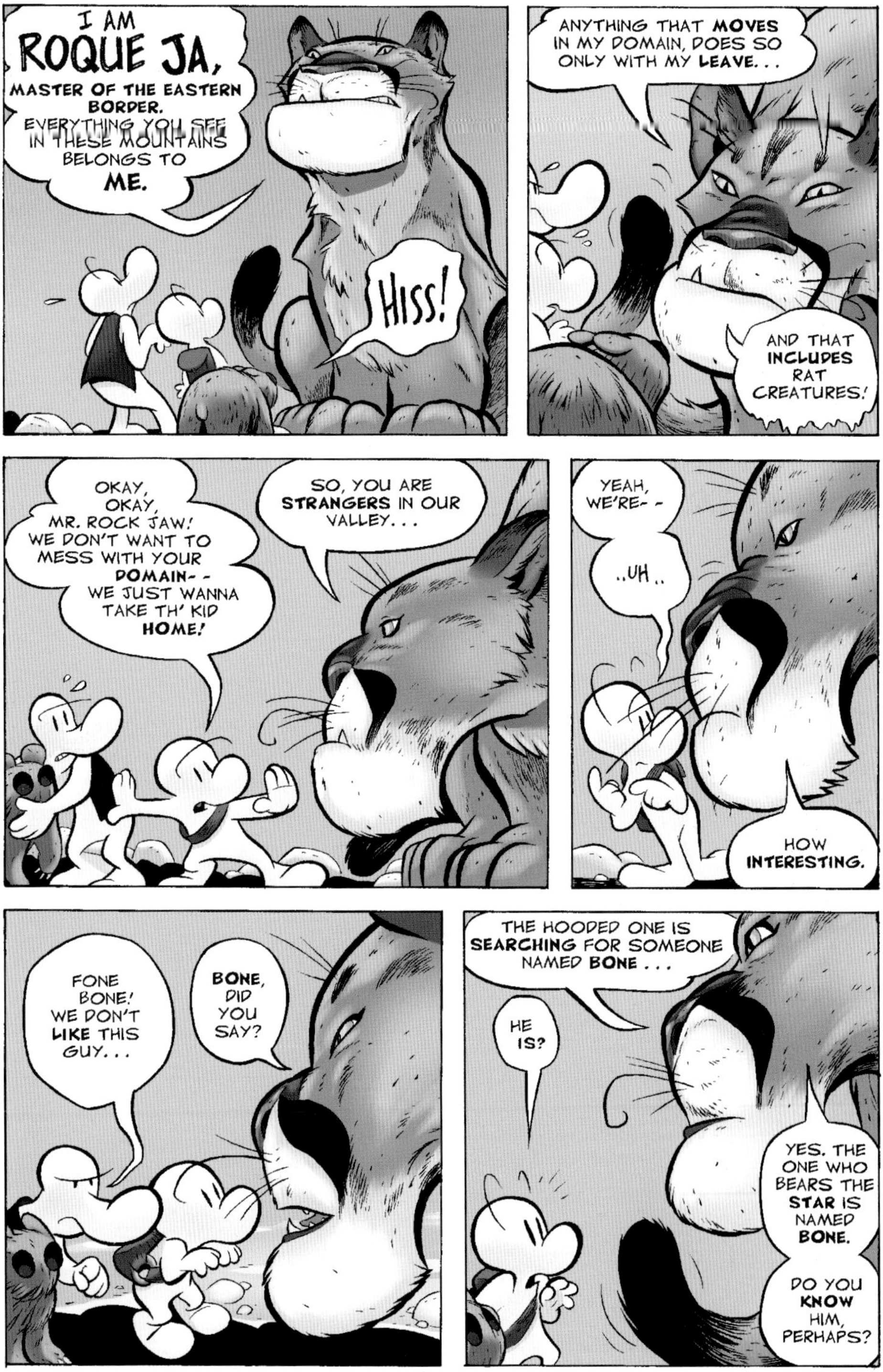
I AM
ROQUE JA,
MASTER OF THE EASTERN BORDER.
EVERYTHING YOU SEE IN THESE MOUNTAINS BELONGS TO ME.
HISS!
ANYTHING THAT MOVES IN MY DOMAIN, DOES SO ONLY WITH MY LEAVE...
AND THAT INCLUDES RAT CREATURES!
OKAY, OKAY, MR. ROCK JAW! WE DON'T WANT TO MESS WITH YOUR DOMAIN- - WE JUST WANNA TAKE TH' KID HOME!
SO, YOU ARE STRANGERS IN OUR VALLEY...
YEAH, WE'RE- -
..UH..
HOW INTERESTING.
FONE BONE! WE DON'T LIKE THIS GUY...
BONE, DID YOU SAY?
THE HOODED ONE IS SEARCHING FOR SOMEONE NAMED BONE...
HE IS?
YES. THE ONE WHO BEARS THE STAR IS NAMED BONE.
DO YOU KNOW HIM, PERHAPS?

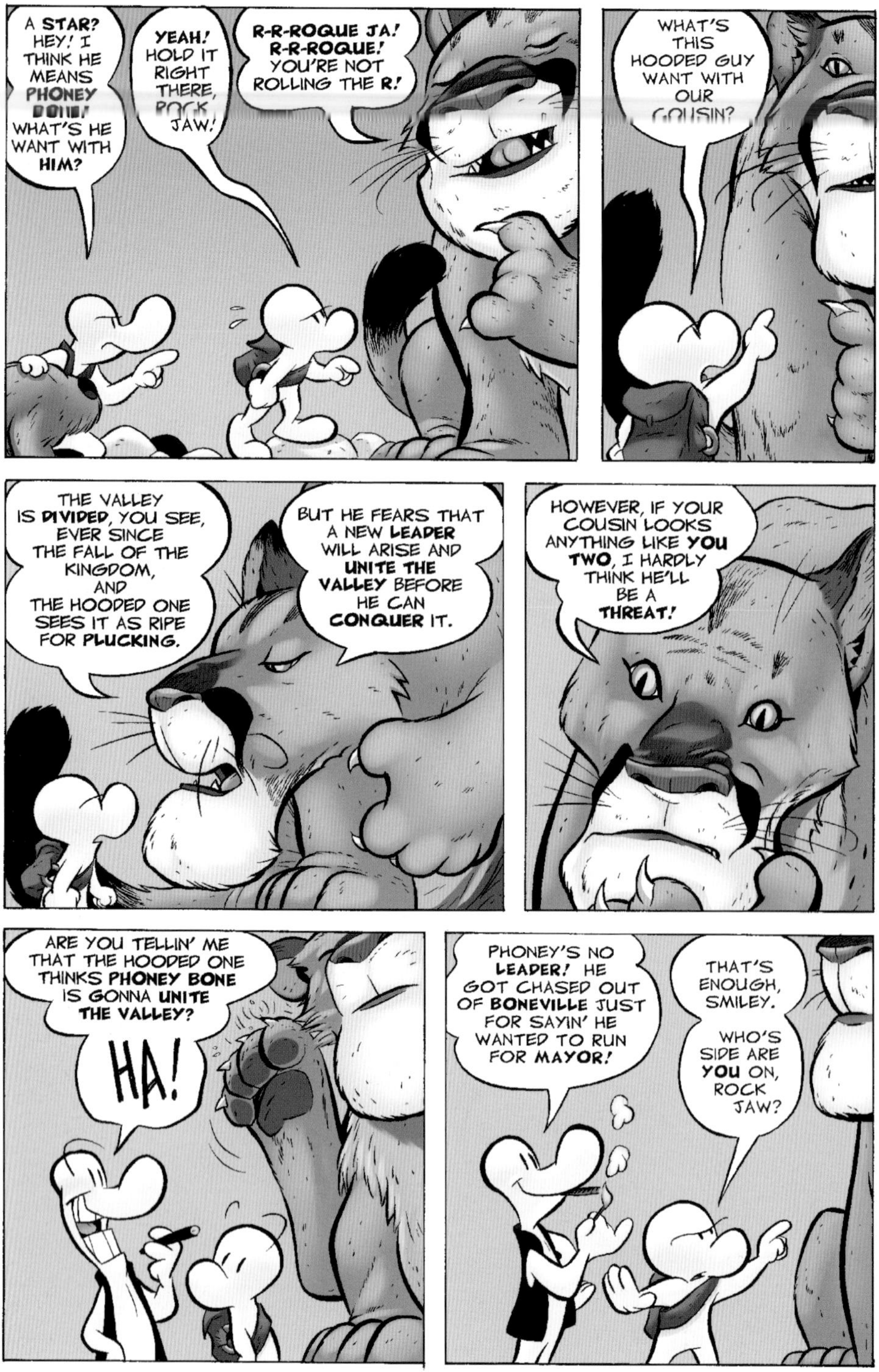
A STAR? HEY! I THINK HE MEANS PHONEY BONE! WHAT'S HE WANT WITH HIM?
YEAH! HOLD IT RIGHT THERE, ROCK JAW!
R-R-ROQUE JA! R-R-ROQUE! YOU'RE NOT ROLLING THE R!
WHAT'S THIS HOODED GUY WANT WITH OUR COUSIN?
THE VALLEY IS DIVIDED, YOU SEE, EVER SINCE THE FALL OF THE KINGDOM, AND THE HOODED ONE SEES IT AS RIPE FOR PLUCKING.
BUT HE FEARS THAT A NEW LEADER WILL ARISE AND UNITE THE VALLEY BEFORE HE CAN CONQUER IT.
HOWEVER, IF YOUR COUSIN LOOKS ANYTHING LIKE YOU TWO, I HARDLY THINK HE'LL BE A THREAT!
ARE YOU TELLIN' ME THAT THE HOODED ONE THINKS PHONEY BONE IS GONNA UNITE THE VALLEY?
HA!
PHONEY'S NO LEADER! HE GOT CHASED OUT OF BONEVILLE JUST FOR SAYIN' HE WANTED TO RUN FOR MAYOR!
THAT'S ENOUGH, SMILEY.
WHO'S SIDE ARE YOU ON, ROCK JAW?

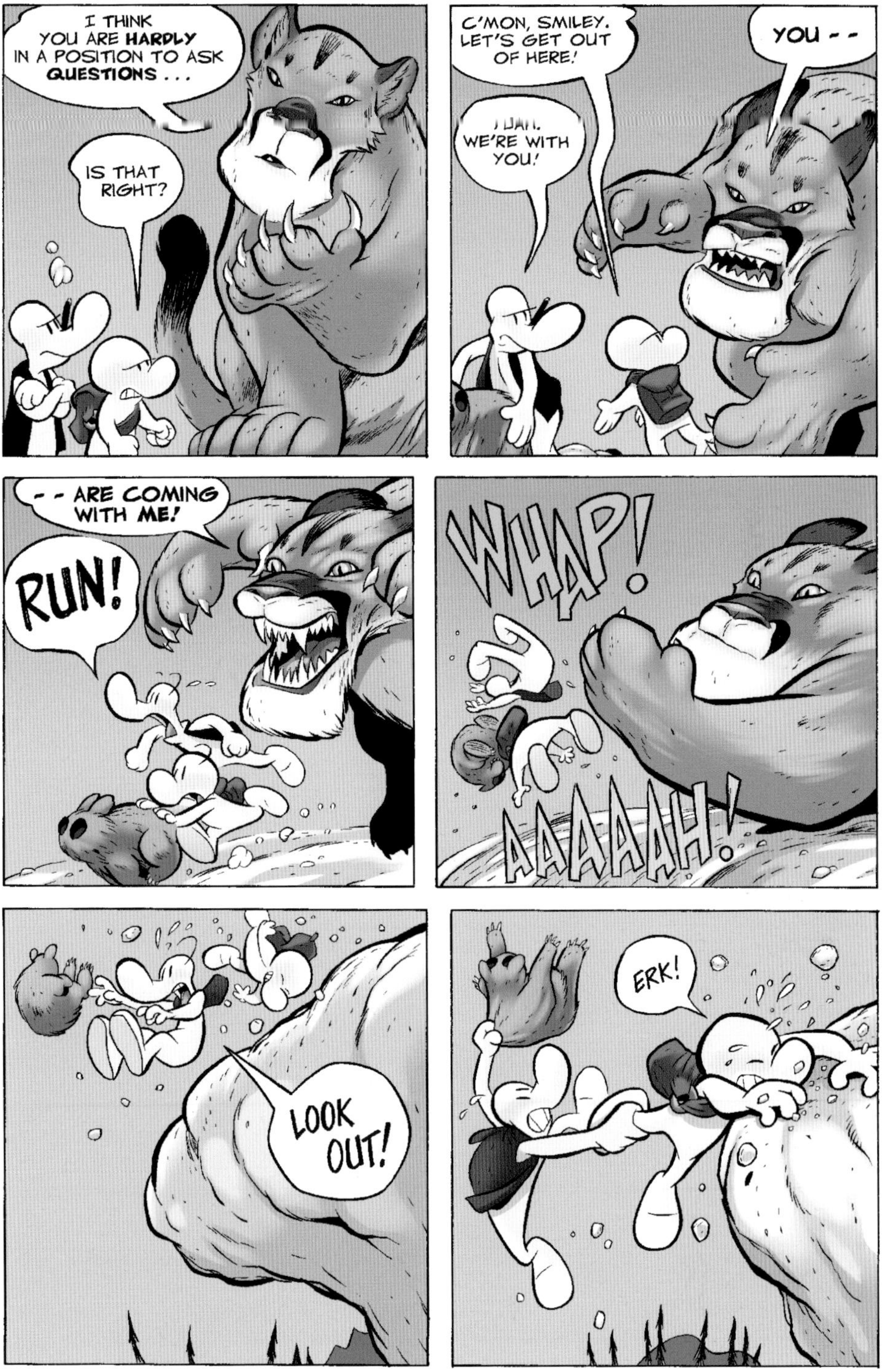
I THINK YOU ARE HARDLY IN A POSITION TO ASK QUESTIONS . . .
IS THAT RIGHT?
C'MON, SMILEY. LET'S GET OUT OF HERE!
WE'RE WITH YOU!
YOU - -
- - ARE COMING WITH ME!
RUN!
WHAP!
AAAAAH!
LOOK OUT!
ERK!

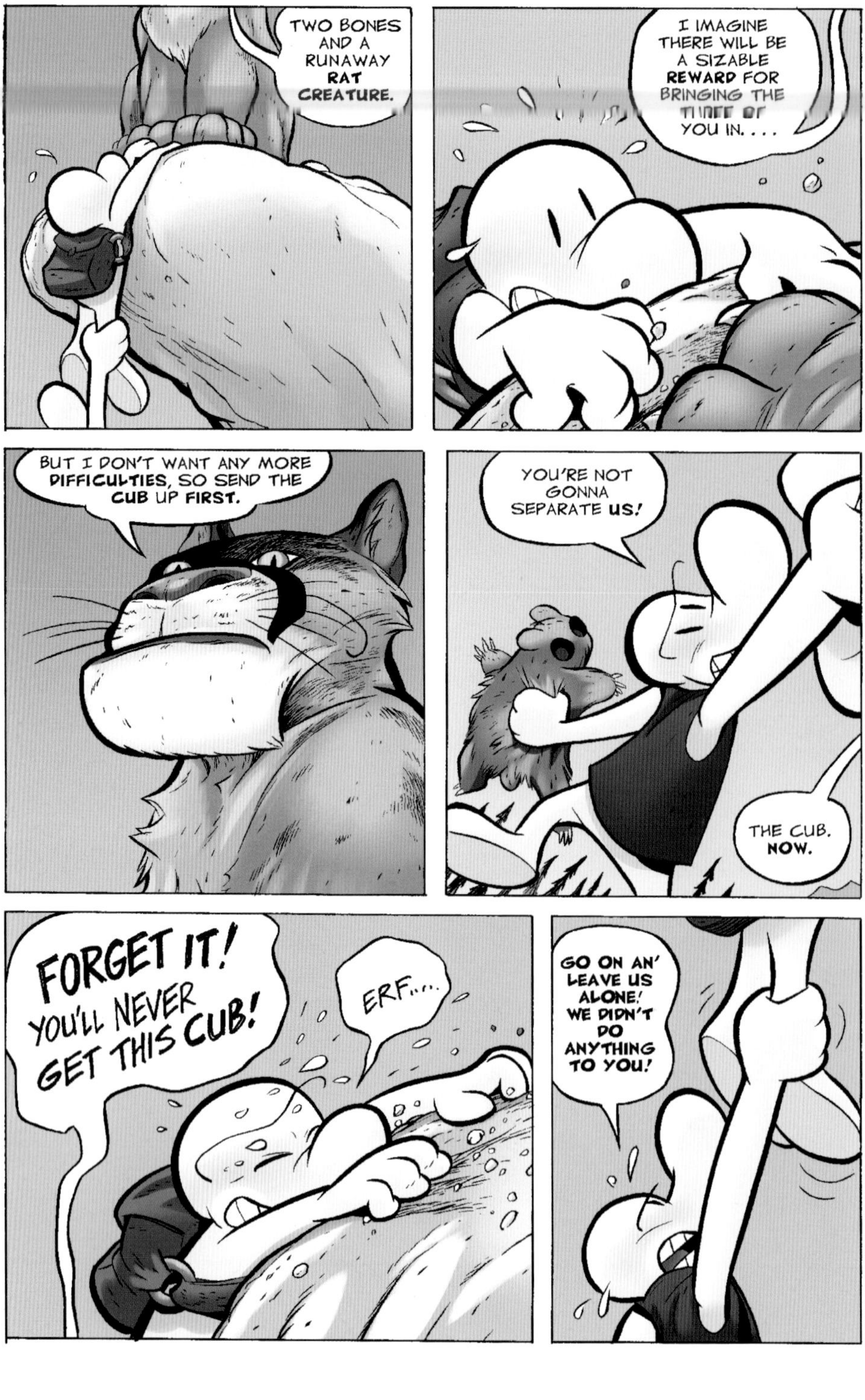
TWO BONES AND A RUNAWAY **RAT CREATURE.**
I IMAGINE THERE WILL BE A SIZABLE **REWARD** FOR BRINGING THE
YOU IN. . . .
BUT I DON'T WANT ANY MORE **DIFFICULTIES**, SO SEND THE **CUB** UP **FIRST.**
YOU'RE NOT GONNA SEPARATE **US!**
THE CUB. **NOW.**
FORGET IT! YOU'LL NEVER GET THIS CUB!
ERF....
GO ON AN' LEAVE US ALONE! WE DIDN'T DO ANYTHING TO YOU!

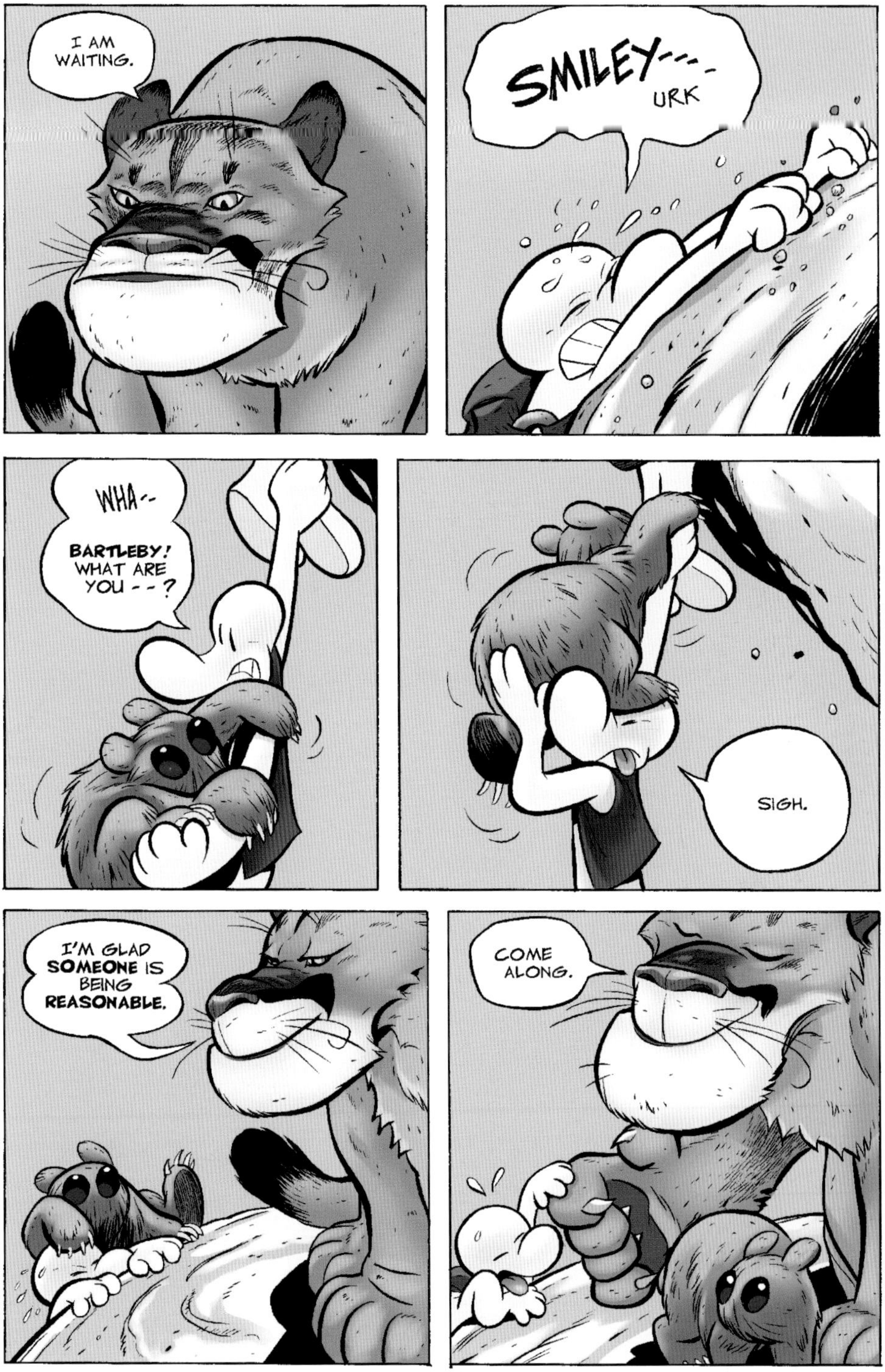
I AM WAITING.
SMILEY----
URK
WHA--
BARTLEBY! WHAT ARE YOU --?
SIGH.
I'M GLAD **SOMEONE** IS BEING **REASONABLE**.
COME ALONG.

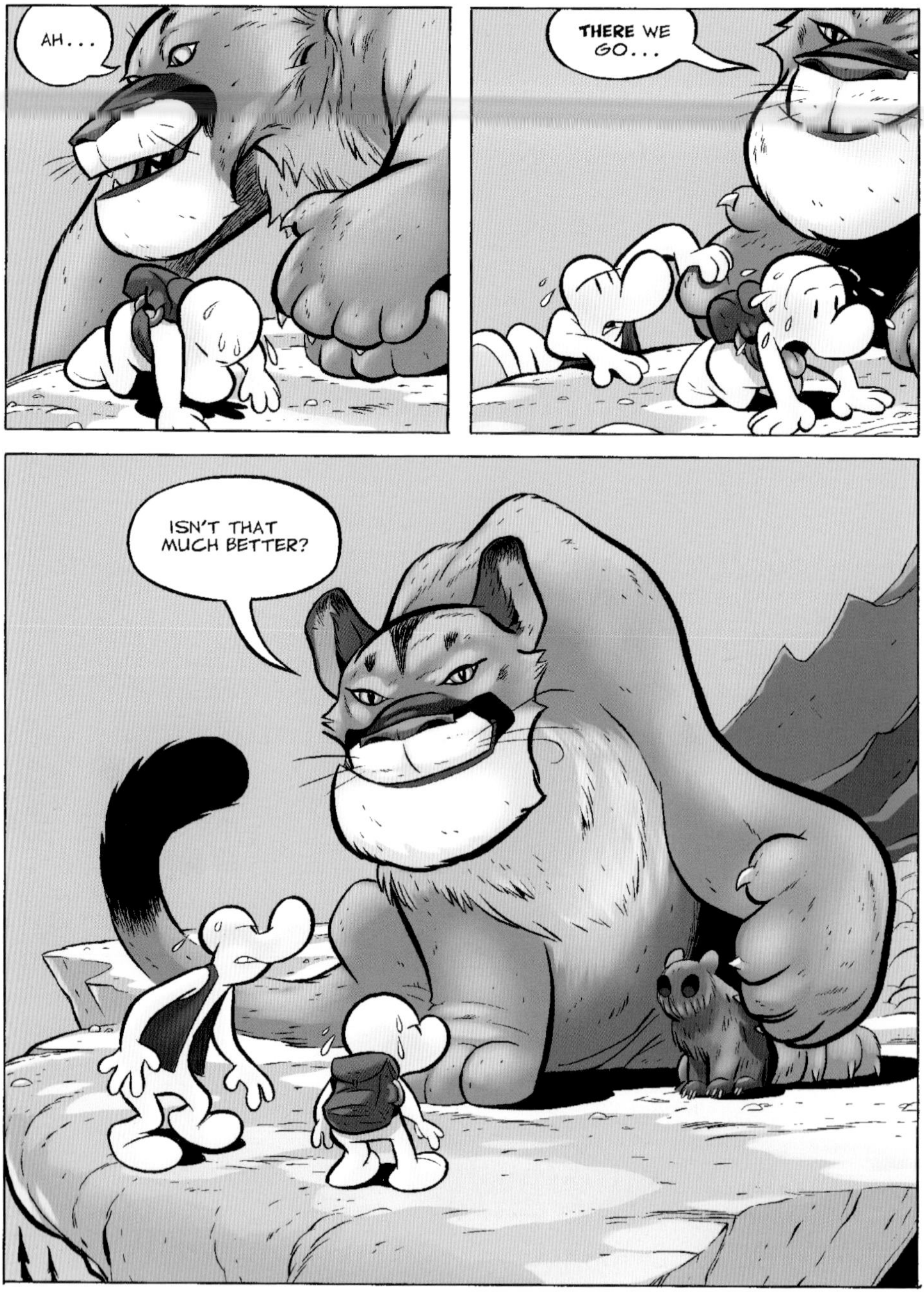
AH...
THERE WE GO...
ISN'T THAT MUCH BETTER?

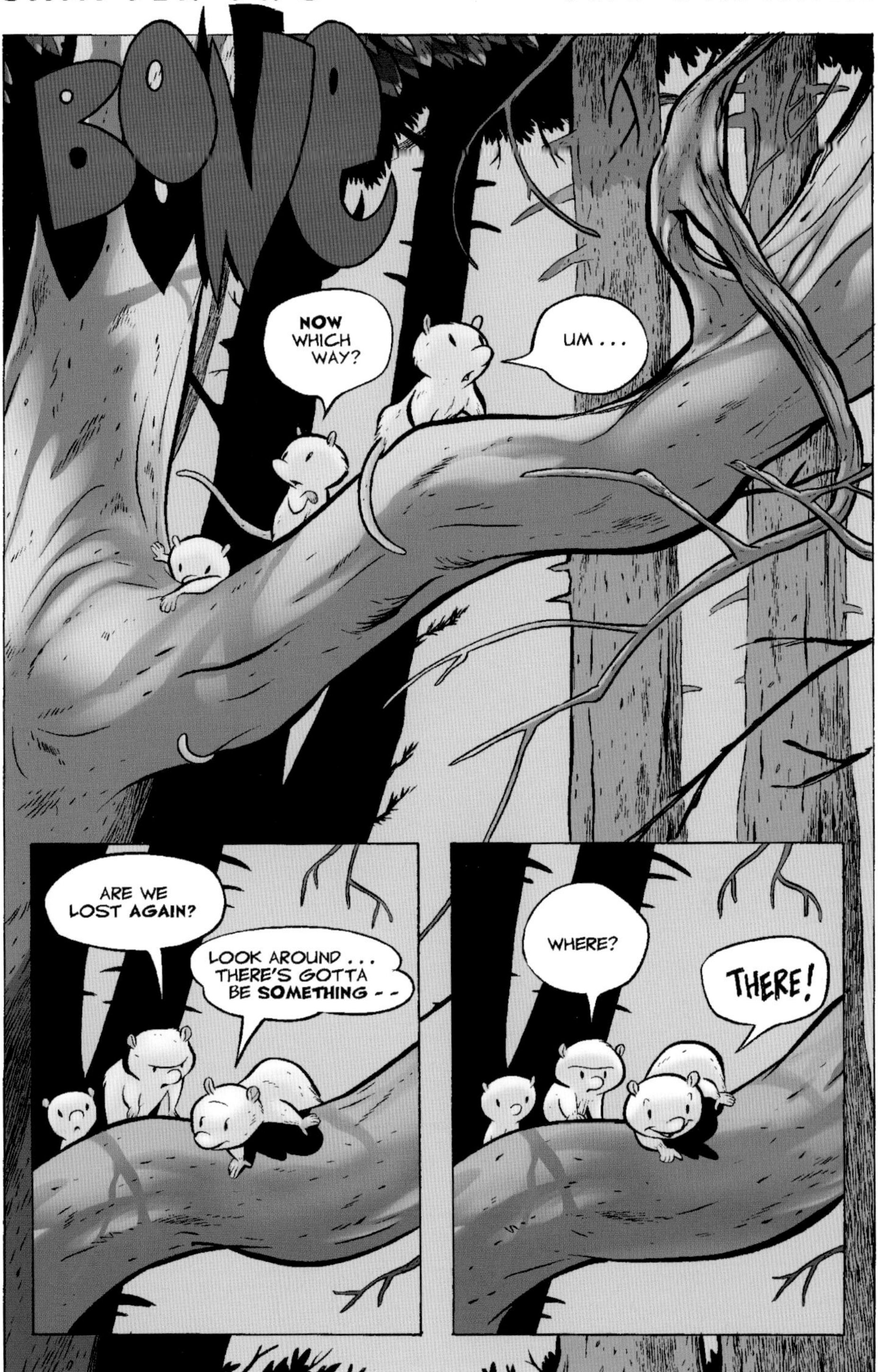
BOMP
NOW WHICH WAY?
UM . . .
ARE WE LOST AGAIN?
LOOK AROUND . . . THERE'S GOTTA BE SOMETHING - -
WHERE?
THERE!

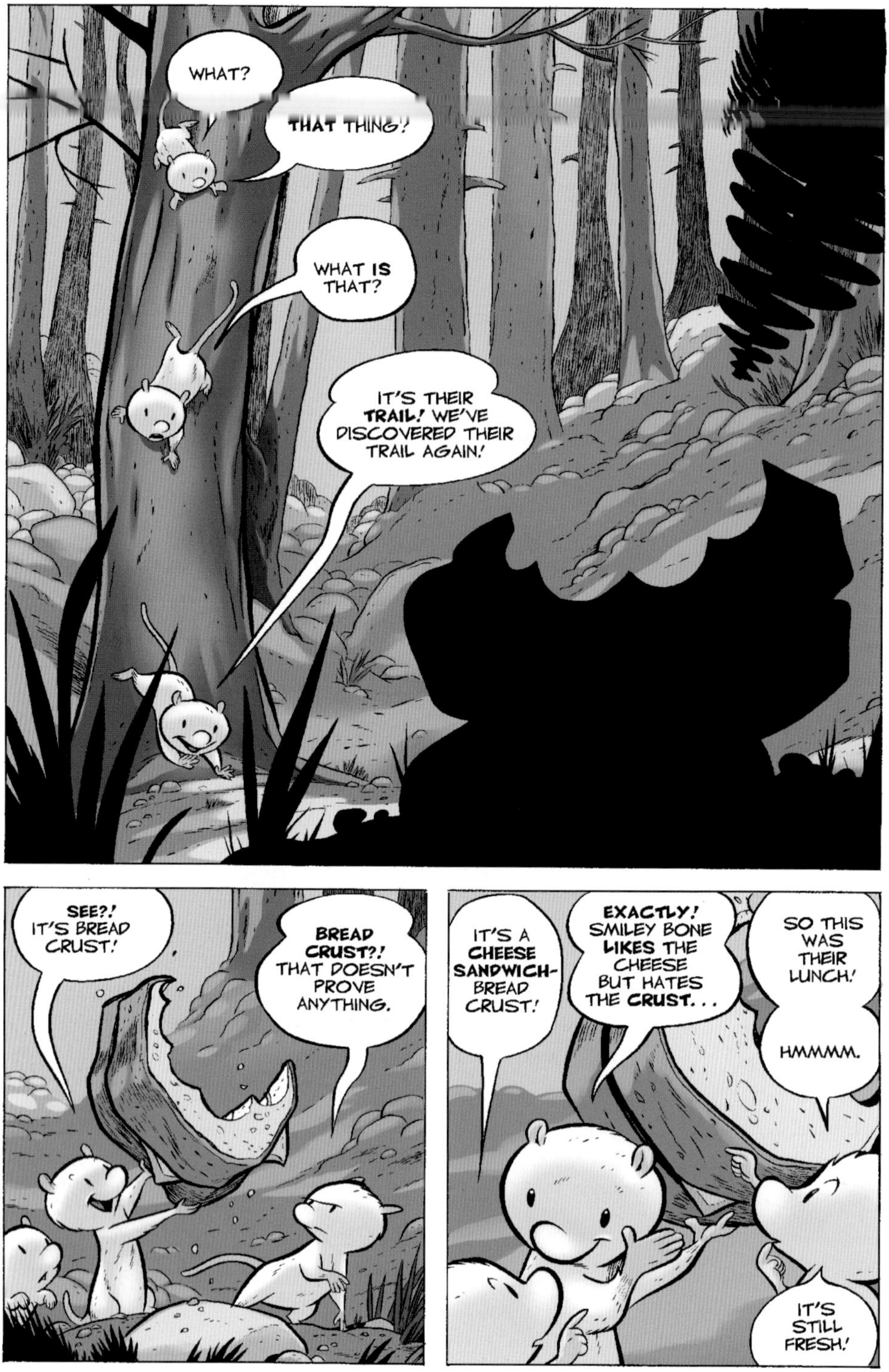
WHAT?
THAT THING?!
WHAT IS THAT?
IT'S THEIR TRAIL! WE'VE DISCOVERED THEIR TRAIL AGAIN!
SEE?! IT'S BREAD CRUST!
BREAD CRUST?! THAT DOESN'T PROVE ANYTHING.
IT'S A CHEESE SANDWICH-BREAD CRUST!
EXACTLY! SMILEY BONE LIKES THE CHEESE BUT HATES THE CRUST...
SO THIS WAS THEIR LUNCH!
HMMMM.
IT'S STILL FRESH!

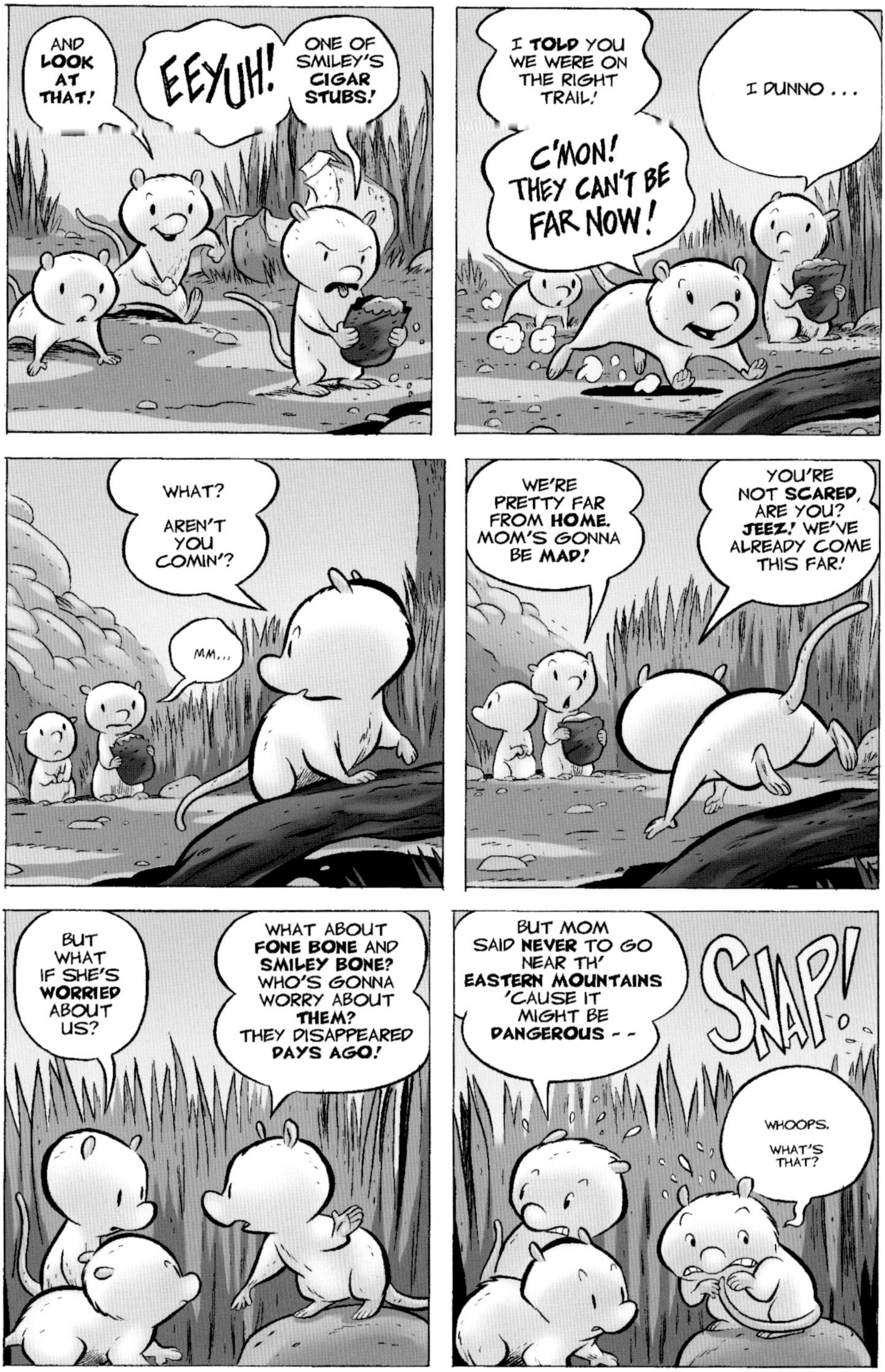
AND LOOK AT THAT!
EEYUH!
ONE OF SMILEY'S CIGAR STUBS!
I TOLD YOU WE WERE ON THE RIGHT TRAIL!
C'MON! THEY CAN'T BE FAR NOW!
I DUNNO . . .
WHAT?
AREN'T YOU COMIN'?
MM...
WE'RE PRETTY FAR FROM HOME. MOM'S GONNA BE MAD!
YOU'RE NOT SCARED, ARE YOU? JEEZ! WE'VE ALREADY COME THIS FAR!
BUT WHAT IF SHE'S WORRIED ABOUT US?
WHAT ABOUT FONE BONE AND SMILEY BONE? WHO'S GONNA WORRY ABOUT THEM? THEY DISAPPEARED DAYS AGO!
BUT MOM SAID NEVER TO GO NEAR TH' EASTERN MOUNTAINS 'CAUSE IT MIGHT BE DANGEROUS - -
SNAP!
WHOOPS.
WHAT'S THAT?

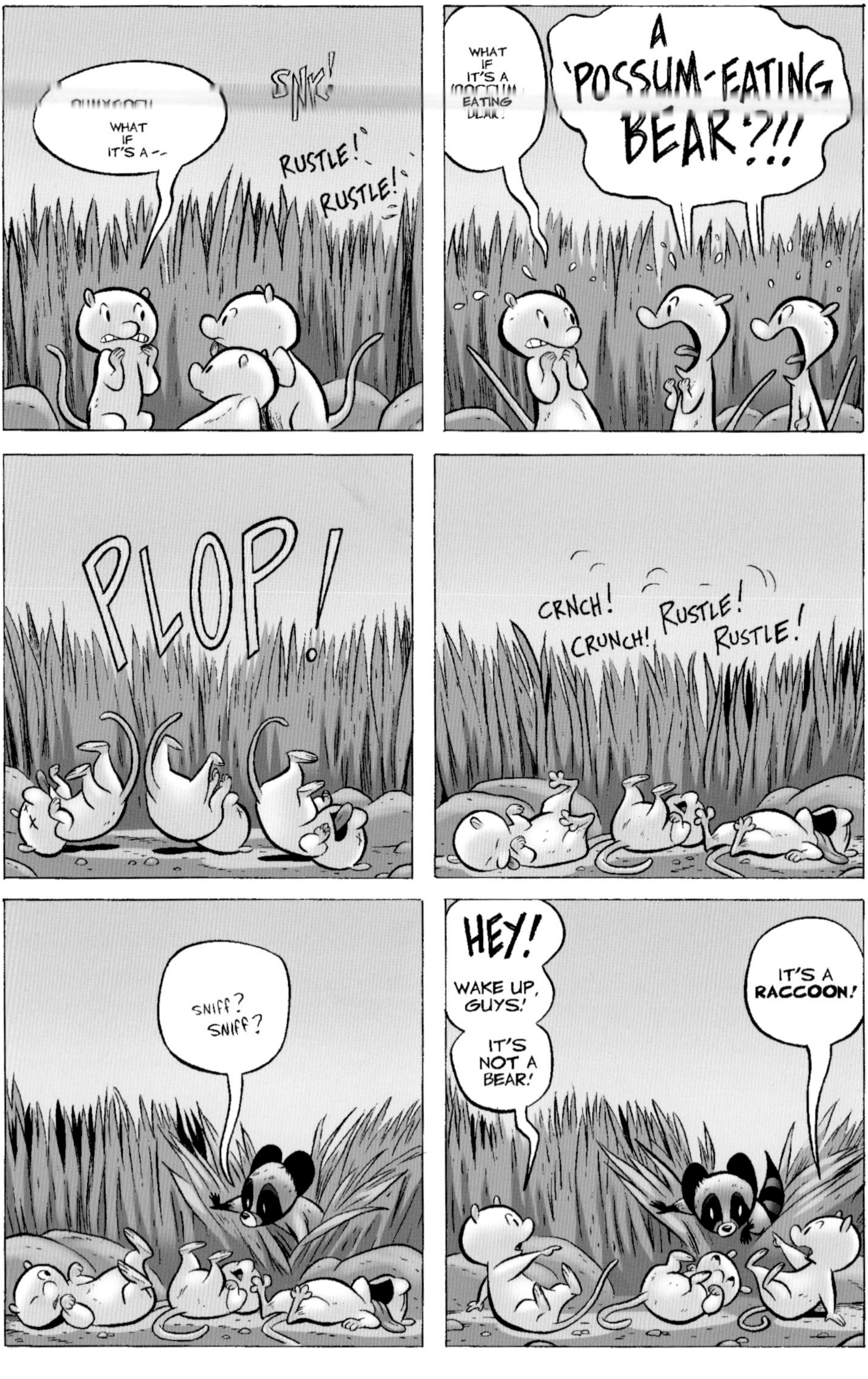
WHAT IF IT'S A --
SNK!
RUSTLE!
RUSTLE!
WHAT IF IT'S A
EATING
A 'POSSUM-EATING BEAR'?!!
PLOP!
CRNCH!
CRUNCH!
RUSTLE!
RUSTLE!
SNIFF? SNIFF?
HEY!
WAKE UP, GUYS!
IT'S NOT A BEAR!
IT'S A RACCOON!

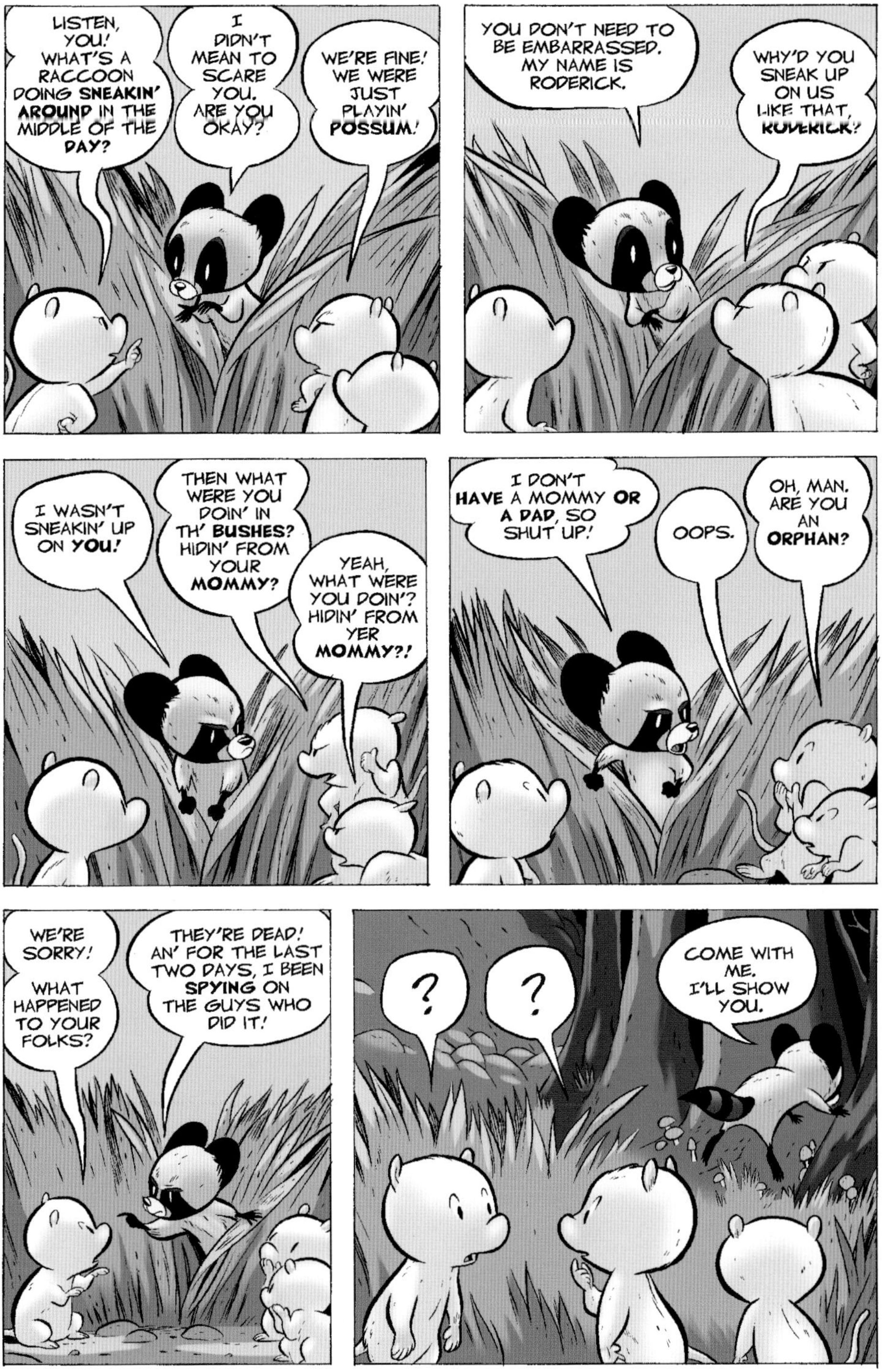
LISTEN, YOU! WHAT'S A RACCOON DOING SNEAKIN' AROUND IN THE MIDDLE OF THE DAY?
I DIDN'T MEAN TO SCARE YOU. ARE YOU OKAY?
WE'RE FINE! WE WERE JUST PLAYIN' POSSUM!
YOU DON'T NEED TO BE EMBARRASSED. MY NAME IS RODERICK.
WHY'D YOU SNEAK UP ON US LIKE THAT, RODERICK?
I WASN'T SNEAKIN' UP ON YOU!
THEN WHAT WERE YOU DOIN' IN TH' BUSHES? HIDIN' FROM YOUR MOMMY?
YEAH, WHAT WERE YOU DOIN'? HIDIN' FROM YER MOMMY?!
I DON'T HAVE A MOMMY OR A DAD, SO SHUT UP!
OOPS.
OH, MAN. ARE YOU AN ORPHAN?
WE'RE SORRY!
WHAT HAPPENED TO YOUR FOLKS?
THEY'RE DEAD! AN' FOR THE LAST TWO DAYS, I BEEN SPYING ON THE GUYS WHO DID IT!
?
?
COME WITH ME. I'LL SHOW YOU.

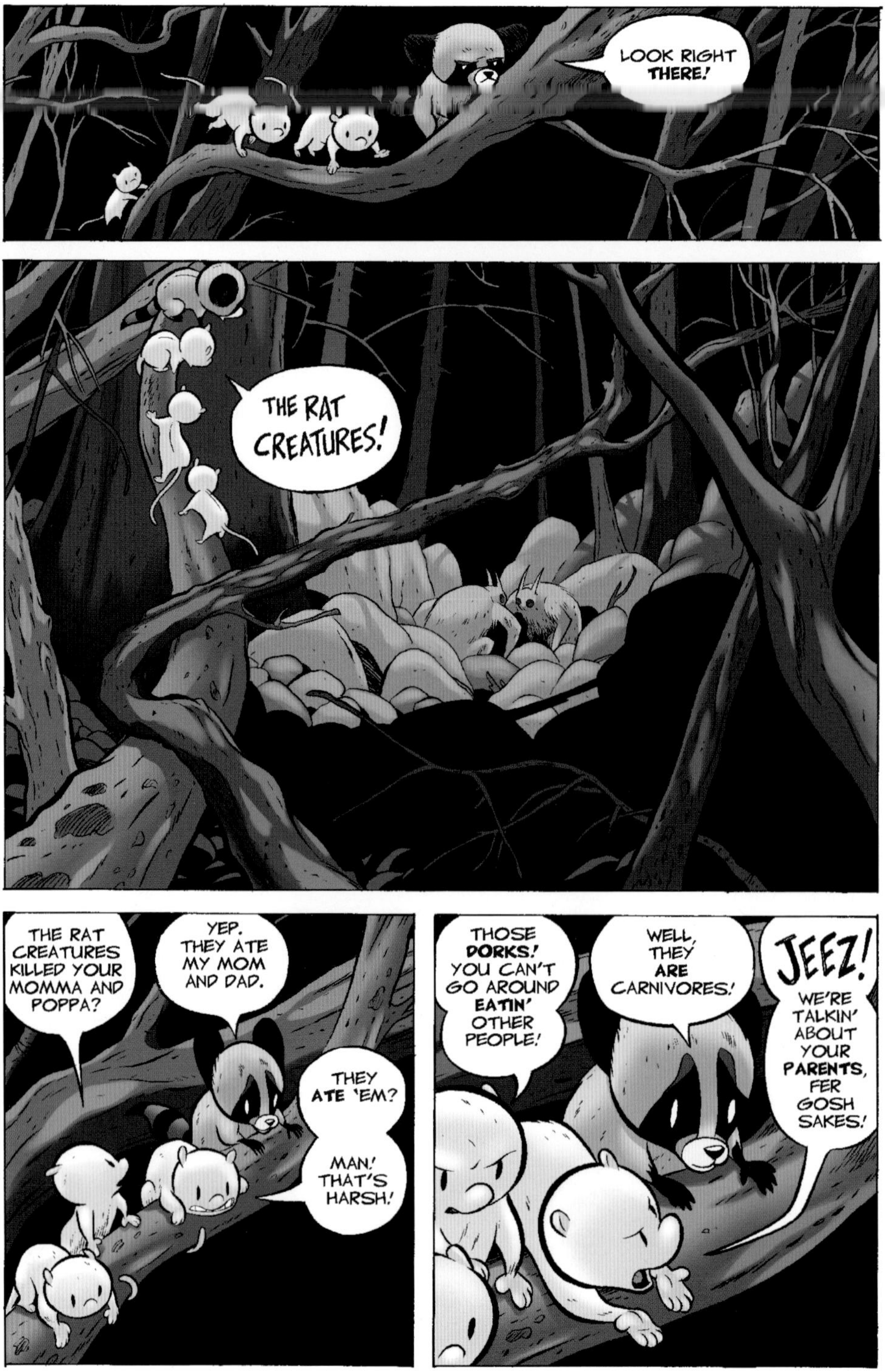
LOOK RIGHT THERE!
THE RAT CREATURES!
THE RAT CREATURES KILLED YOUR MOMMA AND POPPA?
YEP. THEY ATE MY MOM AND DAD.
THEY ATE 'EM?
MAN! THAT'S HARSH!
THOSE DORKS! YOU CAN'T GO AROUND EATIN' OTHER PEOPLE!
WELL, THEY ARE CARNIVORES!
JEEZ!
WE'RE TALKIN' ABOUT YOUR PARENTS, FER GOSH SAKES!

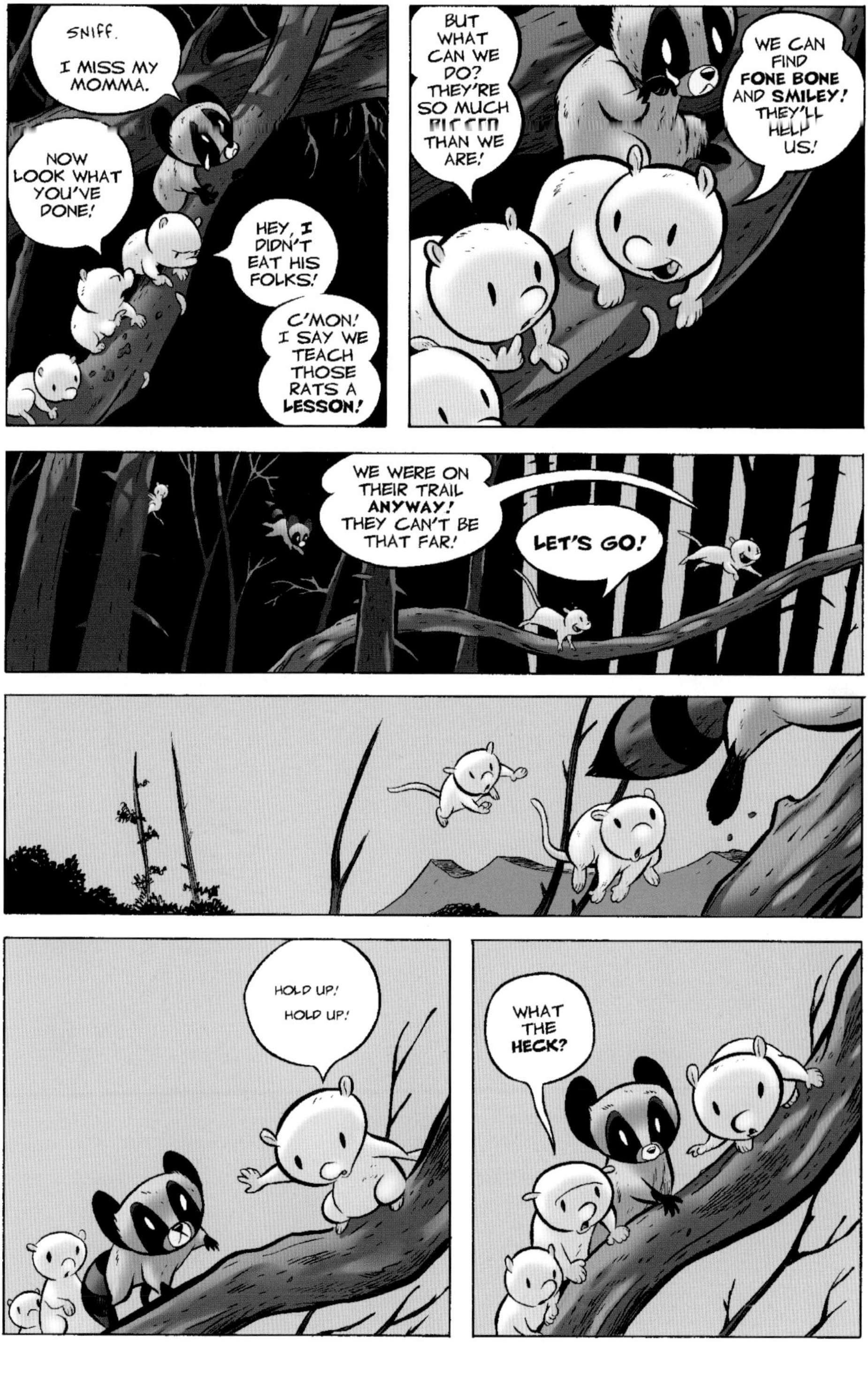
SNIFF.
I MISS MY MOMMA.
NOW LOOK WHAT YOU'VE DONE!
HEY, I DIDN'T EAT HIS FOLKS!
C'MON! I SAY WE TEACH THOSE RATS A **LESSON**!
BUT WHAT CAN WE DO? THEY'RE SO MUCH BIGGER THAN WE ARE!
WE CAN FIND **FONE BONE** AND **SMILEY**! THEY'LL HELP US!
WE WERE ON THEIR TRAIL **ANYWAY**! THEY CAN'T BE THAT FAR!
LET'S GO!
HOLD UP! HOLD UP!
WHAT THE **HECK?**

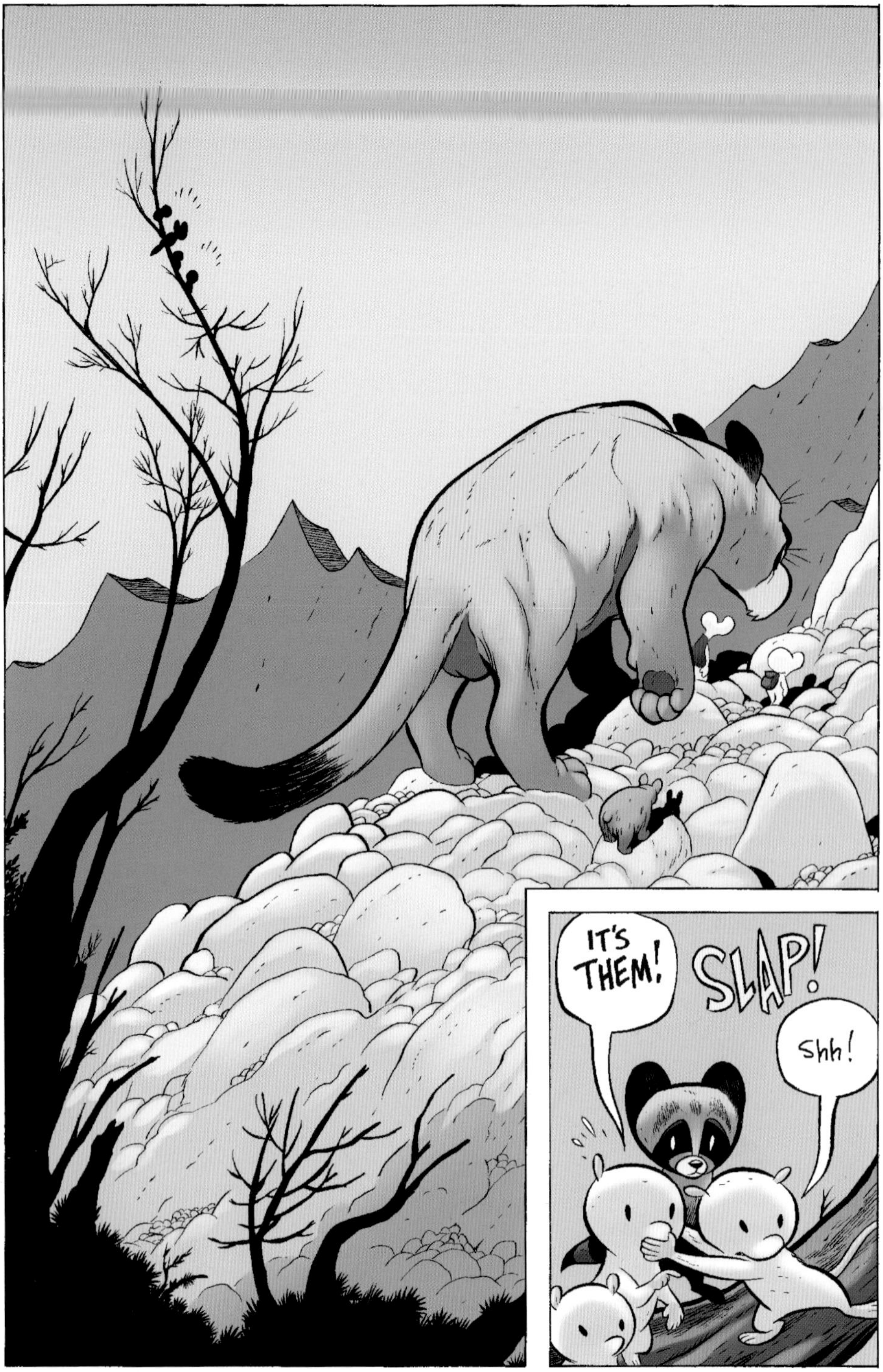
IT'S THEM!
SLAP!
Shh!

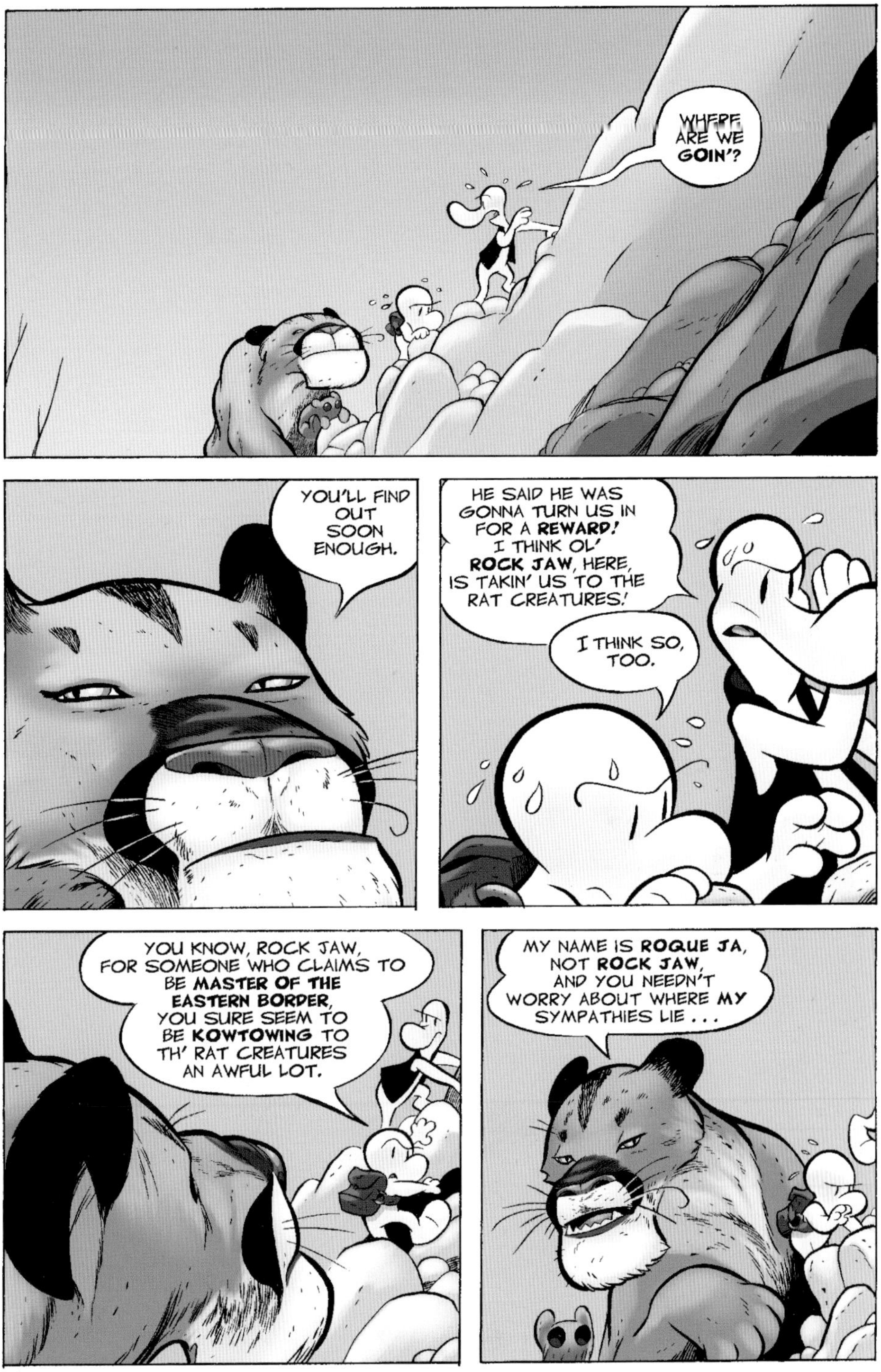
WHERE ARE WE GOIN'?
YOU'LL FIND OUT SOON ENOUGH.
HE SAID HE WAS GONNA TURN US IN FOR A REWARD! I THINK OL' ROCK JAW, HERE, IS TAKIN' US TO THE RAT CREATURES!
I THINK SO, TOO.
YOU KNOW, ROCK JAW, FOR SOMEONE WHO CLAIMS TO BE MASTER OF THE EASTERN BORDER, YOU SURE SEEM TO BE KOWTOWING TO TH' RAT CREATURES AN AWFUL LOT.
MY NAME IS ROQUE JA, NOT ROCK JAW, AND YOU NEEDN'T WORRY ABOUT WHERE MY SYMPATHIES LIE . . .

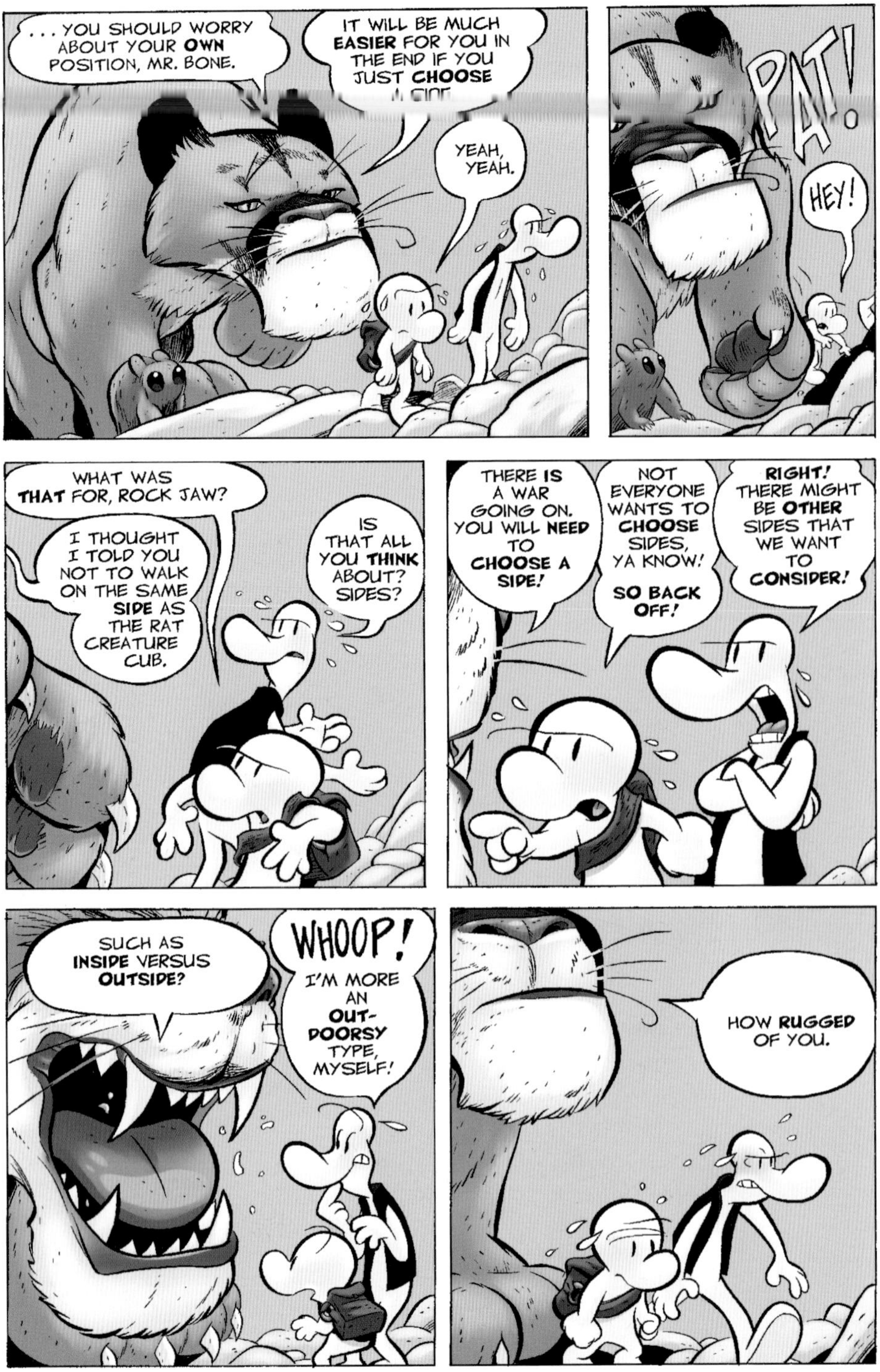
. . . YOU SHOULD WORRY ABOUT YOUR **OWN** POSITION, MR. BONE.
IT WILL BE MUCH **EASIER** FOR YOU IN THE END IF YOU JUST **CHOOSE**
YEAH, YEAH.
PAT!
HEY!
WHAT WAS **THAT** FOR, ROCK JAW?
I THOUGHT I TOLD YOU NOT TO WALK ON THE SAME **SIDE** AS THE RAT CREATURE CUB.
IS THAT ALL YOU **THINK** ABOUT? SIDES?
THERE **IS** A WAR GOING ON. YOU WILL **NEED** TO **CHOOSE A SIDE!**
NOT EVERYONE WANTS TO **CHOOSE** SIDES, YA KNOW! **SO BACK OFF!**
RIGHT! THERE MIGHT BE **OTHER** SIDES THAT WE WANT TO **CONSIDER!**
SUCH AS **INSIDE** VERSUS **OUTSIDE?**
WHOOP! I'M MORE AN **OUT-DOORSY** TYPE, MYSELF!
HOW **RUGGED** OF YOU.

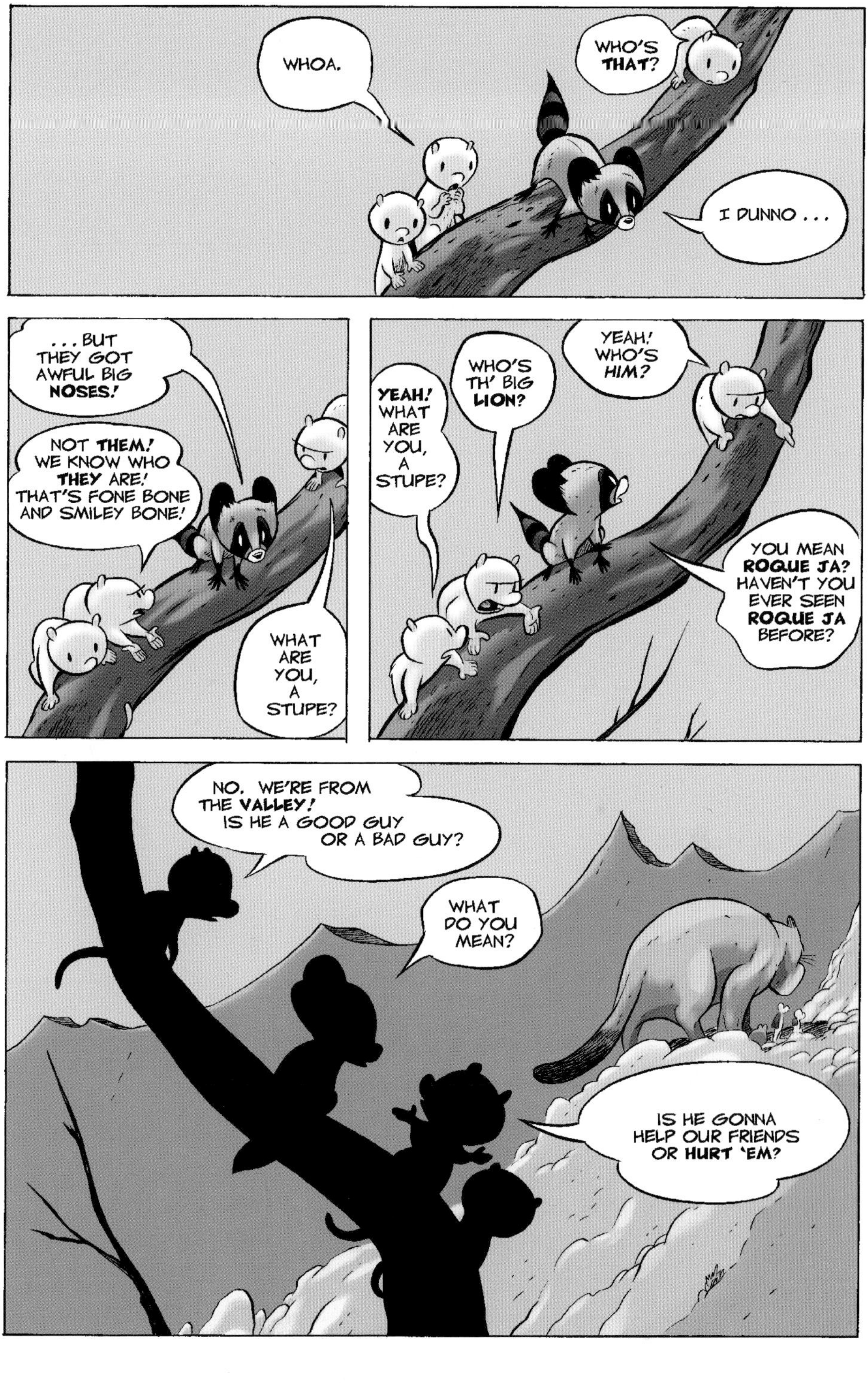
WHOA.
WHO'S **THAT**?
I DUNNO . . .
. . . BUT THEY GOT AWFUL BIG **NOSES**!
NOT **THEM**! WE KNOW WHO **THEY** ARE! THAT'S FONE BONE AND SMILEY BONE!
WHAT ARE YOU, A STUPE?
YEAH! WHO'S *HIM*?
WHO'S TH' BIG **LION**?
YEAH! WHAT ARE YOU, A STUPE?
YOU MEAN **ROQUE JA?** HAVEN'T YOU EVER SEEN **ROQUE JA** BEFORE?
NO. WE'RE FROM THE **VALLEY**! IS HE A GOOD GUY OR A BAD GUY?
WHAT DO YOU MEAN?
IS HE GONNA HELP OUR FRIENDS OR **HURT** 'EM?

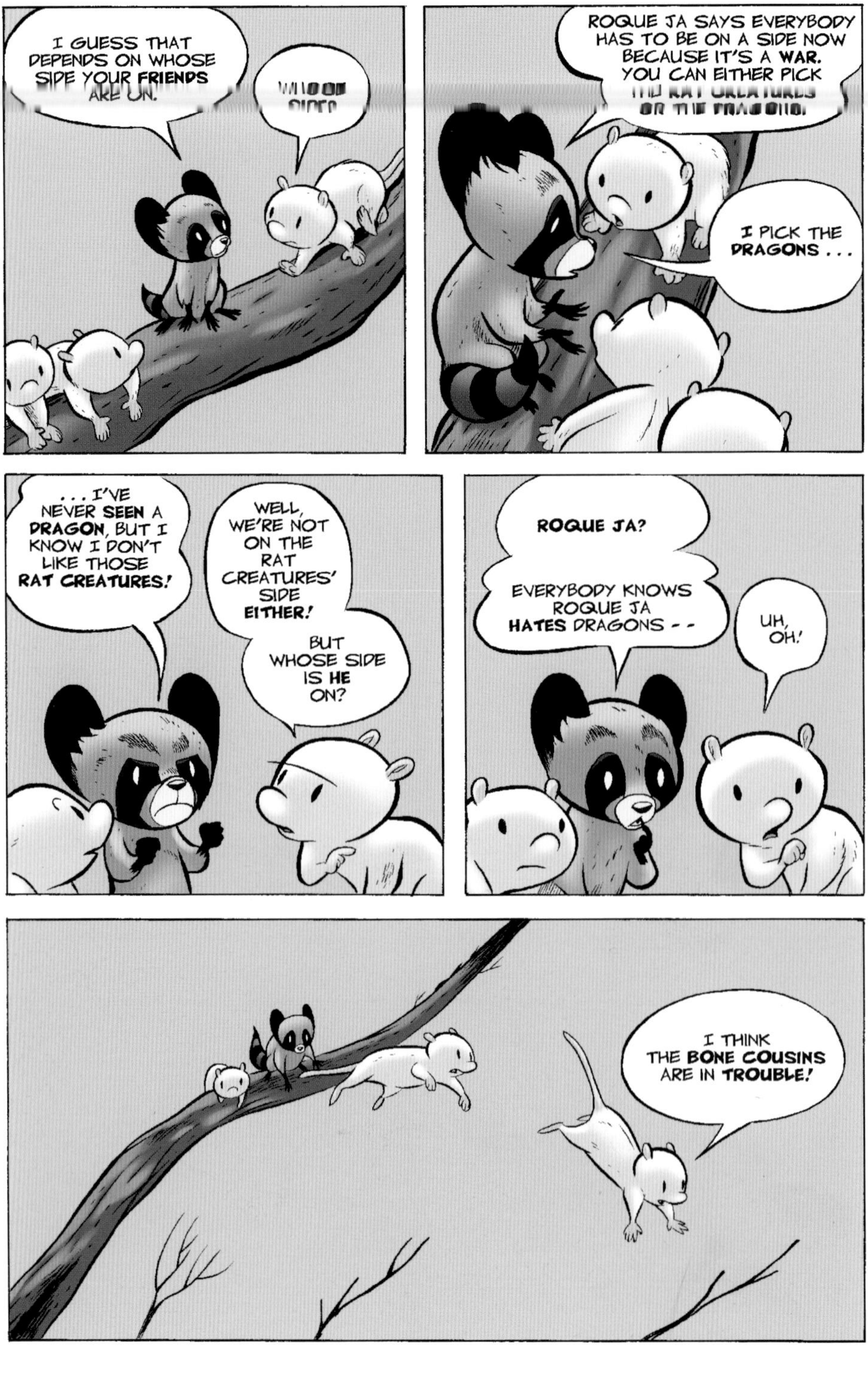
I GUESS THAT DEPENDS ON WHOSE SIDE YOUR **FRIENDS** ARE ON.
ROQUE JA SAYS EVERYBODY HAS TO BE ON A SIDE NOW BECAUSE IT'S A **WAR.** YOU CAN EITHER PICK
I PICK THE **DRAGONS** . . .
. . . I'VE NEVER **SEEN** A **DRAGON**, BUT I KNOW I DON'T LIKE THOSE **RAT CREATURES!**
WELL, WE'RE NOT ON THE RAT CREATURES' SIDE **EITHER!**
BUT WHOSE SIDE IS **HE** ON?
ROQUE JA?
EVERYBODY KNOWS ROQUE JA **HATES** DRAGONS - -
UH, OH!
I THINK THE **BONE COUSINS** ARE IN **TROUBLE!**

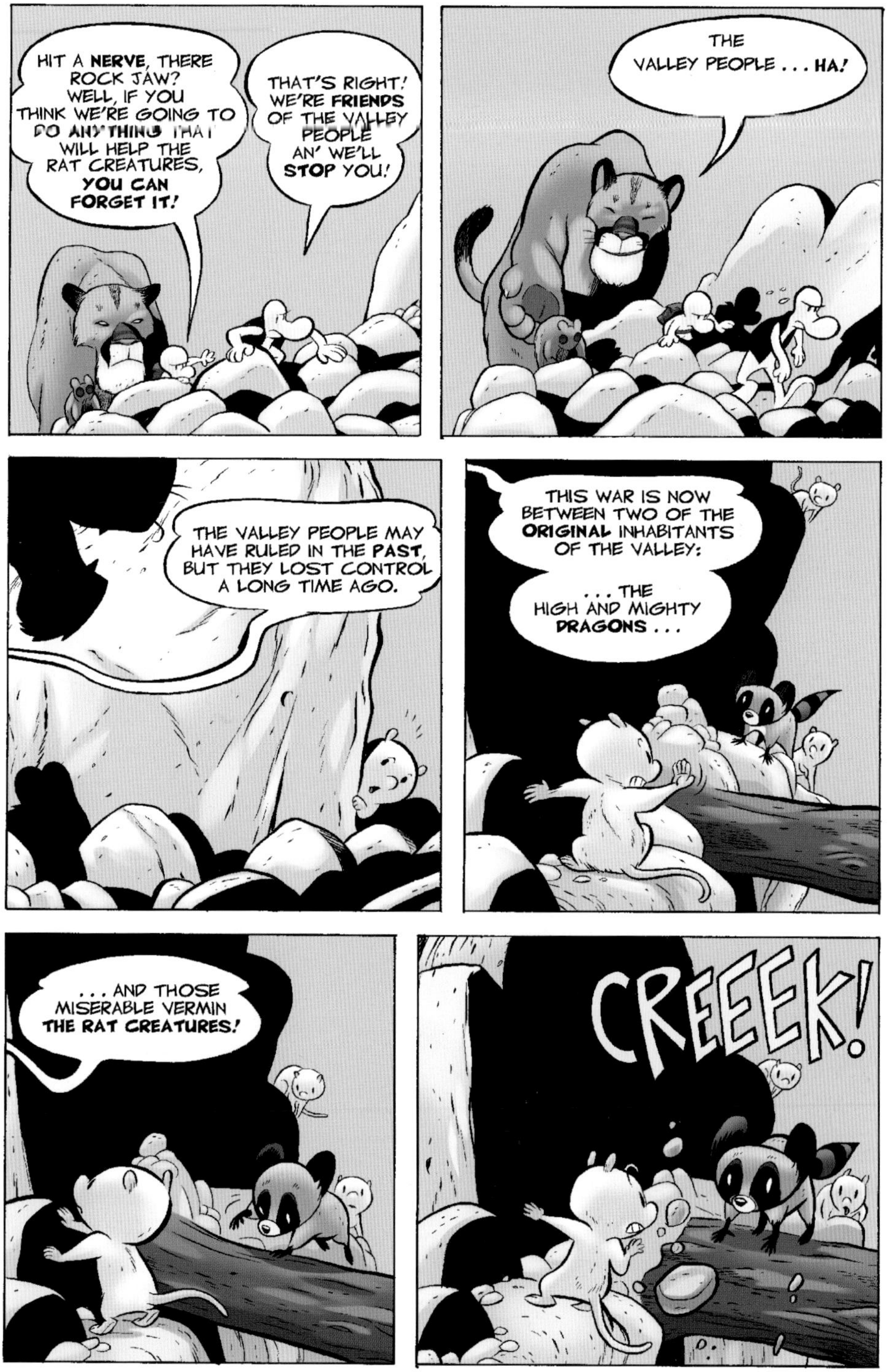
HIT A NERVE, THERE ROCK JAW? WELL, IF YOU THINK WE'RE GOING TO DO ANYTHING THAT WILL HELP THE RAT CREATURES, YOU CAN FORGET IT!
THAT'S RIGHT! WE'RE FRIENDS OF THE VALLEY PEOPLE AN' WE'LL STOP YOU!
THE VALLEY PEOPLE . . . HA!
THE VALLEY PEOPLE MAY HAVE RULED IN THE PAST, BUT THEY LOST CONTROL A LONG TIME AGO.
THIS WAR IS NOW BETWEEN TWO OF THE ORIGINAL INHABITANTS OF THE VALLEY:
. . . THE HIGH AND MIGHTY DRAGONS . . .
. . . AND THOSE MISERABLE VERMIN THE RAT CREATURES!
CREEEK!

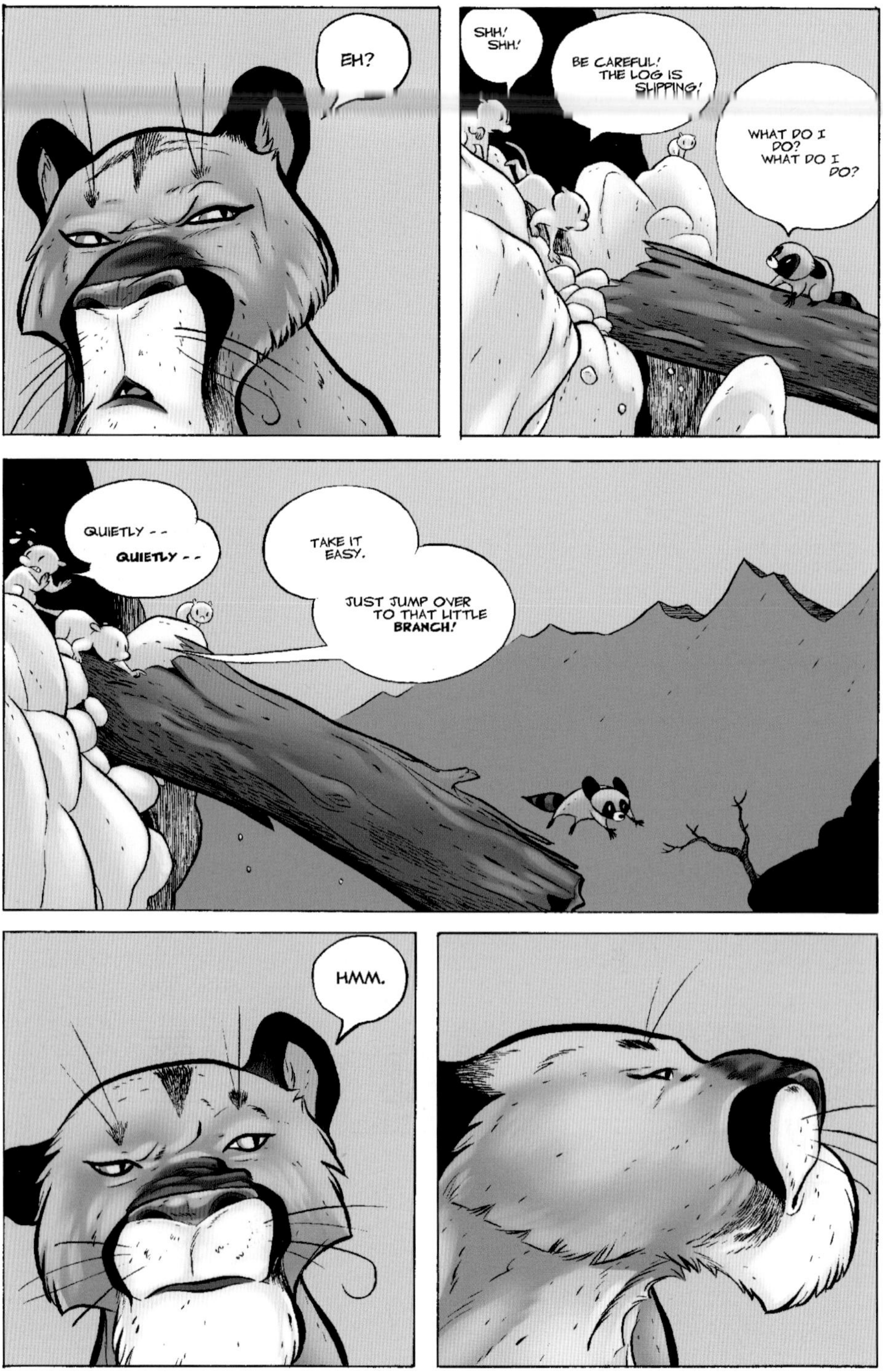
EH?
SHH! SHH!
BE CAREFUL! THE LOG IS SLIPPING!
WHAT DO I DO? WHAT DO I DO?
QUIETLY -- QUIETLY --
TAKE IT EASY.
JUST JUMP OVER TO THAT LITTLE BRANCH!
HMM.

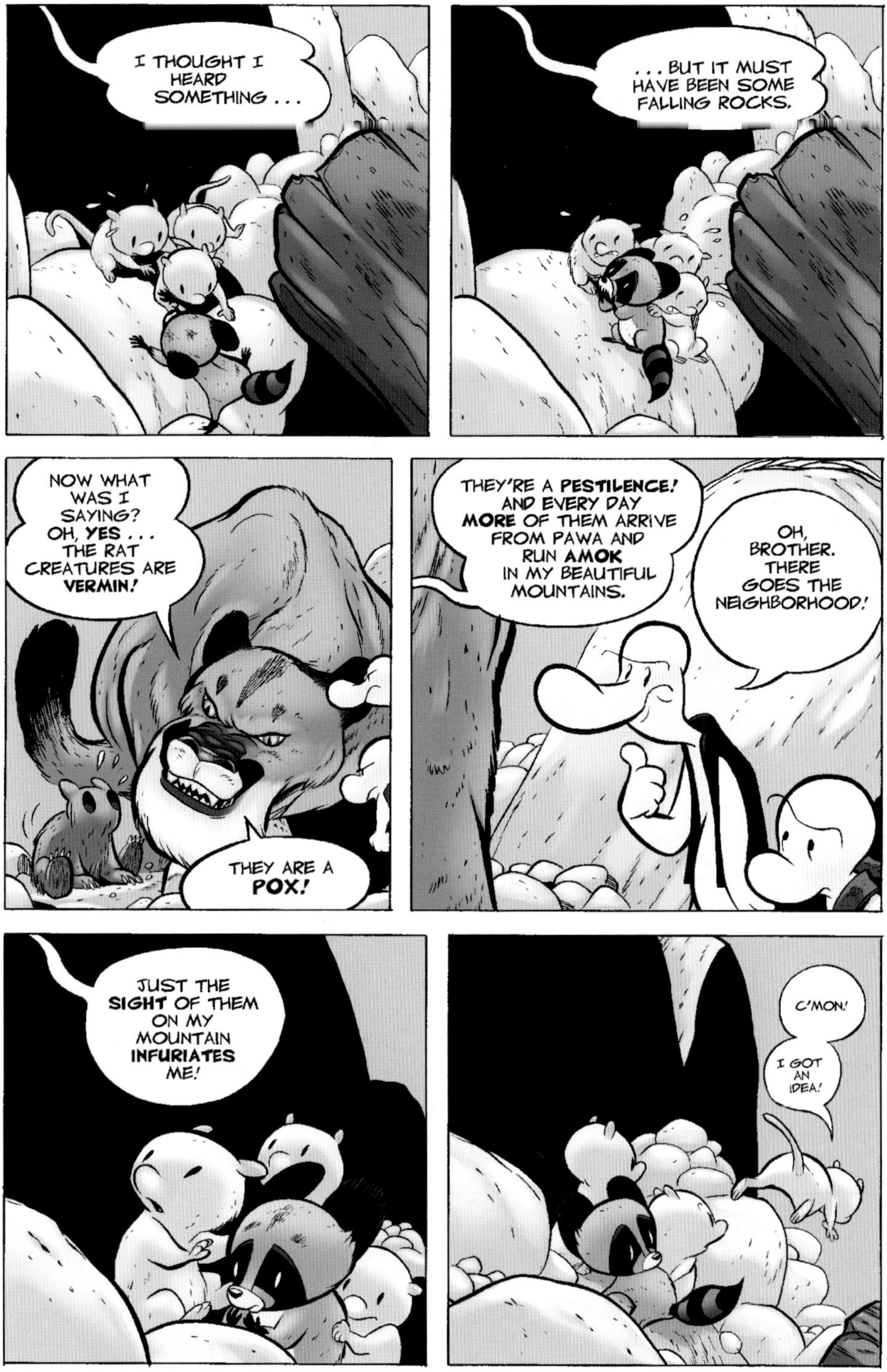
I THOUGHT I HEARD SOMETHING . . .
. . . BUT IT MUST HAVE BEEN SOME FALLING ROCKS.
NOW WHAT WAS I SAYING? OH, YES . . . THE RAT CREATURES ARE VERMIN!
THEY ARE A POX!
THEY'RE A PESTILENCE! AND EVERY DAY MORE OF THEM ARRIVE FROM PAWA AND RUN AMOK IN MY BEAUTIFUL MOUNTAINS.
OH, BROTHER. THERE GOES THE NEIGHBORHOOD!
JUST THE SIGHT OF THEM ON MY MOUNTAIN INFURIATES ME!
C'MON!
I GOT AN IDEA!

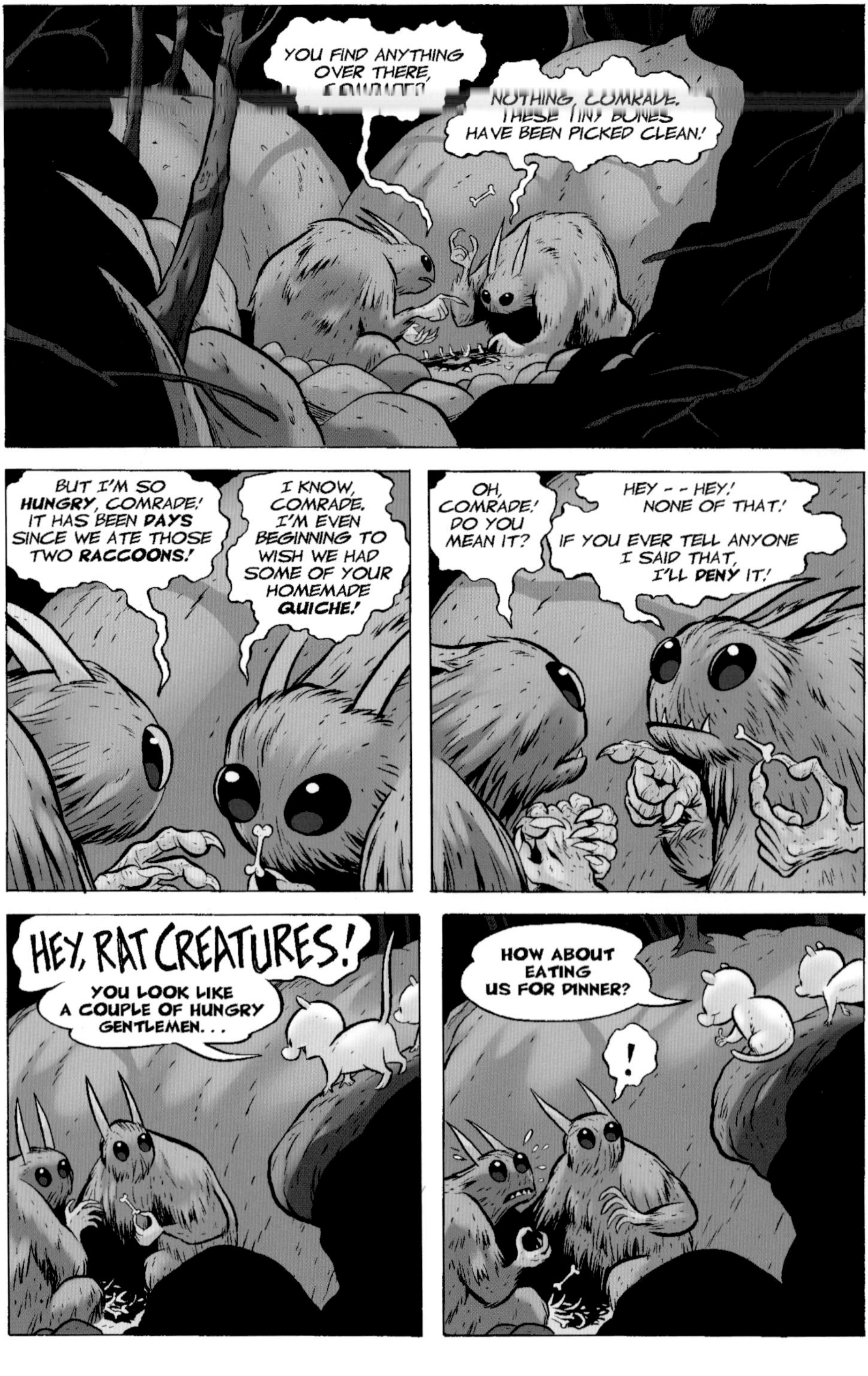
YOU FIND ANYTHING OVER THERE,
NOTHING, COMRADE. THESE TINY BONES HAVE BEEN PICKED CLEAN!
BUT I'M SO HUNGRY, COMRADE! IT HAS BEEN DAYS SINCE WE ATE THOSE TWO RACCOONS!
I KNOW, COMRADE. I'M EVEN BEGINNING TO WISH WE HAD SOME OF YOUR HOMEMADE QUICHE!
OH, COMRADE! DO YOU MEAN IT?
HEY - - HEY! NONE OF THAT!
IF YOU EVER TELL ANYONE I SAID THAT, I'LL DENY IT!
HEY, RAT CREATURES!
YOU LOOK LIKE A COUPLE OF HUNGRY GENTLEMEN. . .
HOW ABOUT EATING US FOR DINNER?
!

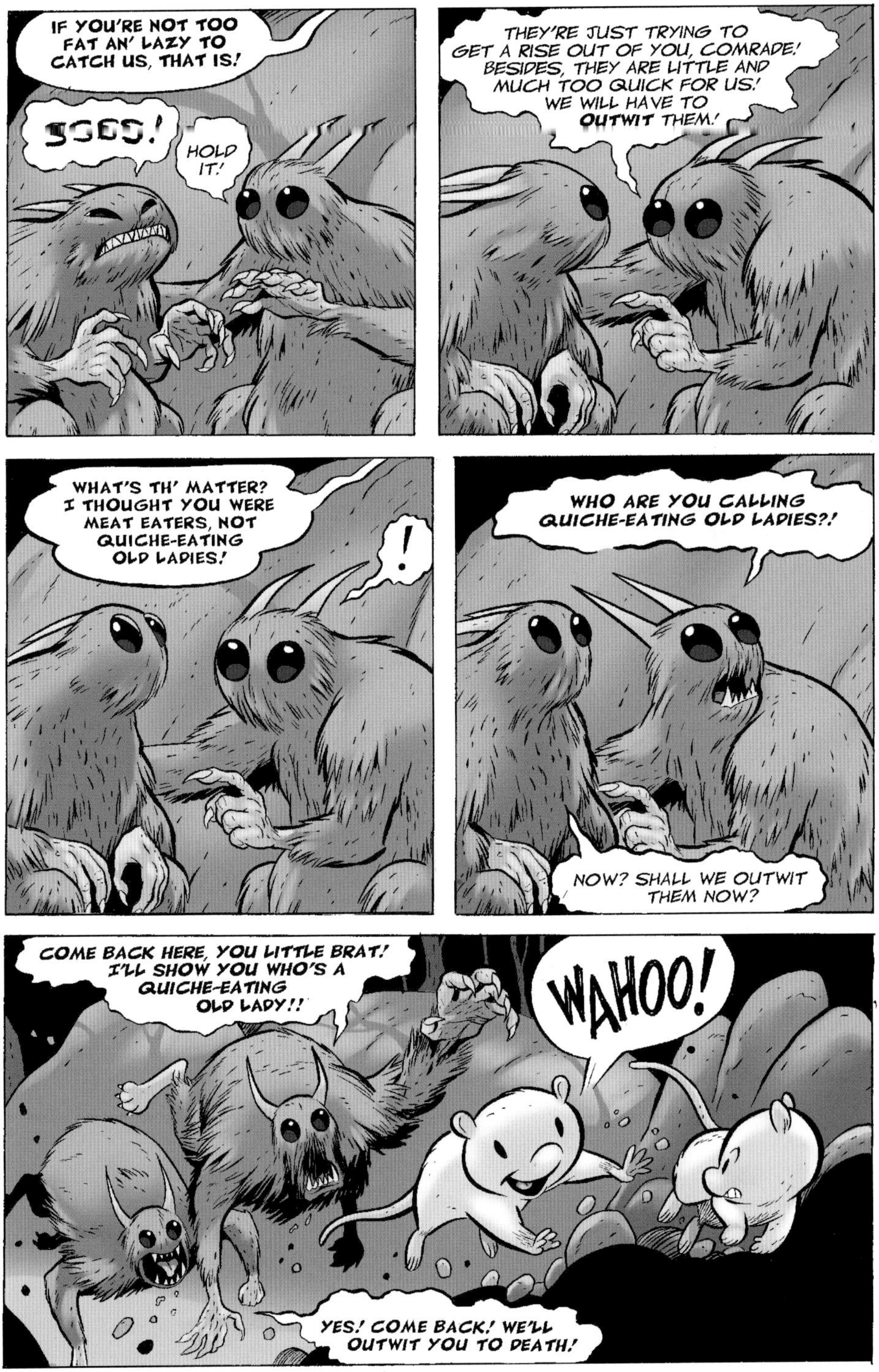
IF YOU'RE NOT TOO FAT AN' LAZY TO CATCH US, THAT IS!
HOLD IT!
THEY'RE JUST TRYING TO GET A RISE OUT OF YOU, COMRADE! BESIDES, THEY ARE LITTLE AND MUCH TOO QUICK FOR US! WE WILL HAVE TO OUTWIT THEM!
WHAT'S TH' MATTER? I THOUGHT YOU WERE MEAT EATERS, NOT QUICHE-EATING OLD LADIES!
!
WHO ARE YOU CALLING QUICHE-EATING OLD LADIES?!
NOW? SHALL WE OUTWIT THEM NOW?
COME BACK HERE, YOU LITTLE BRAT! I'LL SHOW YOU WHO'S A QUICHE-EATING OLD LADY!!
WAHOO!
YES! COME BACK! WE'LL OUTWIT YOU TO DEATH!

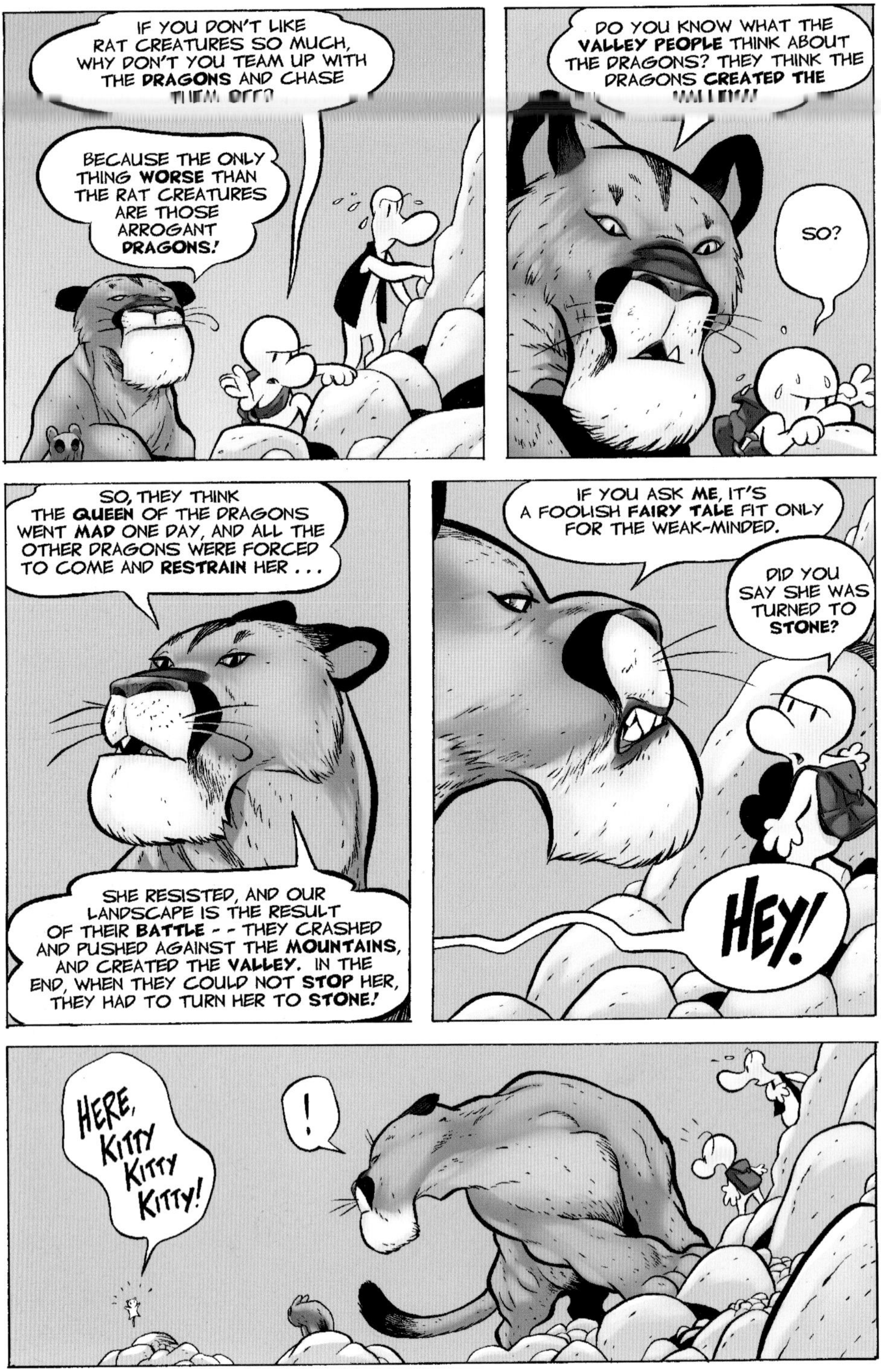
IF YOU DON'T LIKE RAT CREATURES SO MUCH, WHY DON'T YOU TEAM UP WITH THE DRAGONS AND CHASE
BECAUSE THE ONLY THING WORSE THAN THE RAT CREATURES ARE THOSE ARROGANT DRAGONS!
DO YOU KNOW WHAT THE VALLEY PEOPLE THINK ABOUT THE DRAGONS? THEY THINK THE DRAGONS CREATED THE
SO?
SO, THEY THINK THE QUEEN OF THE DRAGONS WENT MAD ONE DAY, AND ALL THE OTHER DRAGONS WERE FORCED TO COME AND RESTRAIN HER . . .
SHE RESISTED, AND OUR LANDSCAPE IS THE RESULT OF THEIR BATTLE - - THEY CRASHED AND PUSHED AGAINST THE MOUNTAINS, AND CREATED THE VALLEY. IN THE END, WHEN THEY COULD NOT STOP HER, THEY HAD TO TURN HER TO STONE!
IF YOU ASK ME, IT'S A FOOLISH FAIRY TALE FIT ONLY FOR THE WEAK-MINDED.
DID YOU SAY SHE WAS TURNED TO STONE?
HEY!
HERE, KITTY KITTY KITTY!
!

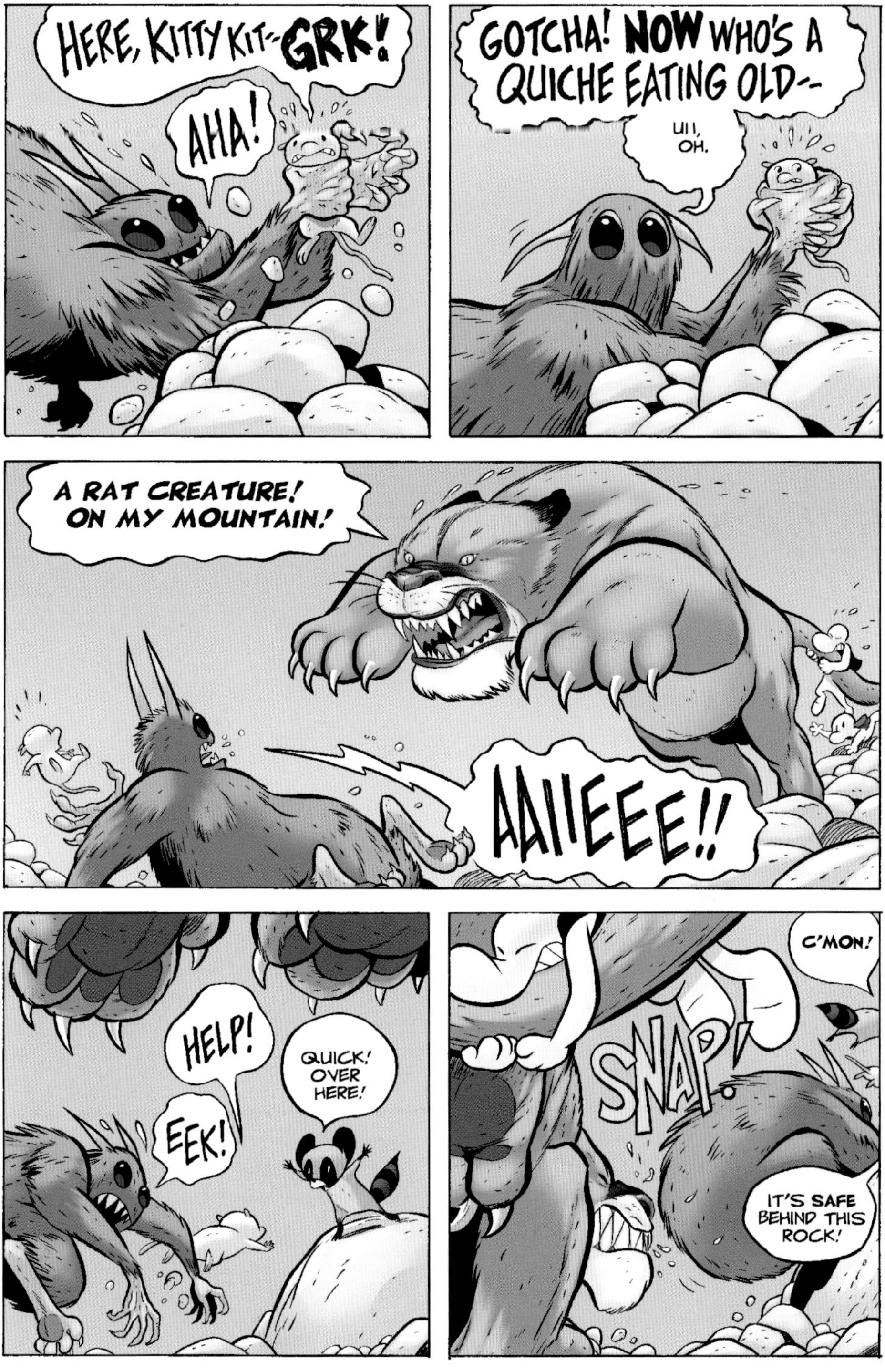
HERE, KITTY KIT-- GRK!
AHA!
GOTCHA! NOW WHO'S A QUICHE EATING OLD--
UH, OH.
A RAT CREATURE! ON MY MOUNTAIN!
AAIIEEEE!!
HELP!
EEK!
QUICK! OVER HERE!
C'MON!
SNAP!
IT'S SAFE BEHIND THIS ROCK!

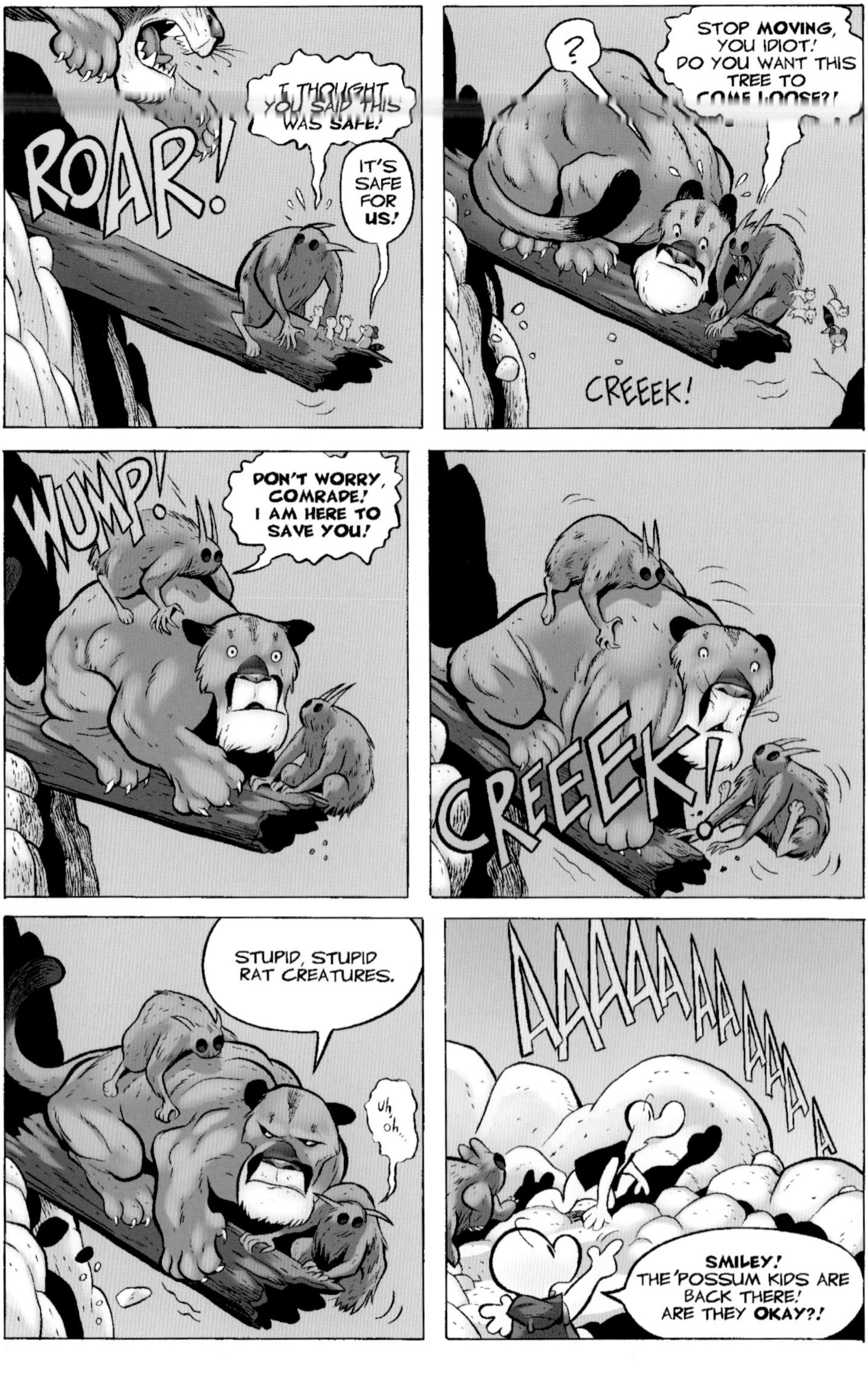
I THOUGHT YOU SAID THIS WAS SAFE!
ROAR!
IT'S SAFE FOR US!
?
STOP MOVING, YOU IDIOT! DO YOU WANT THIS TREE TO COME LOOSE?!
CREEEK!
WUMP!
DON'T WORRY, COMRADE! I AM HERE TO SAVE YOU!
CREEEK!
STUPID, STUPID RAT CREATURES.
Uh, oh...
AAAAAAAAAAAAAA
SMILEY! THE 'POSSUM KIDS ARE BACK THERE! ARE THEY OKAY?!

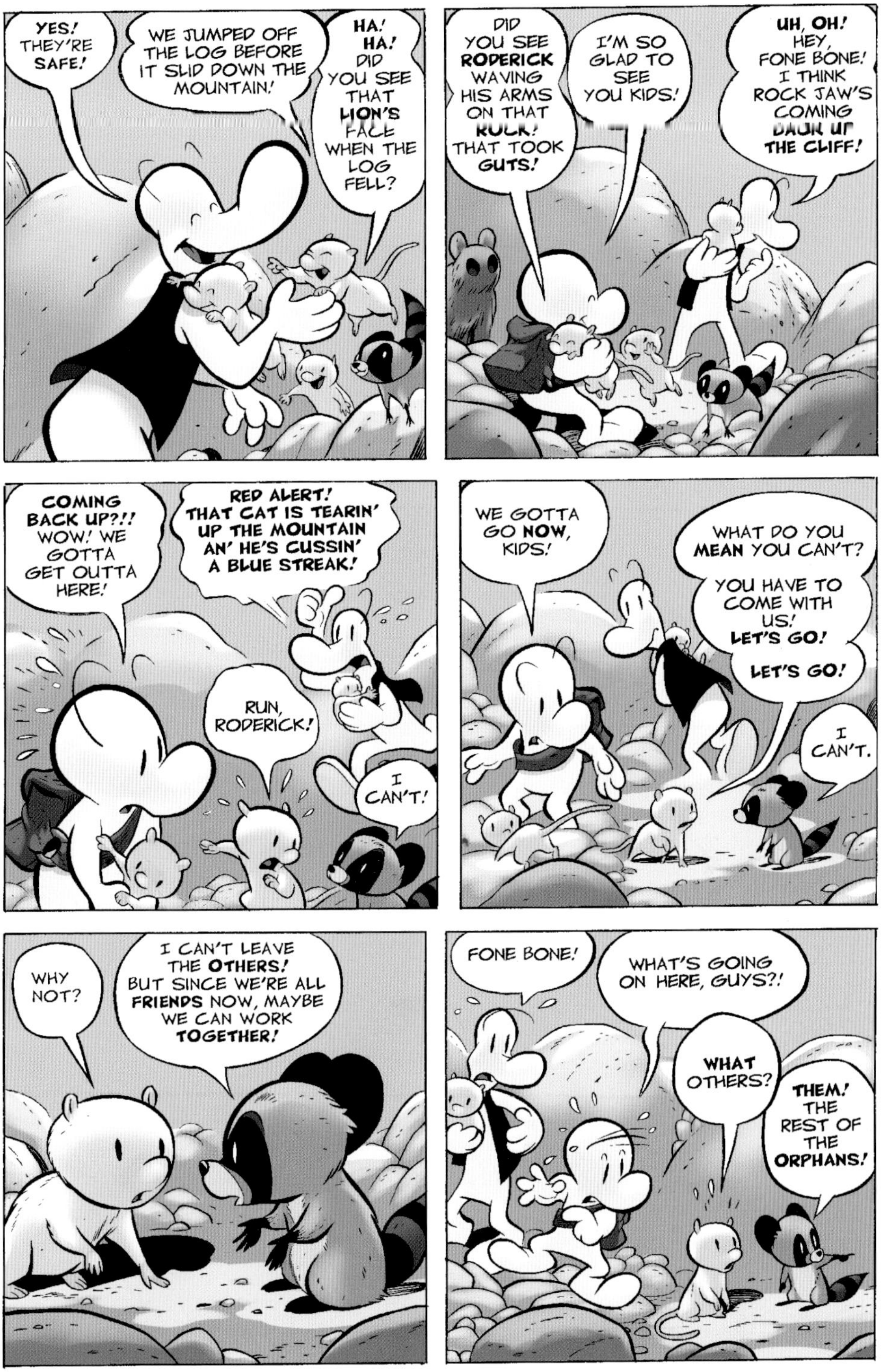
YES! THEY'RE SAFE!
WE JUMPED OFF THE LOG BEFORE IT SLID DOWN THE MOUNTAIN!
HA! HA! DID YOU SEE THAT LION'S FACE WHEN THE LOG FELL?
DID YOU SEE RODERICK WAVING HIS ARMS ON THAT ROCK! THAT TOOK GUTS!
I'M SO GLAD TO SEE YOU KIDS!
UH, OH! HEY, FONE BONE! I THINK ROCK JAW'S COMING BACK UP THE CLIFF!
COMING BACK UP?!! WOW! WE GOTTA GET OUTTA HERE!
RED ALERT! THAT CAT IS TEARIN' UP THE MOUNTAIN AN' HE'S CUSSIN' A BLUE STREAK!
RUN, RODERICK!
I CAN'T!
WE GOTTA GO NOW, KIDS!
WHAT DO YOU MEAN YOU CAN'T?
YOU HAVE TO COME WITH US! LET'S GO!
LET'S GO!
I CAN'T.
WHY NOT?
I CAN'T LEAVE THE OTHERS! BUT SINCE WE'RE ALL FRIENDS NOW, MAYBE WE CAN WORK TOGETHER!
FONE BONE!
WHAT'S GOING ON HERE, GUYS?!
WHAT OTHERS?
THEM! THE REST OF THE ORPHANS!

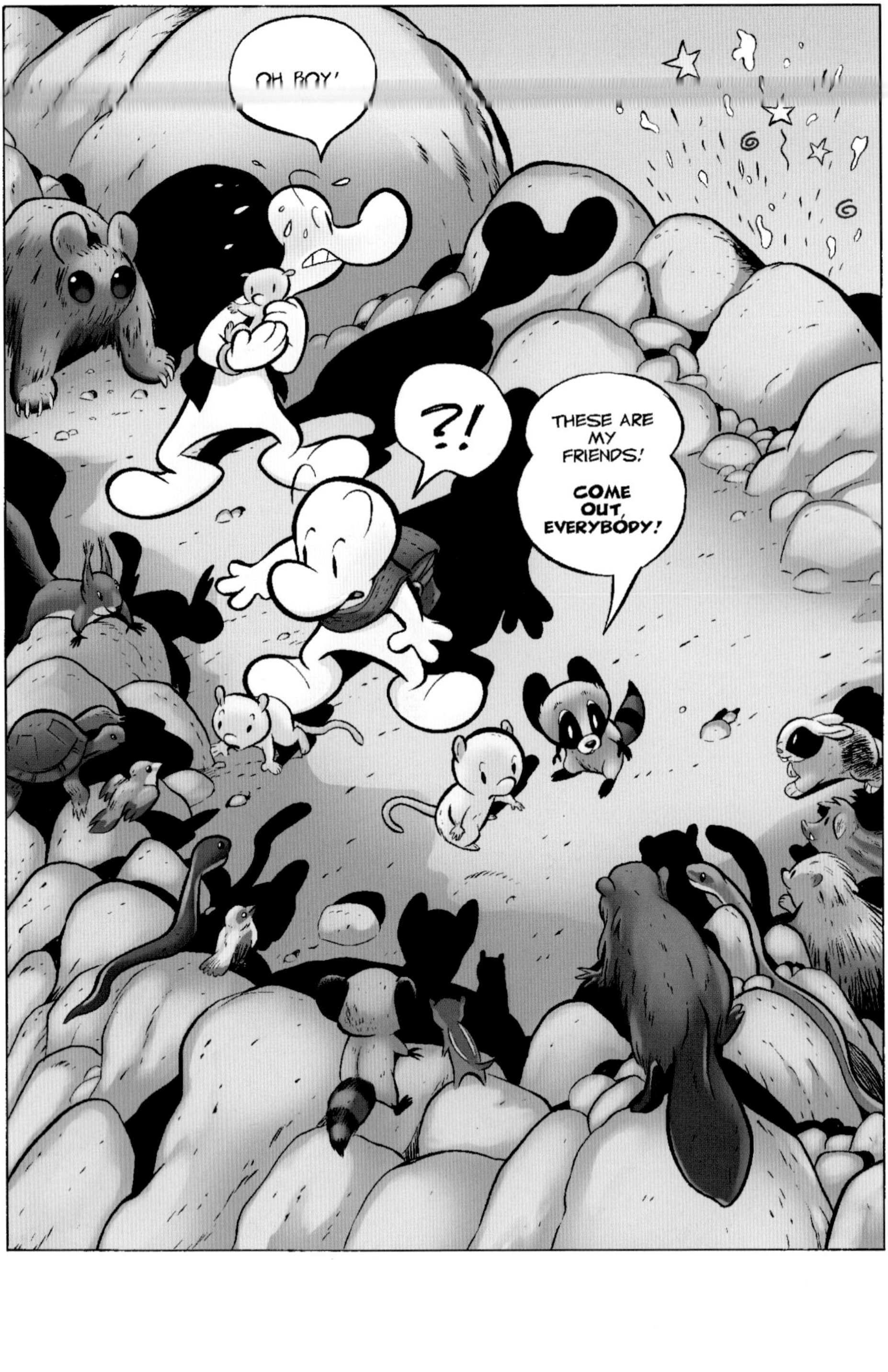
OH BOY!
?!
THESE ARE MY FRIENDS!
COME OUT, EVERYBODY!

CHAPTER THREE RAT CREATURE TEMPLE

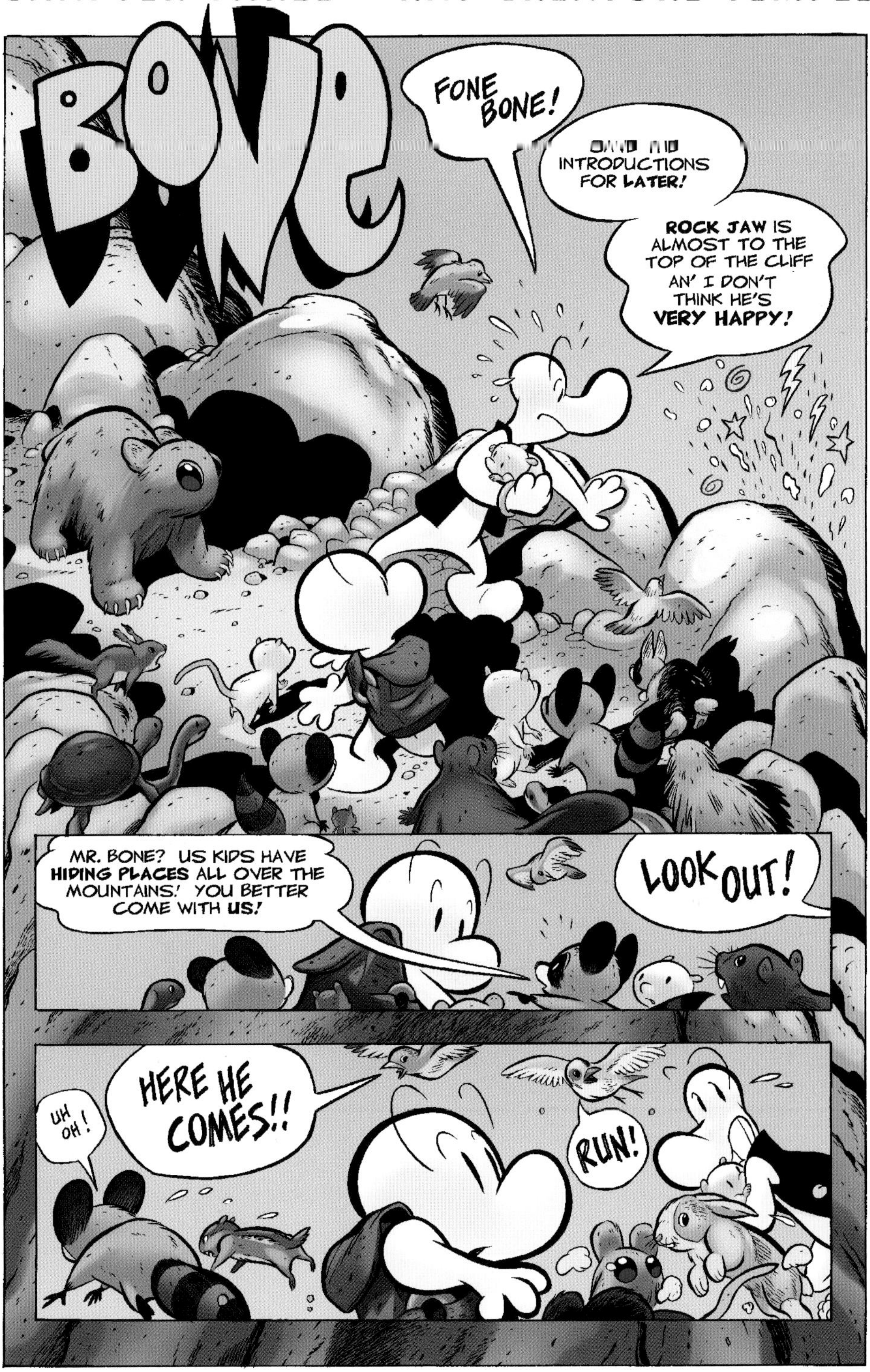
BONE
FONE BONE!
INTRODUCTIONS FOR LATER!
ROCK JAW IS ALMOST TO THE TOP OF THE CLIFF AN' I DON'T THINK HE'S VERY HAPPY!
MR. BONE? US KIDS HAVE HIDING PLACES ALL OVER THE MOUNTAINS! YOU BETTER COME WITH US!
LOOK OUT!
UH OH!
HERE HE COMES!!
RUN!

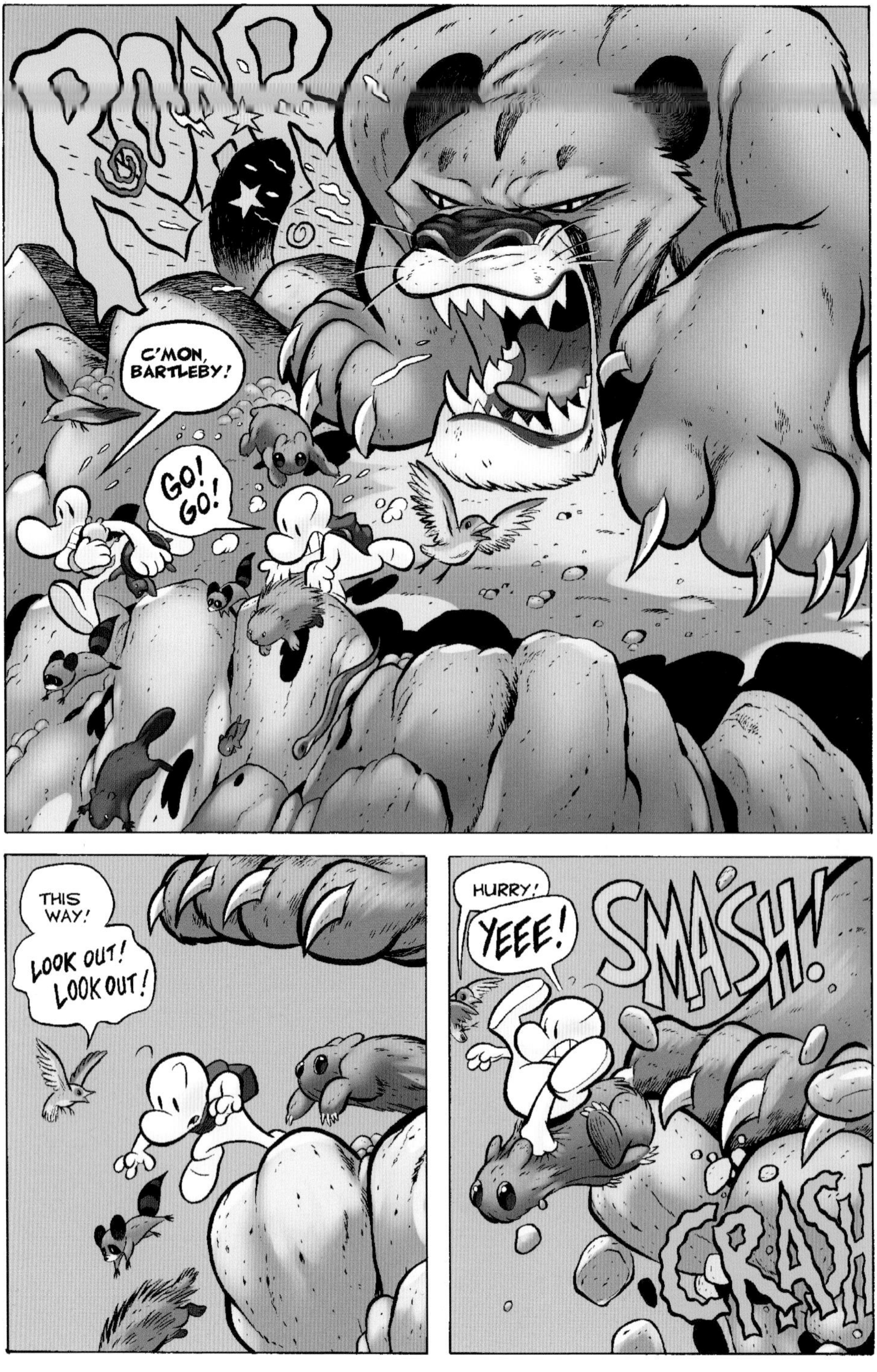
ROAR
C'MON, BARTLEBY!
GO! GO!
THIS WAY!
LOOK OUT! LOOK OUT!
HURRY!
YEEE!
SMASH!

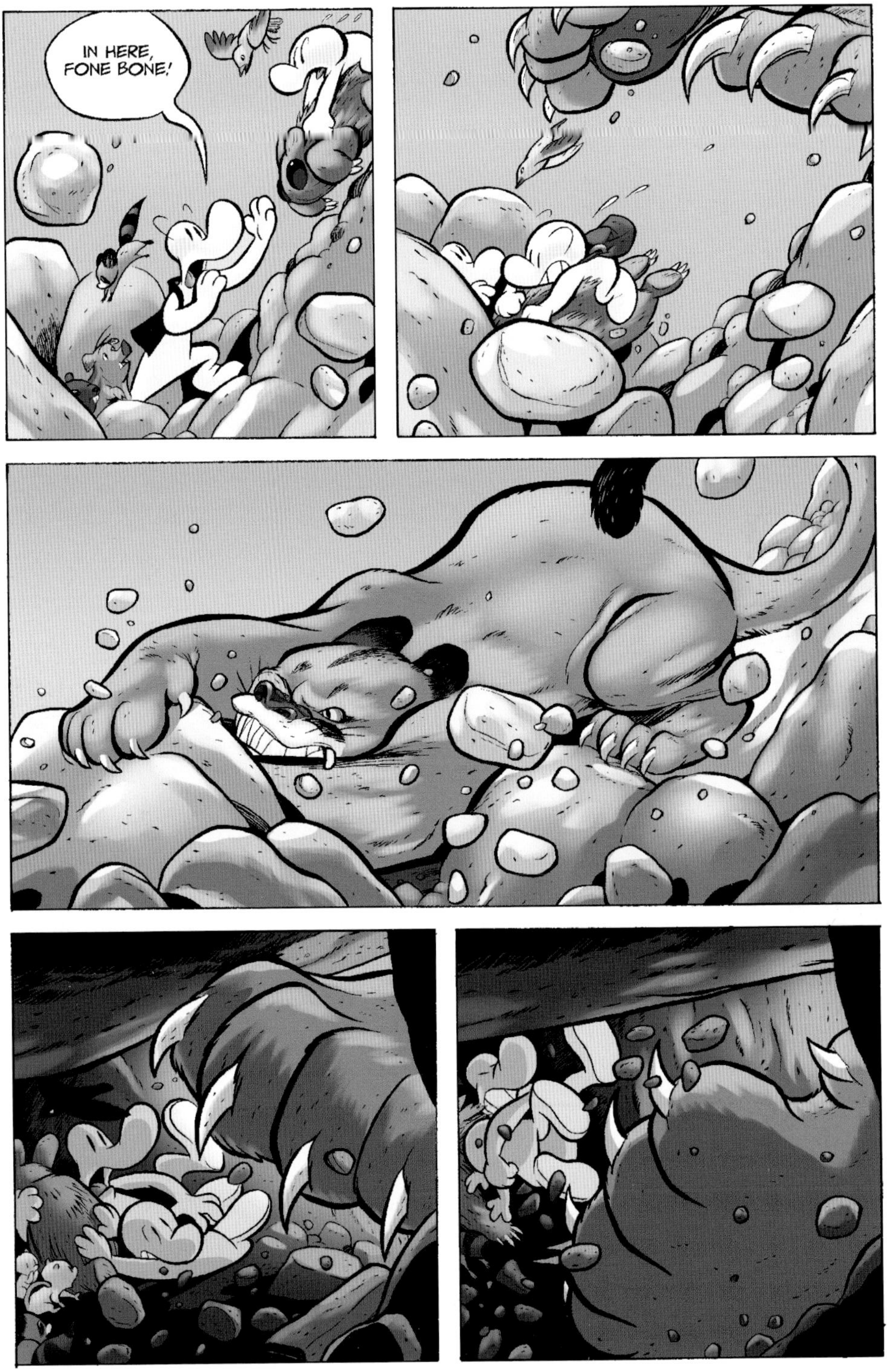
IN HERE, FONE BONE!

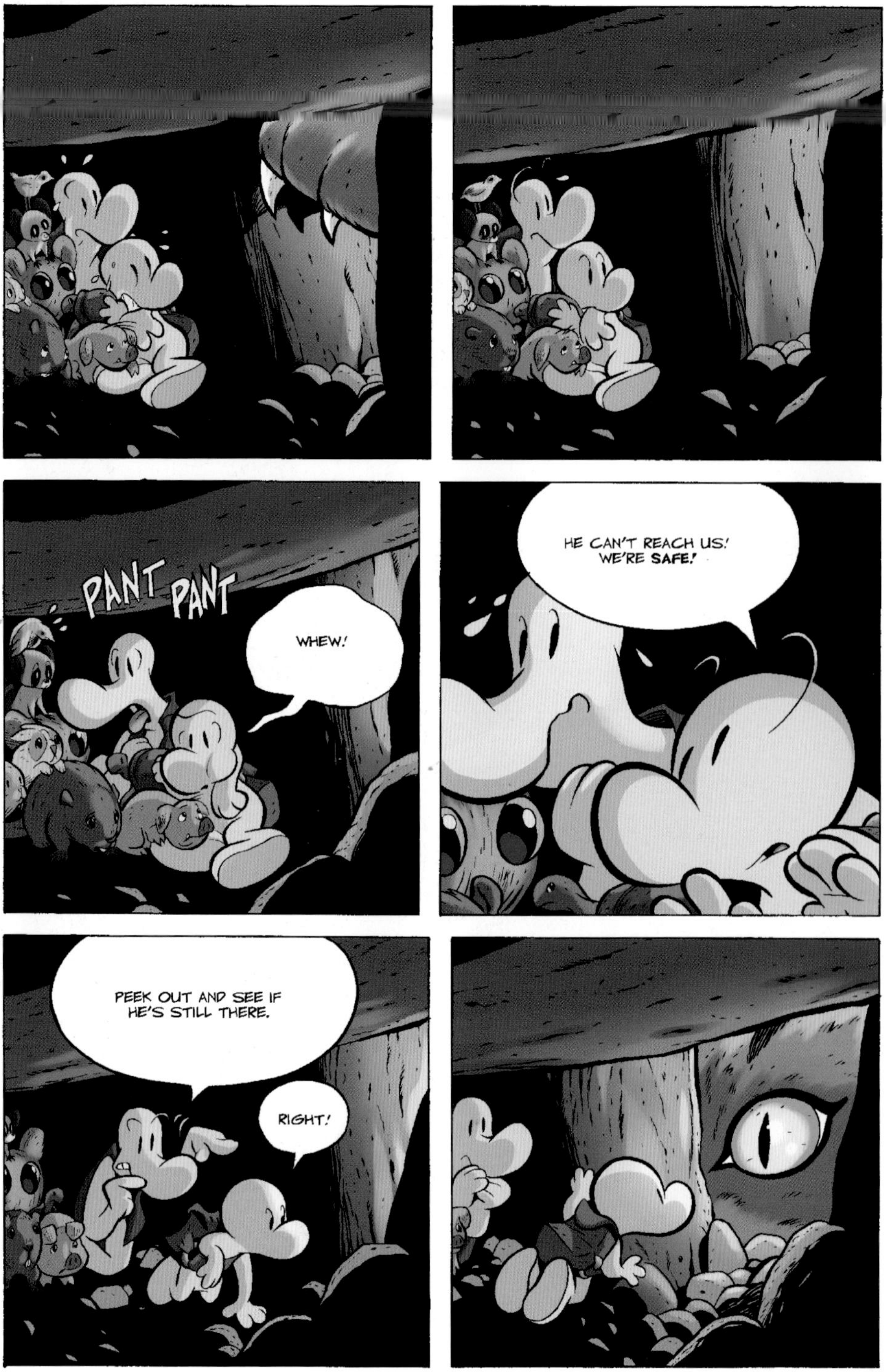
PANT PANT
WHEW!
HE CAN'T REACH US! WE'RE SAFE!
PEEK OUT AND SEE IF HE'S STILL THERE.
RIGHT!

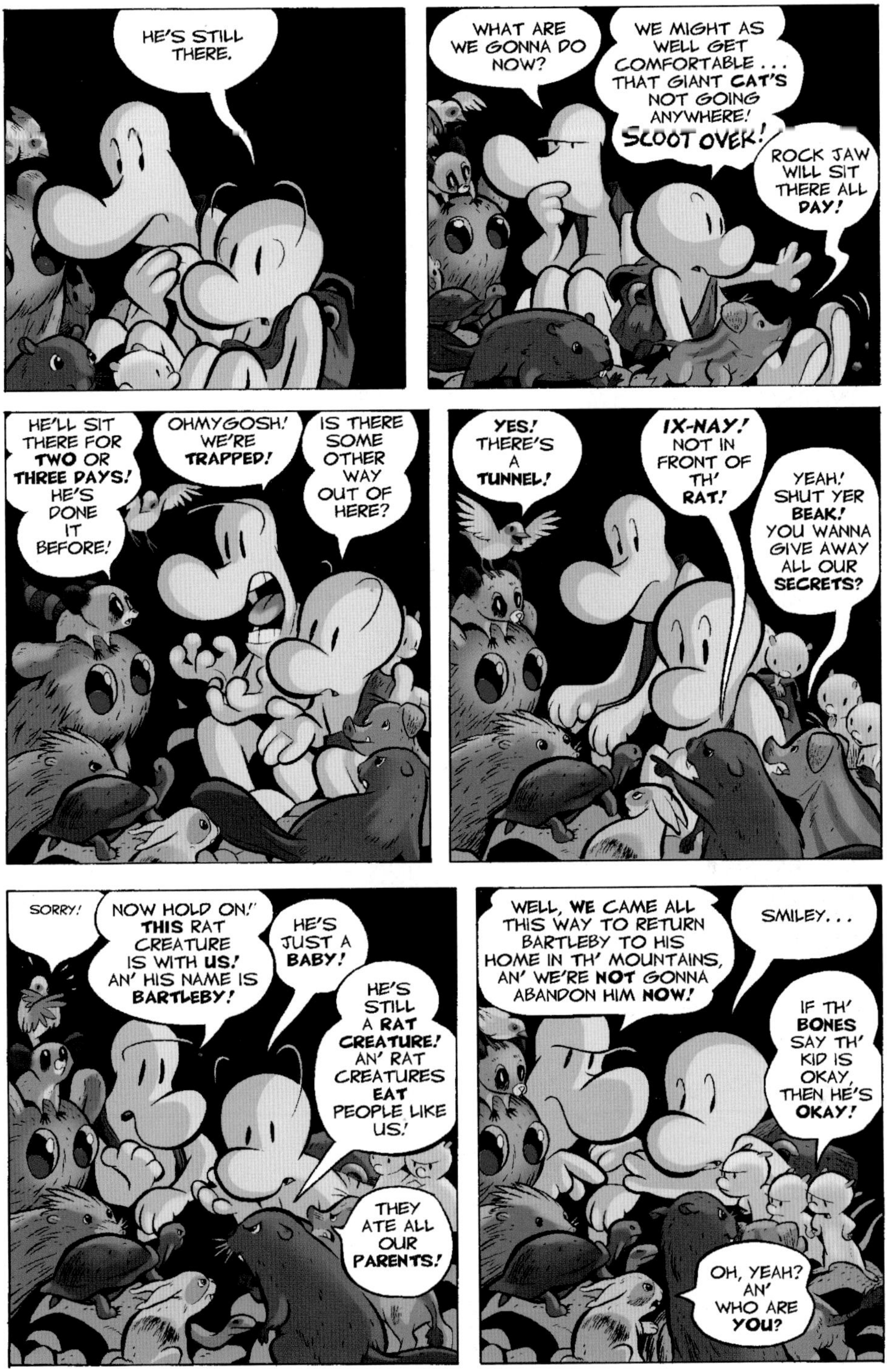
HE'S STILL THERE.
WHAT ARE WE GONNA DO NOW?
WE MIGHT AS WELL GET COMFORTABLE . . . THAT GIANT CAT'S NOT GOING ANYWHERE!
SCOOT OVER!
ROCK JAW WILL SIT THERE ALL DAY!
HE'LL SIT THERE FOR TWO OR THREE DAYS! HE'S DONE IT BEFORE!
OHMYGOSH! WE'RE TRAPPED!
IS THERE SOME OTHER WAY OUT OF HERE?
YES! THERE'S A TUNNEL!
IX-NAY! NOT IN FRONT OF TH' RAT!
YEAH! SHUT YER BEAK! YOU WANNA GIVE AWAY ALL OUR SECRETS?
SORRY!
NOW HOLD ON! THIS RAT CREATURE IS WITH US! AN' HIS NAME IS BARTLEBY!
HE'S JUST A BABY!
HE'S STILL A RAT CREATURE! AN' RAT CREATURES EAT PEOPLE LIKE US!
THEY ATE ALL OUR PARENTS!
WELL, WE CAME ALL THIS WAY TO RETURN BARTLEBY TO HIS HOME IN TH' MOUNTAINS, AN' WE'RE NOT GONNA ABANDON HIM NOW!
SMILEY. . .
IF TH' BONES SAY TH' KID IS OKAY, THEN HE'S OKAY!
OH, YEAH? AN' WHO ARE YOU?

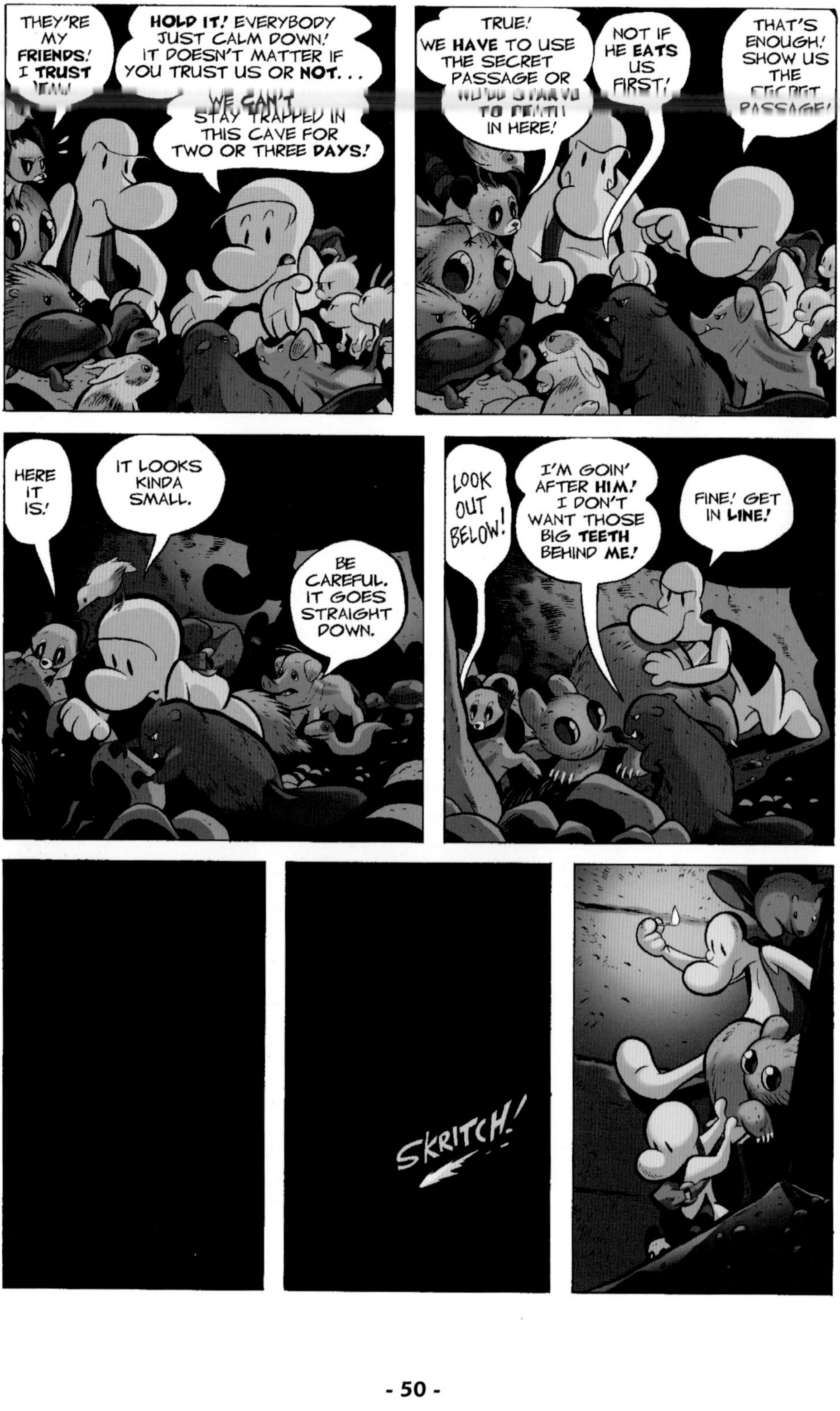
THEY'RE MY FRIENDS! I TRUST
HOLD IT! EVERYBODY JUST CALM DOWN! IT DOESN'T MATTER IF YOU TRUST US OR NOT...
WE CAN'T STAY TRAPPED IN THIS CAVE FOR TWO OR THREE DAYS!
TRUE! WE HAVE TO USE THE SECRET PASSAGE OR
IN HERE!
NOT IF HE EATS US FIRST!
THAT'S ENOUGH! SHOW US THE
PASSAGE!
HERE IT IS!
IT LOOKS KINDA SMALL.
BE CAREFUL. IT GOES STRAIGHT DOWN.
LOOK OUT BELOW!
I'M GOIN' AFTER HIM! I DON'T WANT THOSE BIG TEETH BEHIND ME!
FINE! GET IN LINE!
SKRITCH!

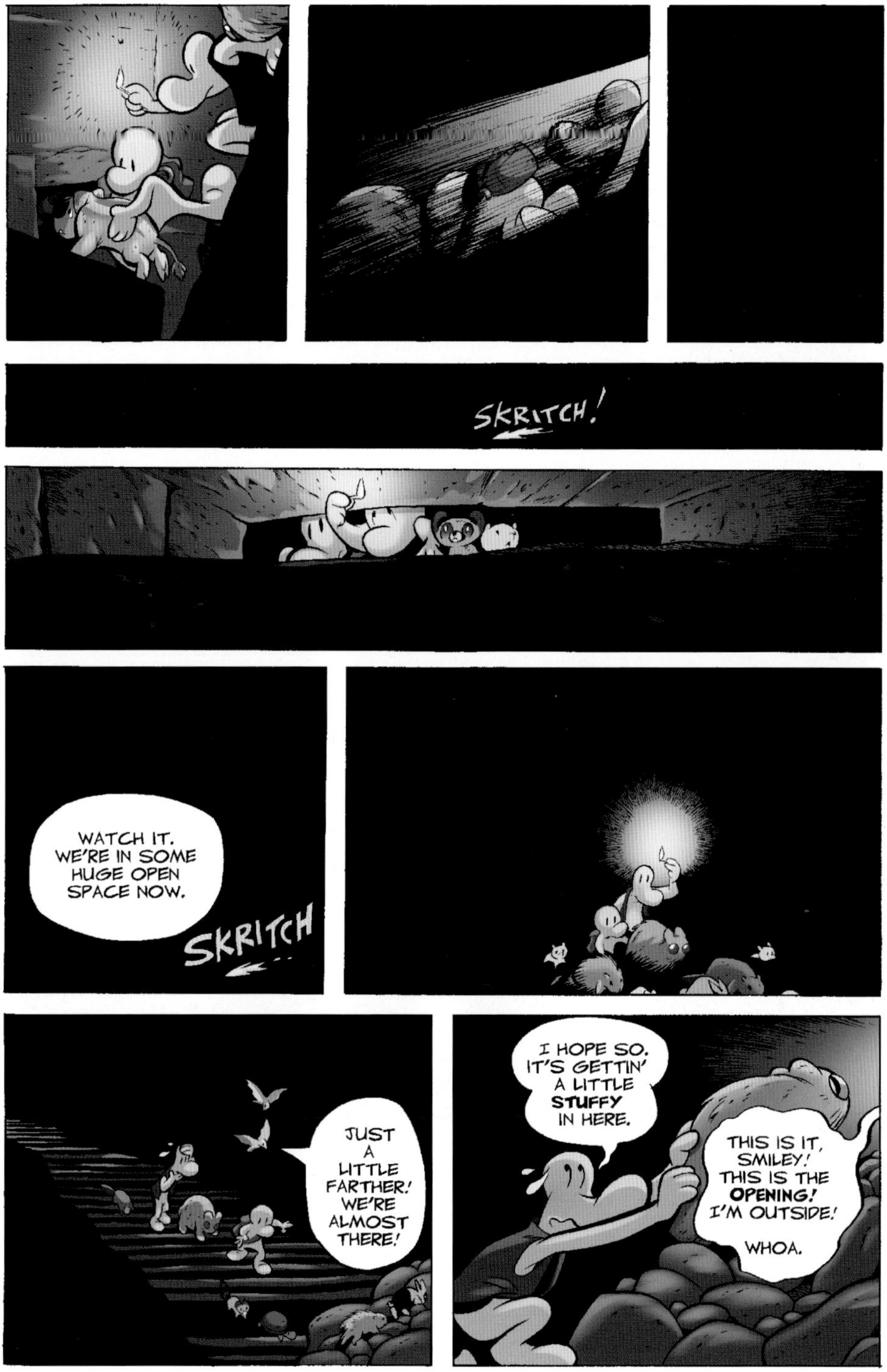
SKRITCH!
WATCH IT. WE'RE IN SOME HUGE OPEN SPACE NOW.
SKRITCH
JUST A LITTLE FARTHER! WE'RE ALMOST THERE!
I HOPE SO. IT'S GETTIN' A LITTLE STUFFY IN HERE.
THIS IS IT, SMILEY! THIS IS THE OPENING! I'M OUTSIDE!
WHOA.

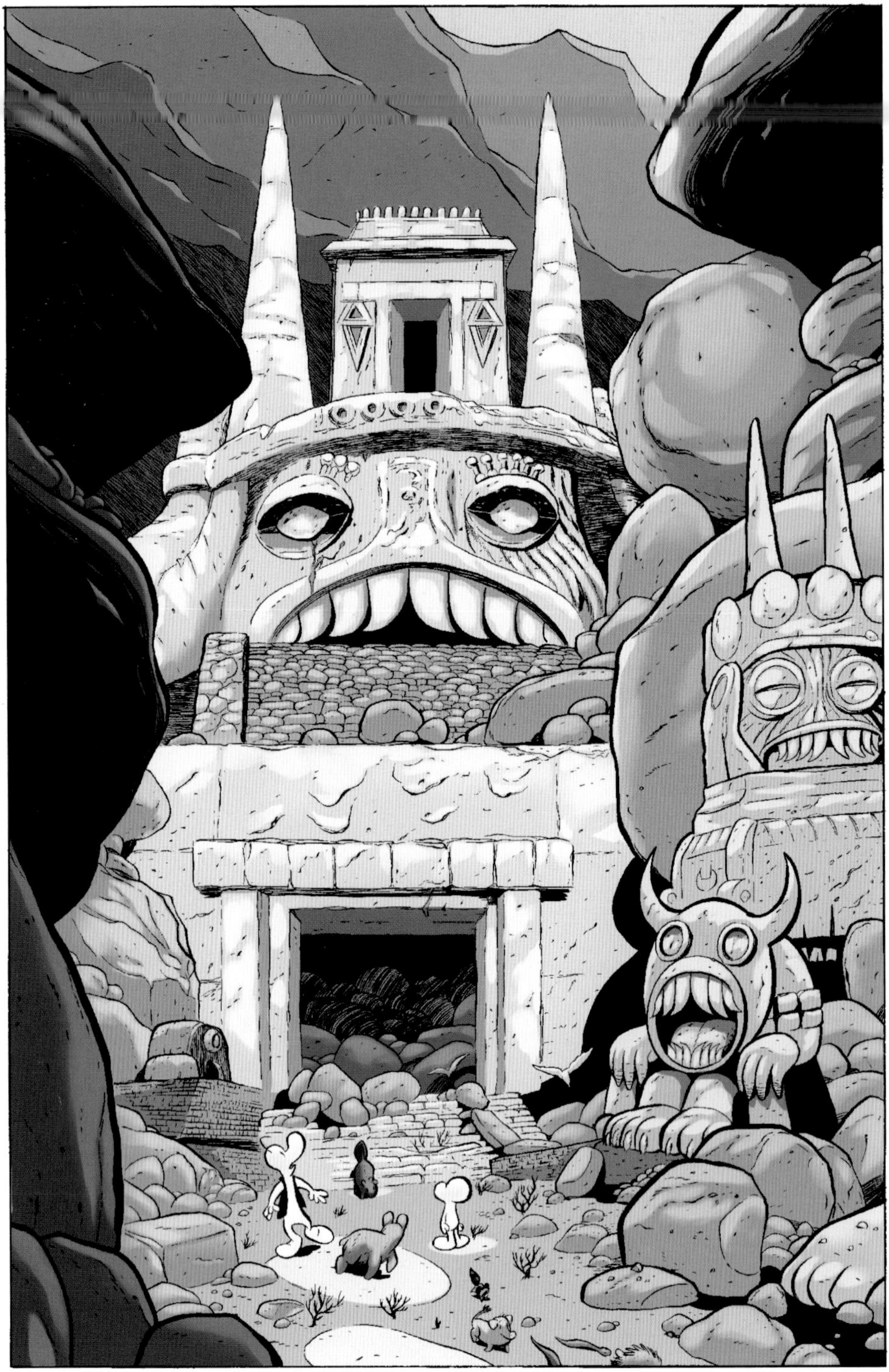

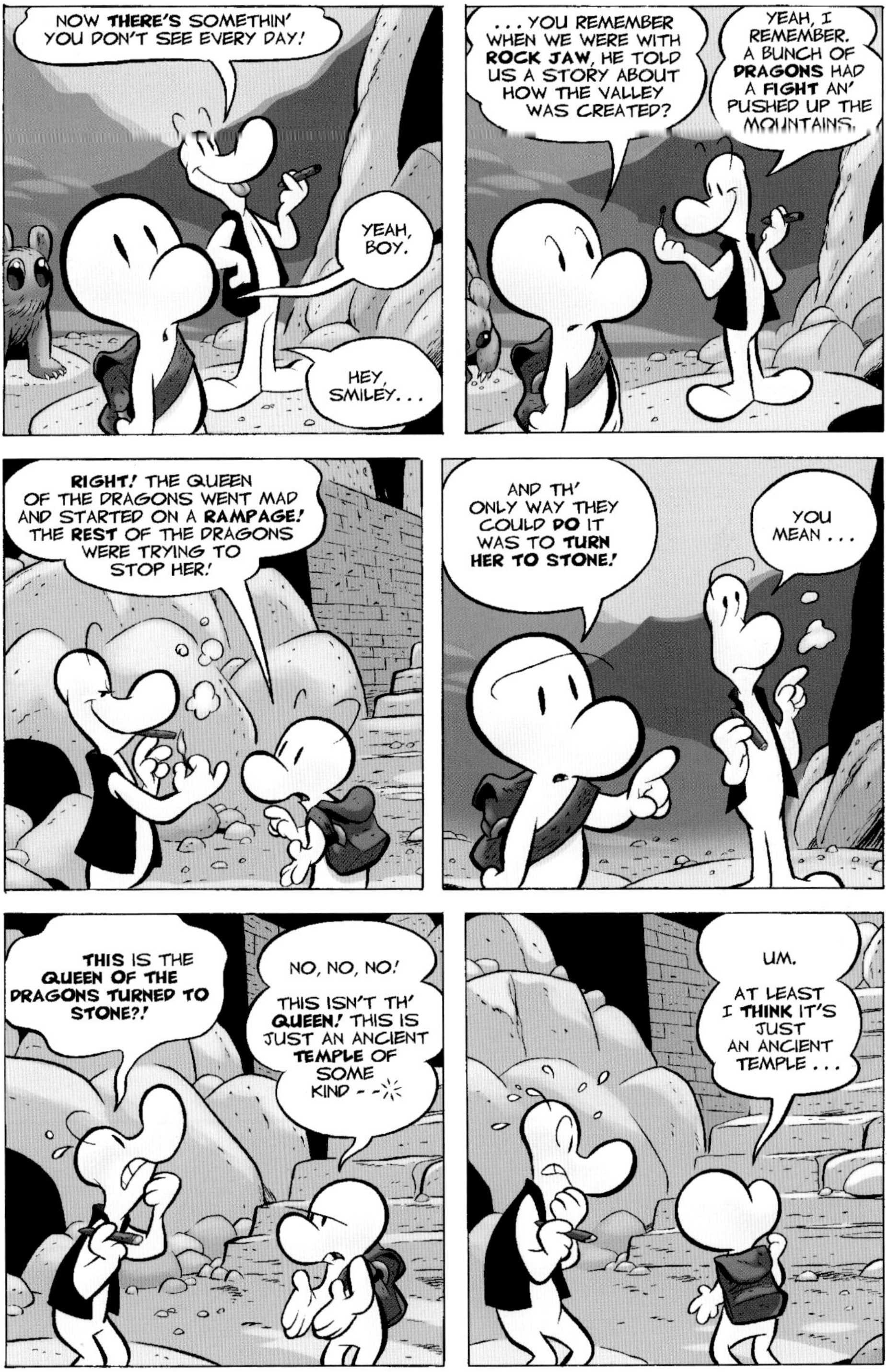
NOW THERE'S SOMETHIN' YOU DON'T SEE EVERY DAY!
YEAH, BOY.
HEY, SMILEY . . .
. . . YOU REMEMBER WHEN WE WERE WITH ROCK JAW, HE TOLD US A STORY ABOUT HOW THE VALLEY WAS CREATED?
YEAH, I REMEMBER. A BUNCH OF DRAGONS HAD A FIGHT AN' PUSHED UP THE MOUNTAINS.
RIGHT! THE QUEEN OF THE DRAGONS WENT MAD AND STARTED ON A RAMPAGE! THE REST OF THE DRAGONS WERE TRYING TO STOP HER!
AND TH' ONLY WAY THEY COULD DO IT WAS TO TURN HER TO STONE!
YOU MEAN . . .
THIS IS THE QUEEN OF THE DRAGONS TURNED TO STONE?!
NO, NO, NO! THIS ISN'T TH' QUEEN! THIS IS JUST AN ANCIENT TEMPLE OF SOME KIND - -
UM.
AT LEAST I THINK IT'S JUST AN ANCIENT TEMPLE . . .

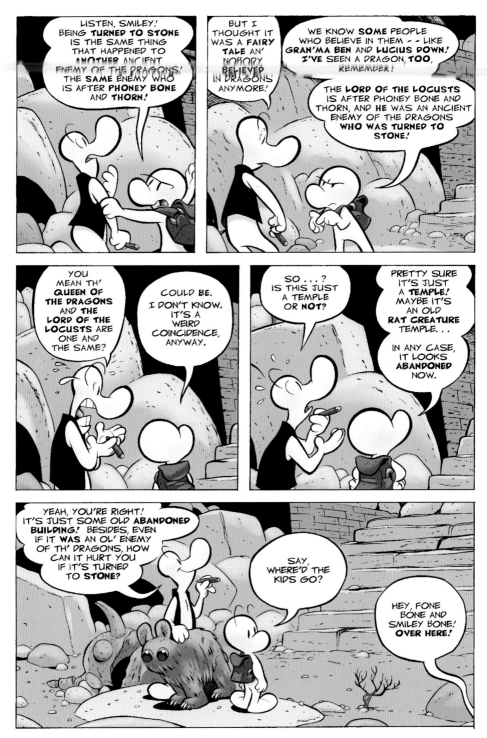

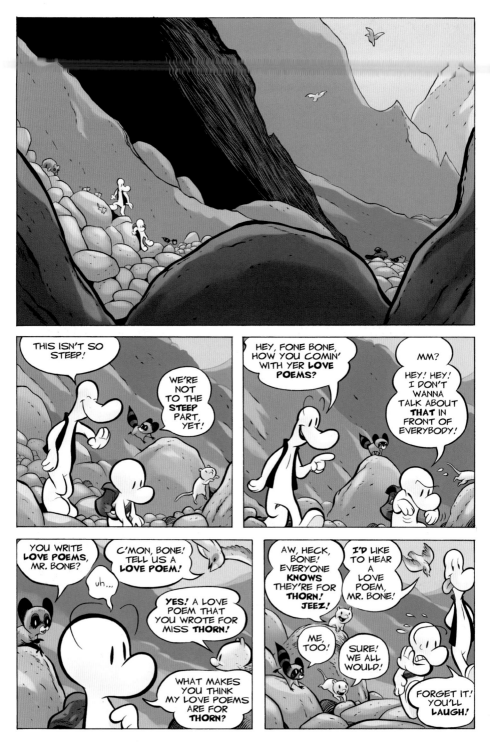

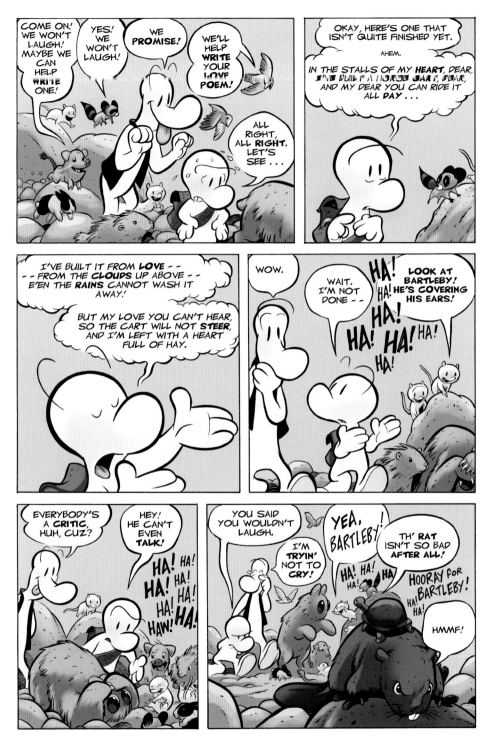

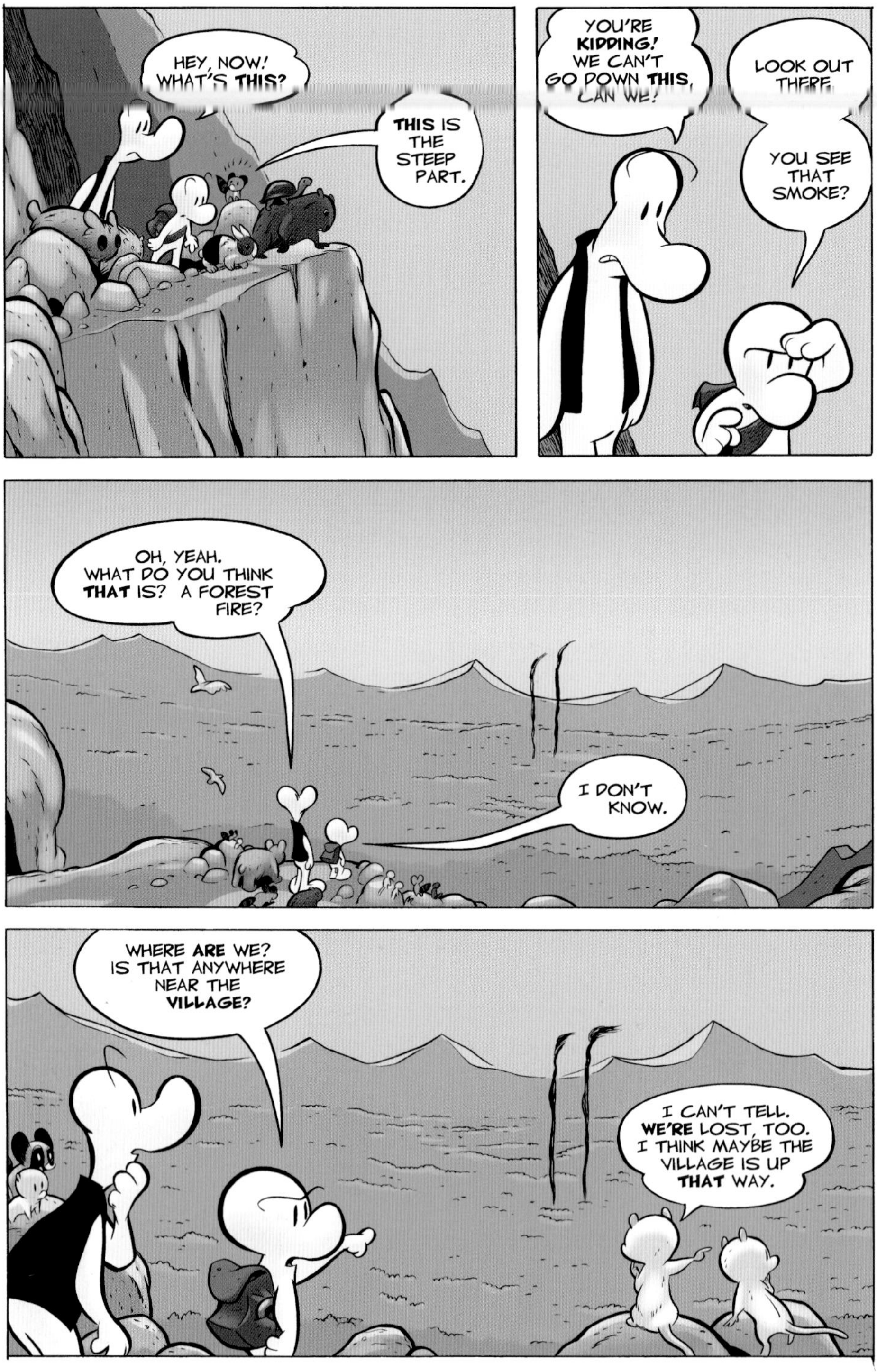
HEY, NOW! WHAT'S THIS?
THIS IS THE STEEP PART.
YOU'RE KIDDING! WE CAN'T GO DOWN THIS, CAN WE?
LOOK OUT THERE.
YOU SEE THAT SMOKE?
OH, YEAH. WHAT DO YOU THINK THAT IS? A FOREST FIRE?
I DON'T KNOW.
WHERE ARE WE? IS THAT ANYWHERE NEAR THE VILLAGE?
I CAN'T TELL. WE'RE LOST, TOO. I THINK MAYBE THE VILLAGE IS UP THAT WAY.

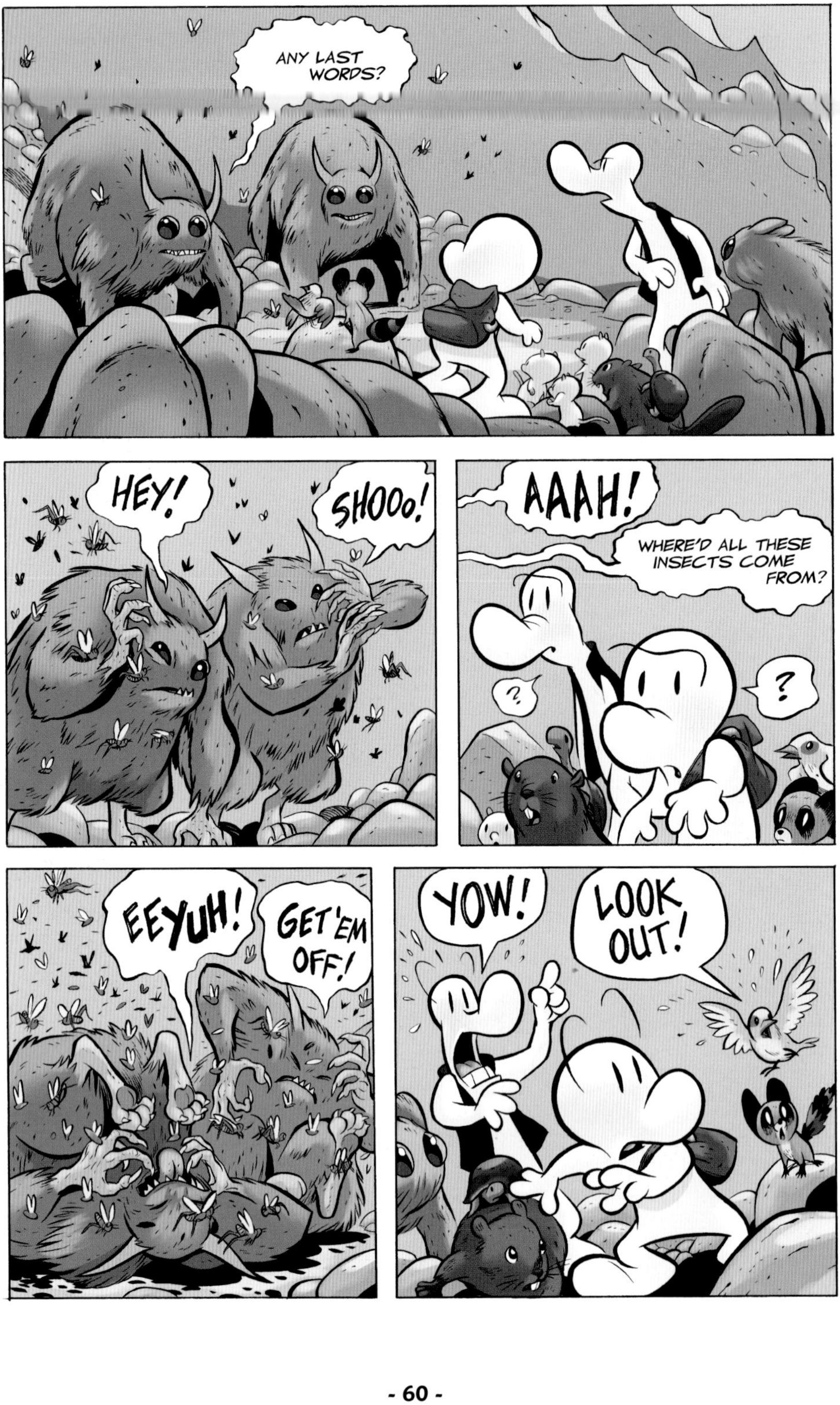
ANY LAST WORDS?
HEY!
SHOOo!
AAAH!
WHERE'D ALL THESE INSECTS COME FROM?
?
?
EEYUH!
GET 'EM OFF!
YOW!
LOOK OUT!

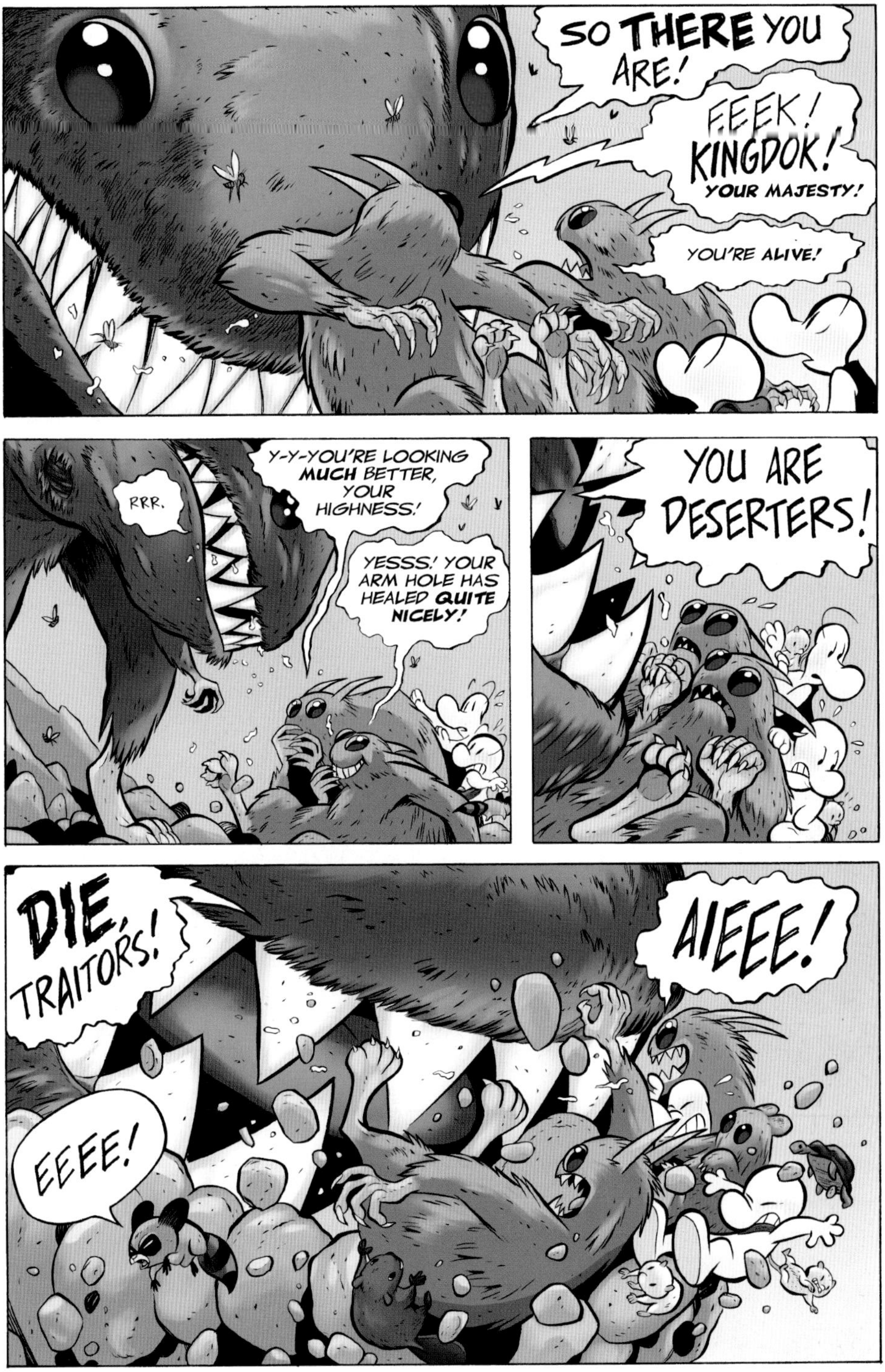
SO THERE YOU ARE!
EEEK! KINGDOK! YOUR MAJESTY!
YOU'RE ALIVE!
RRR.
Y-Y-YOU'RE LOOKING MUCH BETTER, YOUR HIGHNESS!
YESSS! YOUR ARM HOLE HAS HEALED QUITE NICELY!
YOU ARE DESERTERS!
DIE, TRAITORS!
AIEEE!
EEEE!

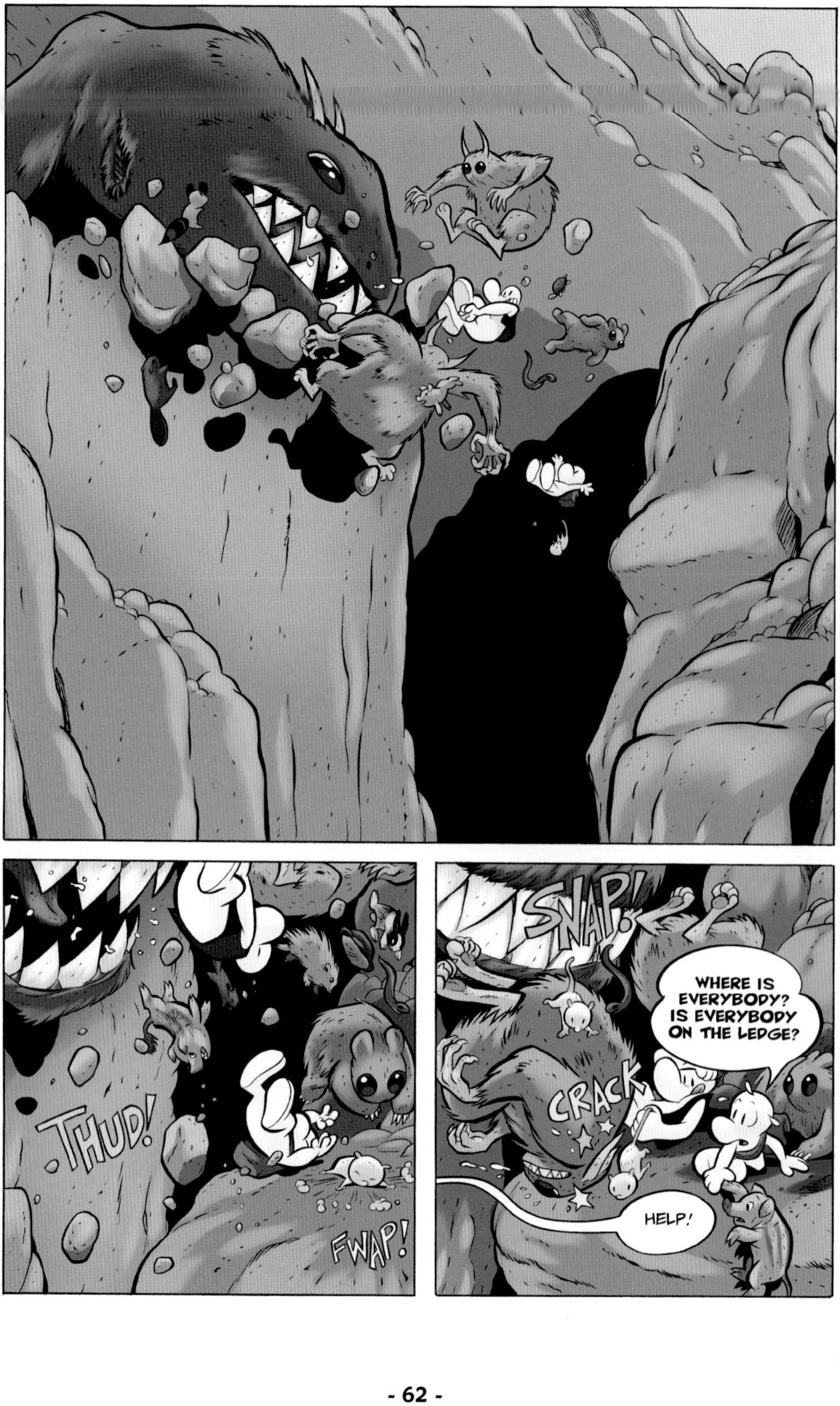
THUD!
FWAP!
SNAP!
WHERE IS EVERYBODY? IS EVERYBODY ON THE LEDGE?
CRACK
HELP!

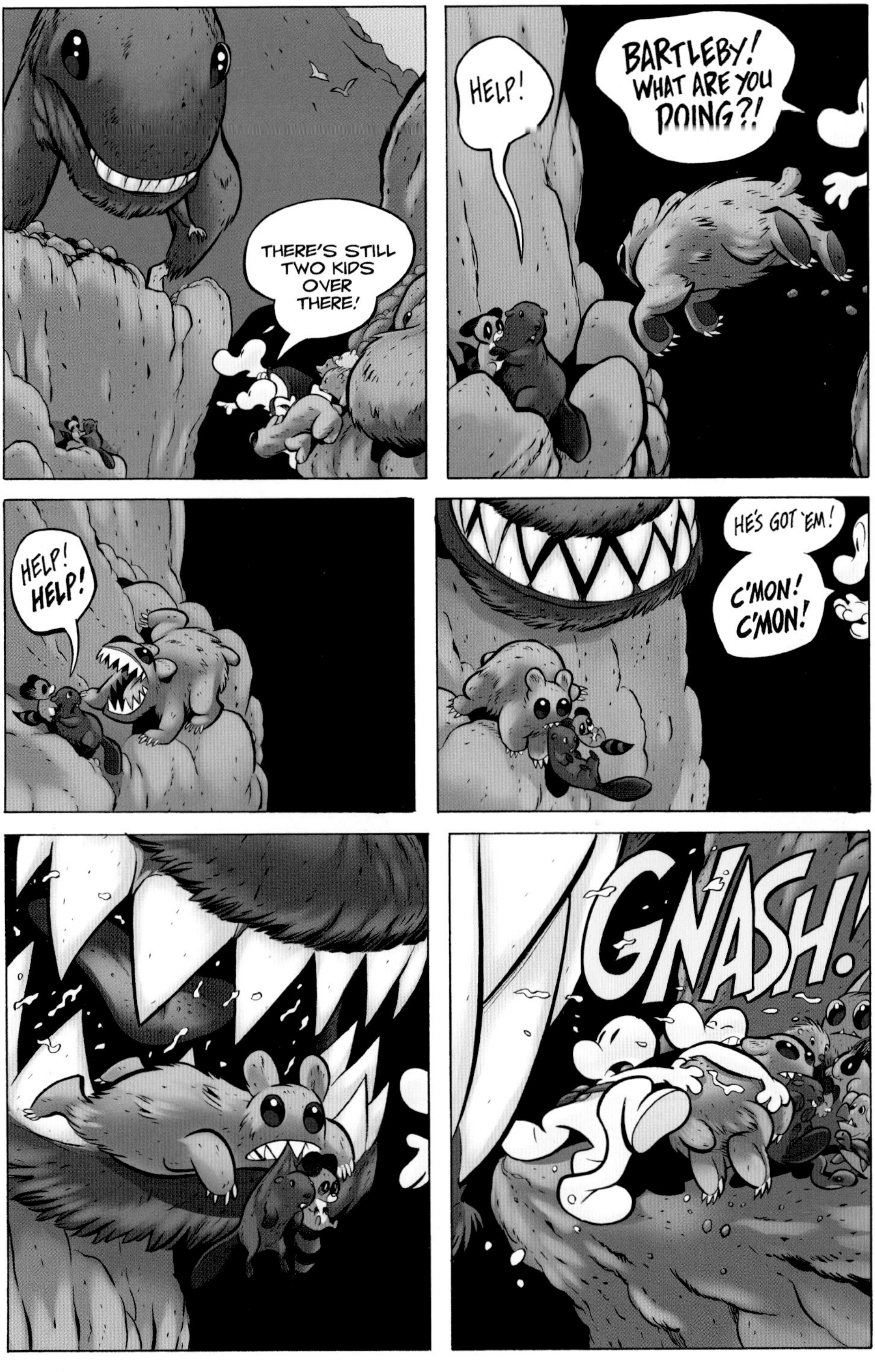
THERE'S STILL TWO KIDS OVER THERE!
HELP!
BARTLEBY! WHAT ARE YOU DOING?!
HELP! HELP!
HE'S GOT 'EM!
C'MON! C'MON!
GNASH!

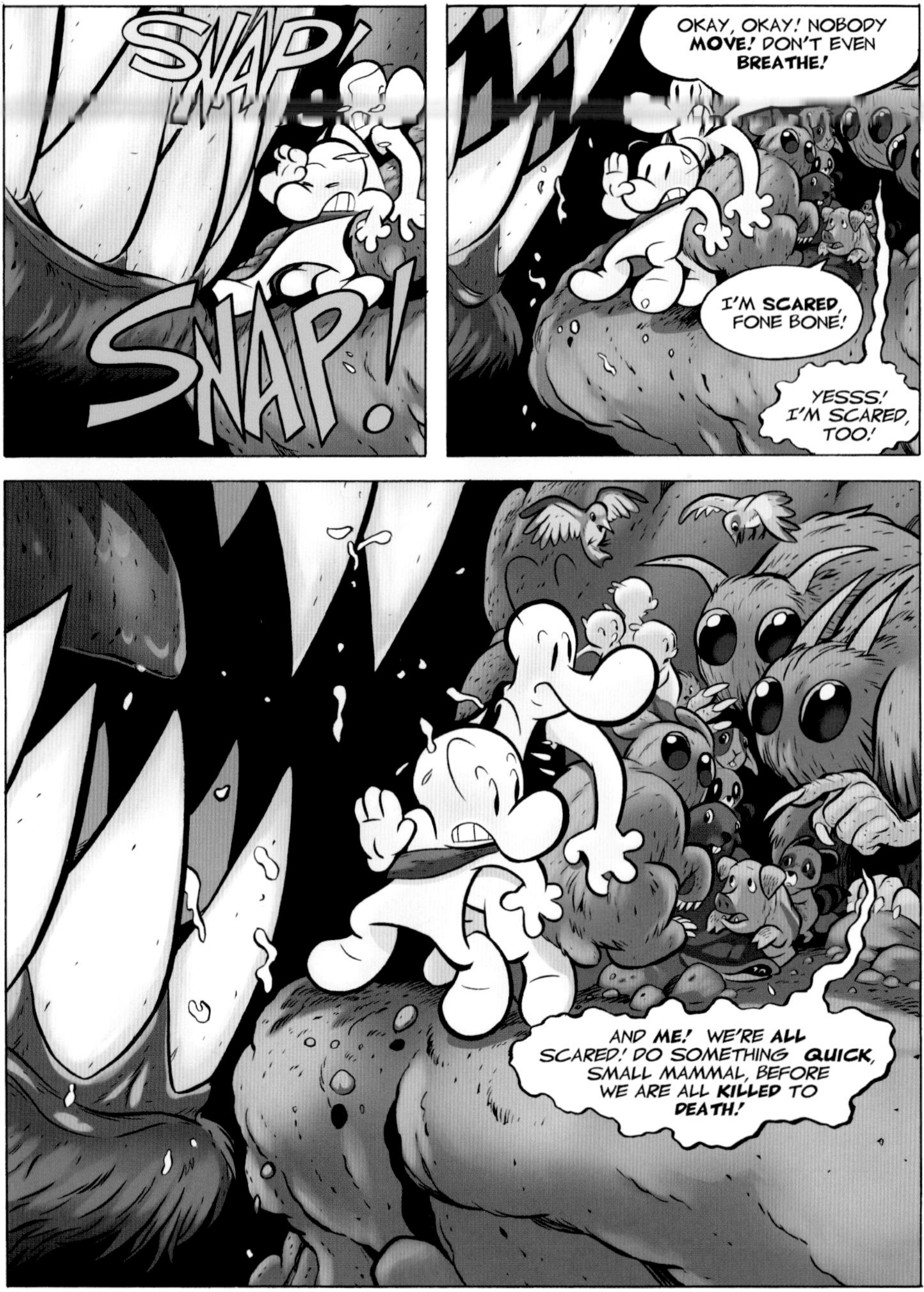
SNAP!
SNAP!
OKAY, OKAY! NOBODY MOVE! DON'T EVEN BREATHE!
I'M SCARED, FONE BONE!
YESSS! I'M SCARED, TOO!
AND ME! WE'RE ALL SCARED! DO SOMETHING QUICK, SMALL MAMMAL, BEFORE WE ARE ALL KILLED TO DEATH!

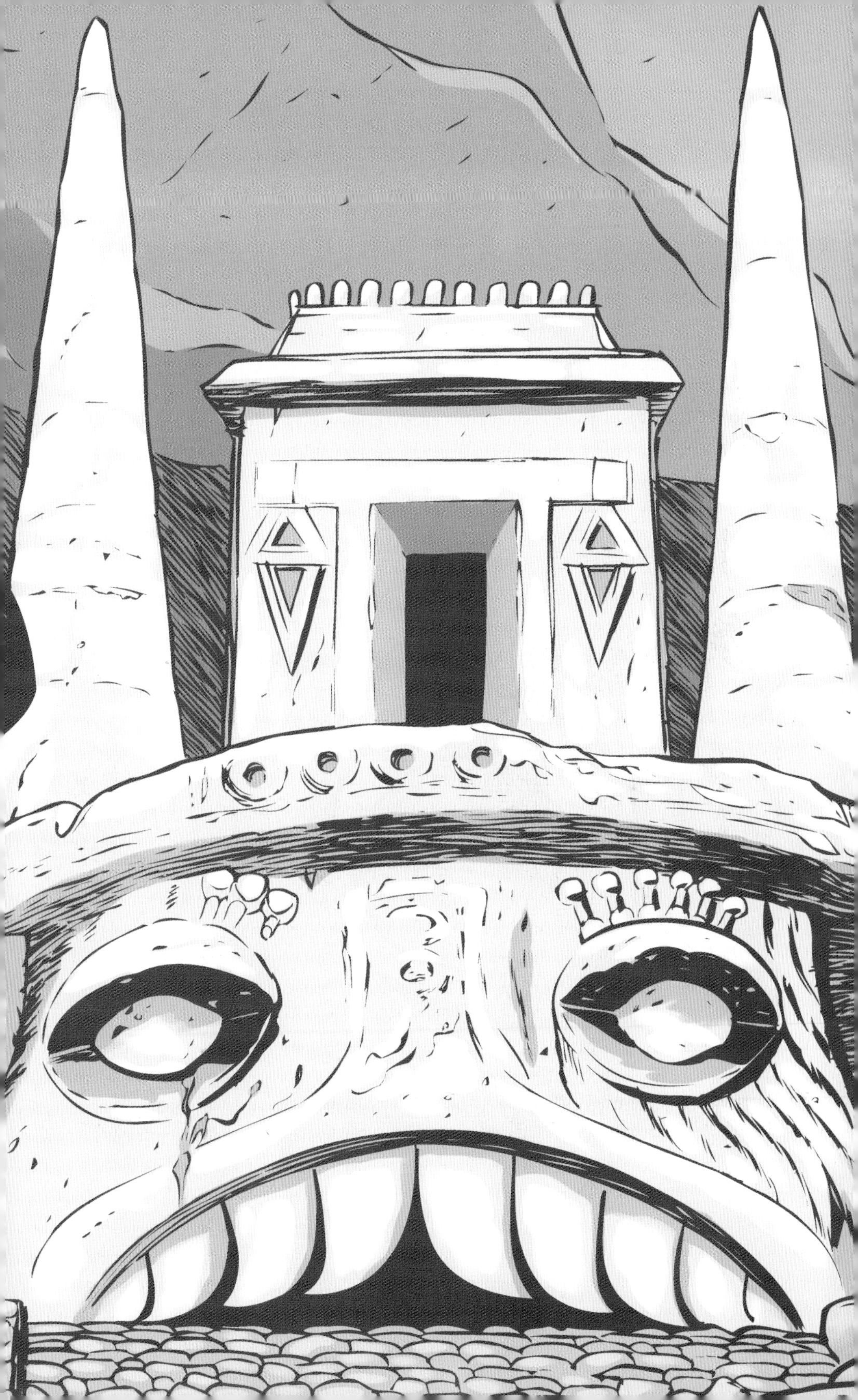

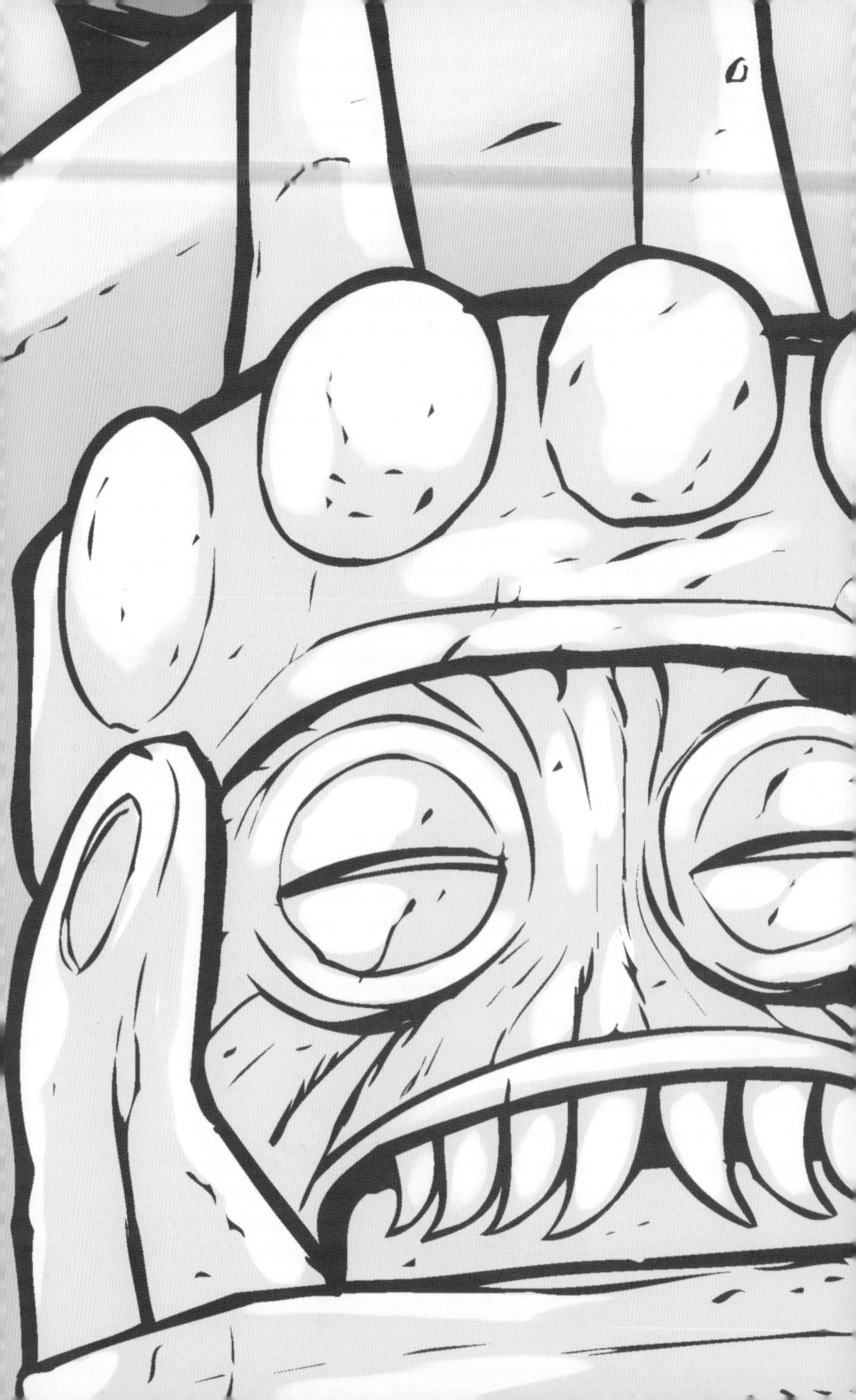

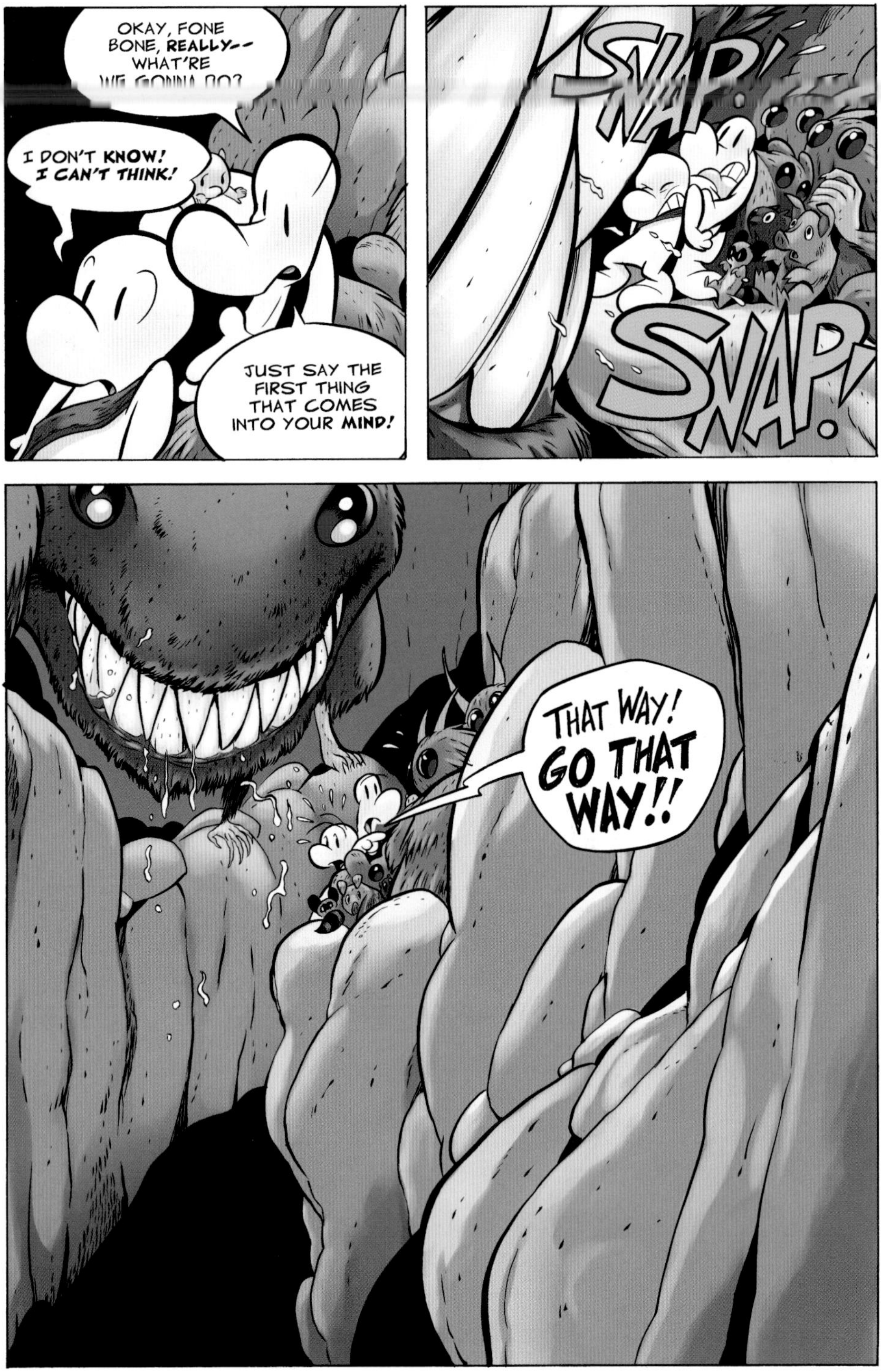
OKAY, FONE BONE, REALLY-- WHAT'RE WE GONNA DO?
I DON'T KNOW! I CAN'T THINK!
JUST SAY THE FIRST THING THAT COMES INTO YOUR MIND!
SNAP!
SNAP!
THAT WAY! GO THAT WAY!!

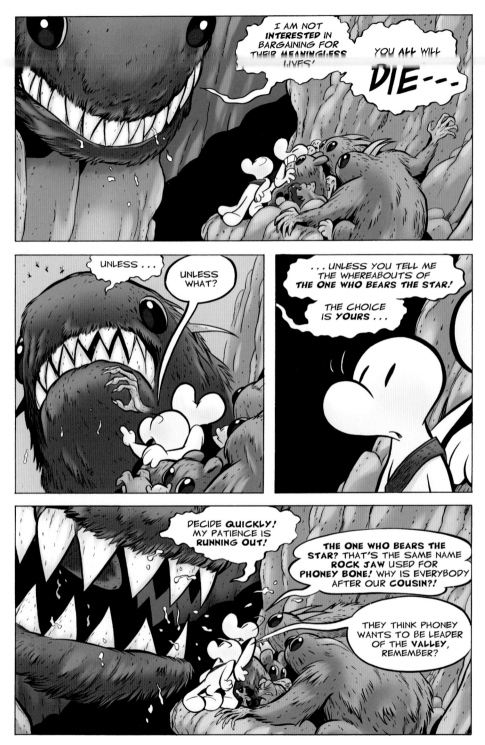

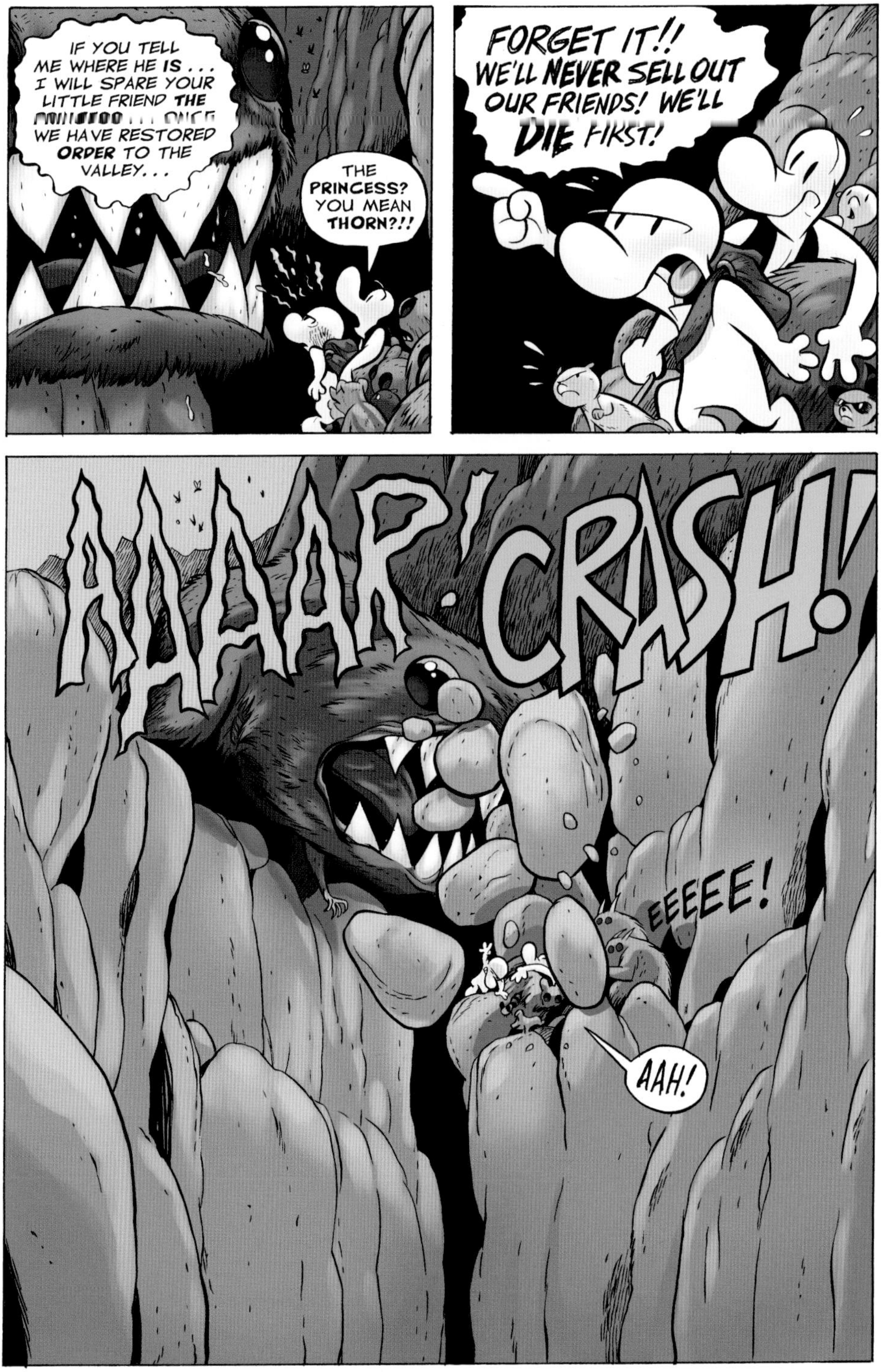
IF YOU TELL ME WHERE HE **IS** . . . I WILL SPARE YOUR LITTLE FRIEND **THE** ONCE WE HAVE RESTORED **ORDER** TO THE VALLEY . . .
THE **PRINCESS?** YOU MEAN **THORN?!!**
FORGET IT!! WE'LL **NEVER** SELL OUT OUR FRIENDS! WE'LL **DIE** FIRST!
AAAAR!
CRASH!
EEEEE!
AAH!

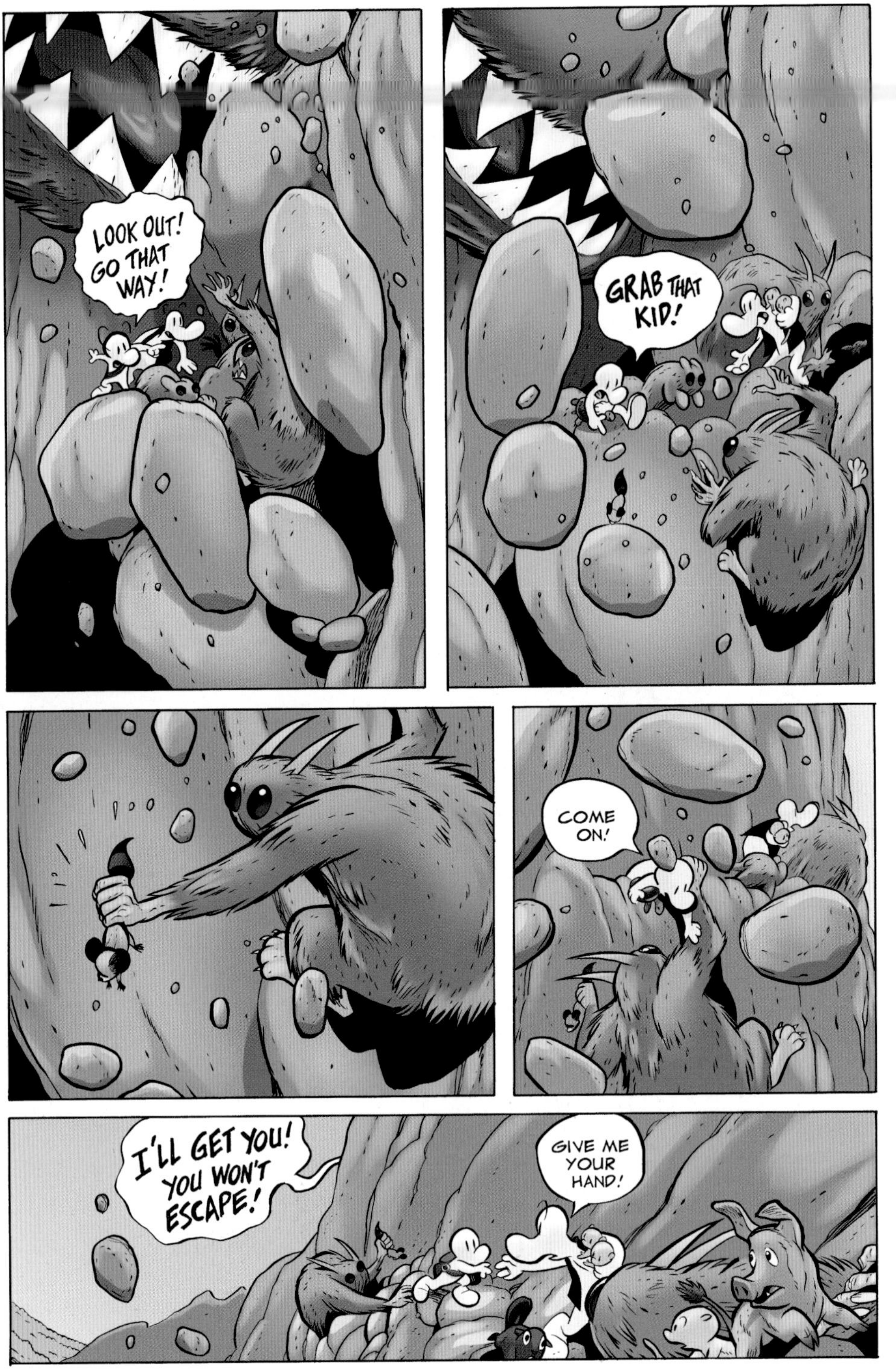
LOOK OUT! GO THAT WAY!
GRAB THAT KID!
COME ON!
I'LL GET YOU! YOU WON'T ESCAPE!
GIVE ME YOUR HAND!

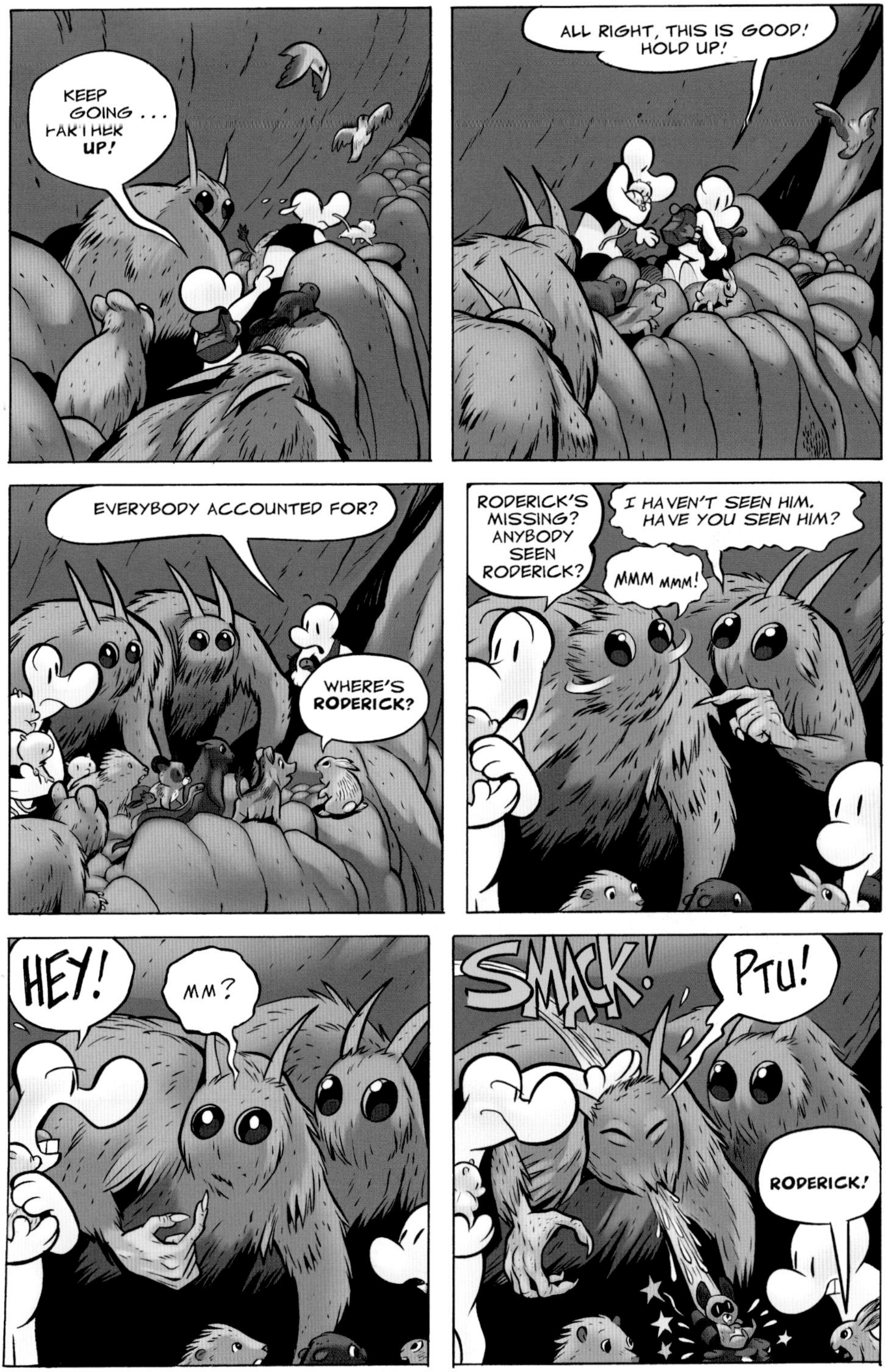
KEEP GOING . . . FARTHER UP!
ALL RIGHT, THIS IS GOOD! HOLD UP!
EVERYBODY ACCOUNTED FOR?
WHERE'S RODERICK?
RODERICK'S MISSING? ANYBODY SEEN RODERICK?
I HAVEN'T SEEN HIM. HAVE YOU SEEN HIM?
MMM MMM!
HEY!
MM?
SMACK!
PTU!
RODERICK!

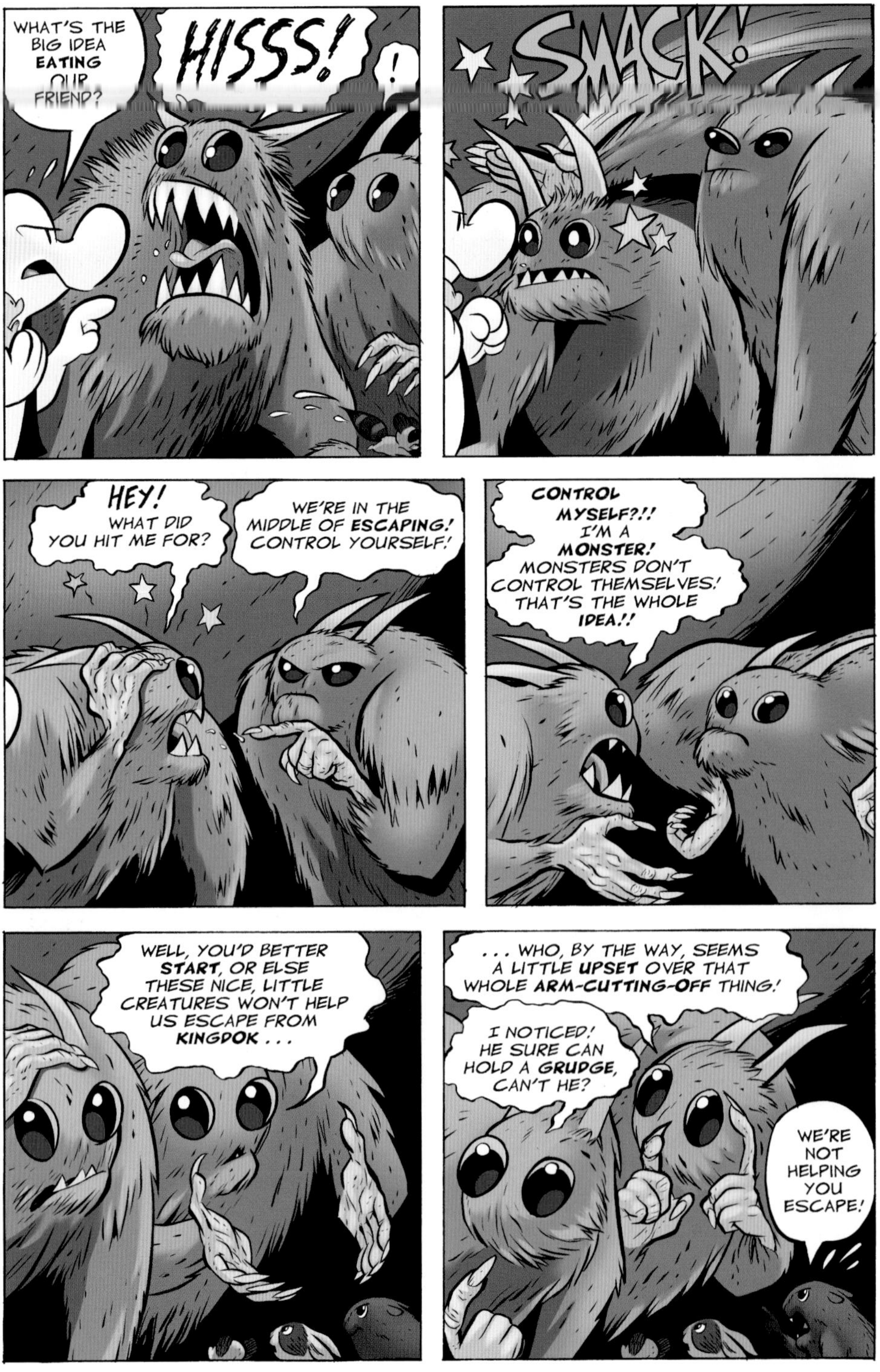
WHAT'S THE BIG IDEA EATING OUR FRIEND?
HISSS!
!
SMACK!
HEY! WHAT DID YOU HIT ME FOR?
WE'RE IN THE MIDDLE OF ESCAPING! CONTROL YOURSELF!
CONTROL MYSELF?!! I'M A MONSTER! MONSTERS DON'T CONTROL THEMSELVES! THAT'S THE WHOLE IDEA!!
WELL, YOU'D BETTER START, OR ELSE THESE NICE, LITTLE CREATURES WON'T HELP US ESCAPE FROM KINGDOK . . .
. . . WHO, BY THE WAY, SEEMS A LITTLE UPSET OVER THAT WHOLE ARM-CUTTING-OFF THING!
I NOTICED! HE SURE CAN HOLD A GRUDGE, CAN'T HE?
WE'RE NOT HELPING YOU ESCAPE!

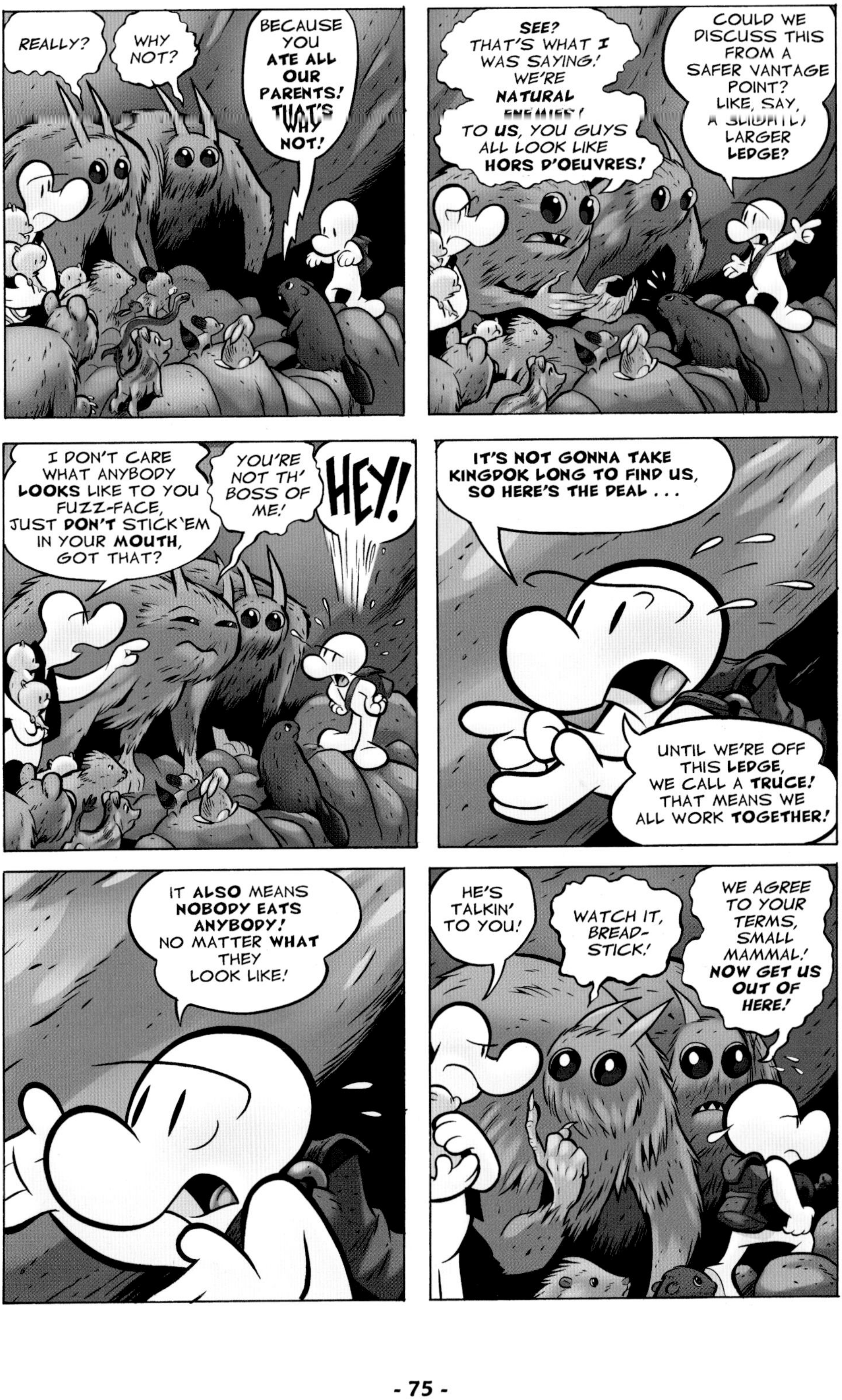
REALLY?
WHY NOT?
BECAUSE YOU ATE ALL OUR PARENTS! THAT'S WHY NOT!
SEE? THAT'S WHAT I WAS SAYING! WE'RE NATURAL
TO US, YOU GUYS ALL LOOK LIKE HORS D'OEUVRES!
COULD WE DISCUSS THIS FROM A SAFER VANTAGE POINT? LIKE, SAY,
LARGER LEDGE?
I DON'T CARE WHAT ANYBODY LOOKS LIKE TO YOU FUZZ-FACE, JUST DON'T STICK 'EM IN YOUR MOUTH, GOT THAT?
YOU'RE NOT TH' BOSS OF ME!
HEY!
IT'S NOT GONNA TAKE KINGDOK LONG TO FIND US, SO HERE'S THE DEAL . . .
UNTIL WE'RE OFF THIS LEDGE, WE CALL A TRUCE! THAT MEANS WE ALL WORK TOGETHER!
IT ALSO MEANS NOBODY EATS ANYBODY! NO MATTER WHAT THEY LOOK LIKE!
HE'S TALKIN' TO YOU!
WATCH IT, BREAD-STICK!
WE AGREE TO YOUR TERMS, SMALL MAMMAL! NOW GET US OUT OF HERE!

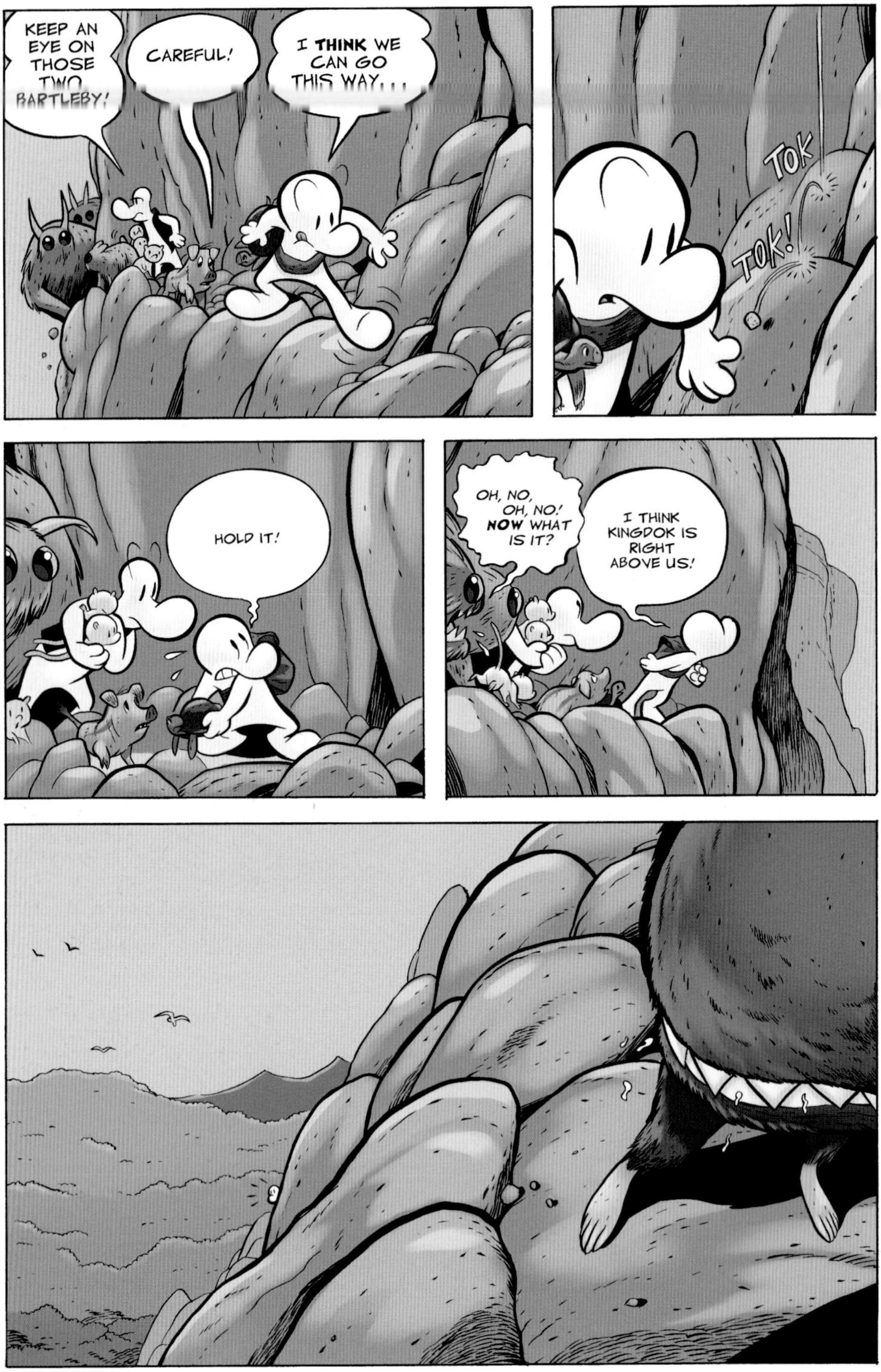
KEEP AN EYE ON THOSE TWO, BARTLEBY!
CAREFUL!
I THINK WE CAN GO THIS WAY...
TOK
TOK!
HOLD IT!
OH, NO, OH, NO! NOW WHAT IS IT?
I THINK KINGDOK IS RIGHT ABOVE US!

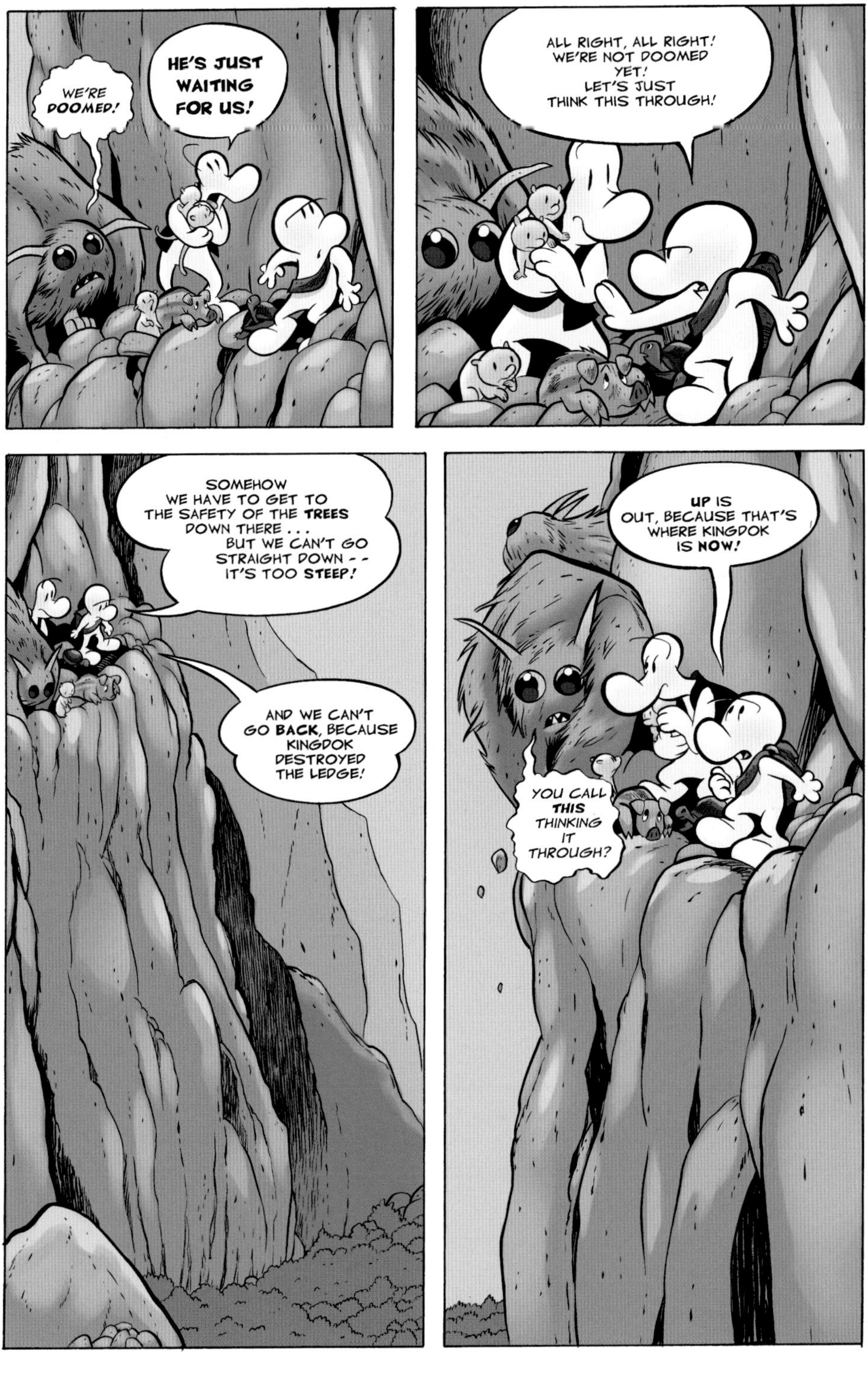
WE'RE DOOMED!
HE'S JUST WAITING FOR US!
ALL RIGHT, ALL RIGHT! WE'RE NOT DOOMED YET! LET'S JUST THINK THIS THROUGH!
SOMEHOW WE HAVE TO GET TO THE SAFETY OF THE TREES DOWN THERE . . . BUT WE CAN'T GO STRAIGHT DOWN - - IT'S TOO STEEP!
AND WE CAN'T GO BACK, BECAUSE KINGDOK DESTROYED THE LEDGE!
UP IS OUT, BECAUSE THAT'S WHERE KINGDOK IS NOW!
YOU CALL THIS THINKING IT THROUGH?

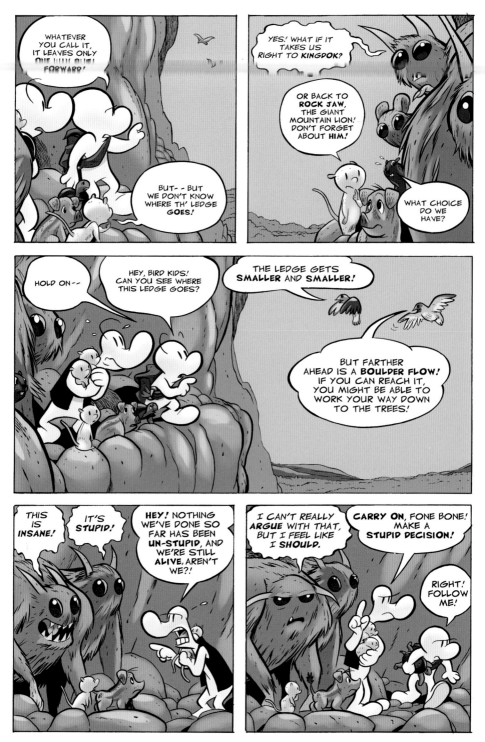

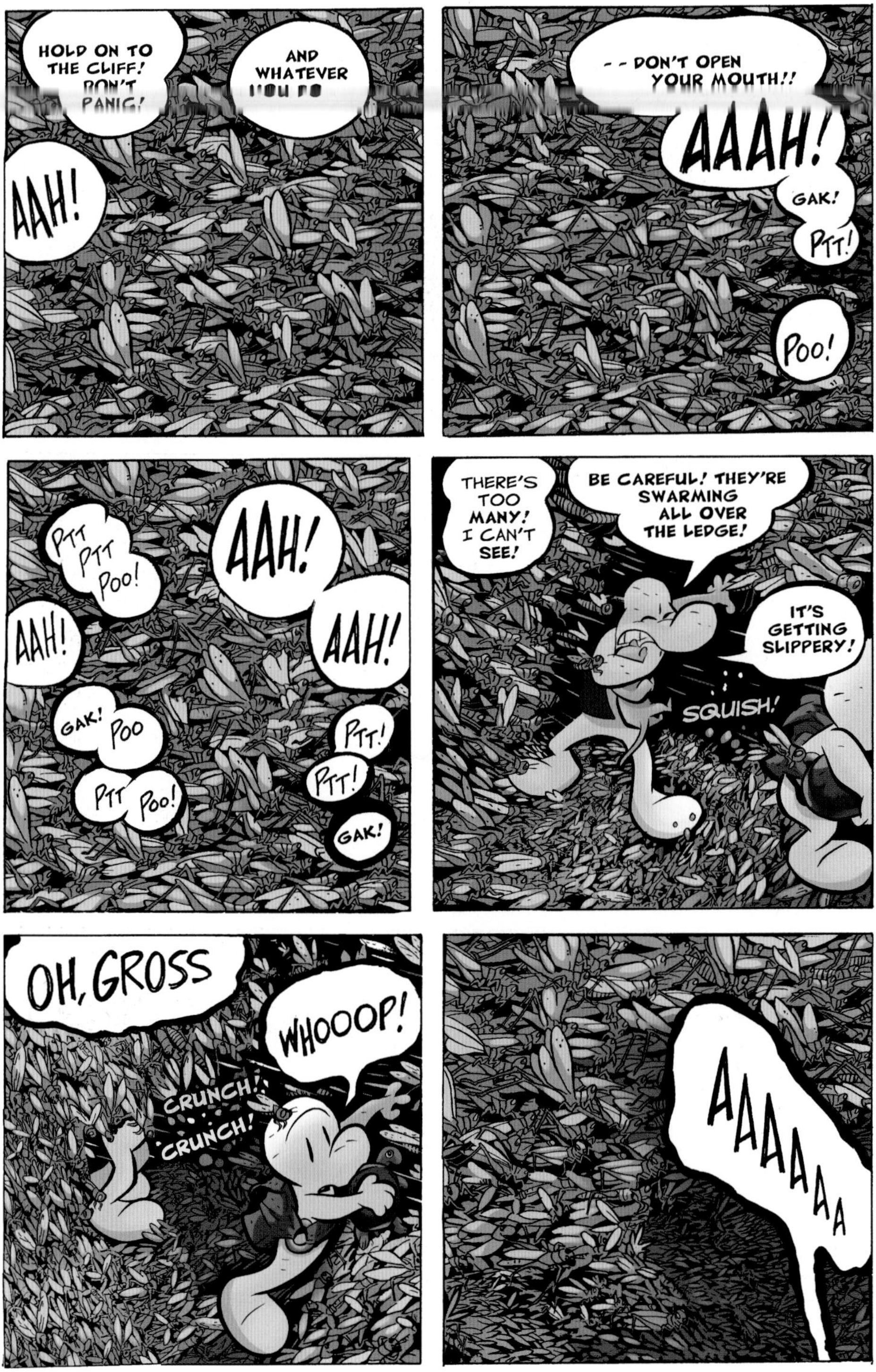
HOLD ON TO THE CLIFF! DON'T PANIC!
AND WHATEVER
AAH!
- - DON'T OPEN YOUR MOUTH!!
AAAH!
GAK!
PTT!
POO!
PTT PTT POO!
AAH!
AAH!
AAH!
GAK! POO
PTT POO!
PTT!
PTT!
GAK!
THERE'S TOO MANY! I CAN'T SEE!
BE CAREFUL! THEY'RE SWARMING ALL OVER THE LEDGE!
IT'S GETTING SLIPPERY!
SQUISH!
OH, GROSS
WHOOOP!
CRUNCH!
CRUNCH!
AAAAAAA

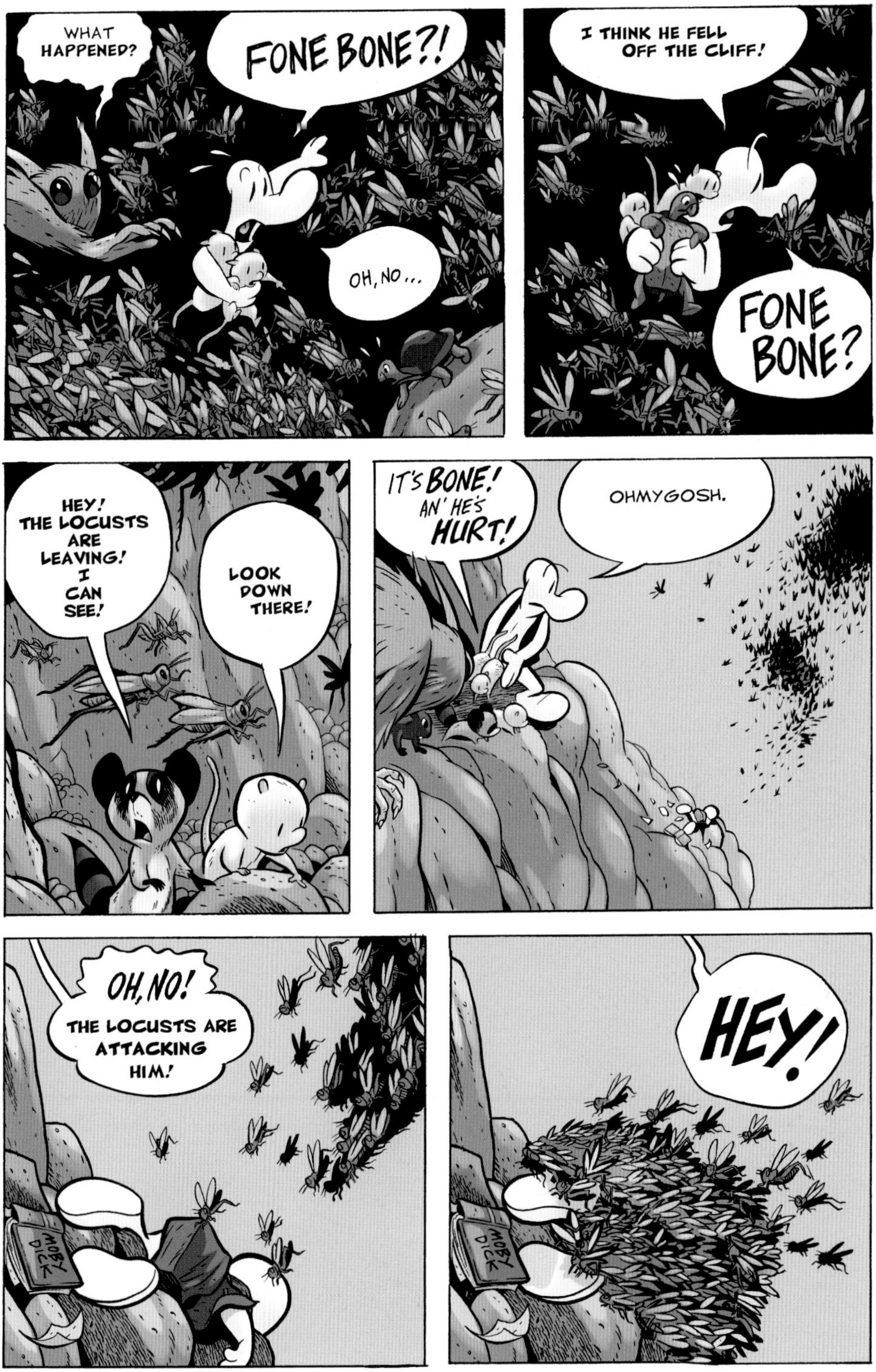
WHAT HAPPENED?
FONE BONE?!
OH, NO...
I THINK HE FELL OFF THE CLIFF!
FONE BONE?
HEY! THE LOCUSTS ARE LEAVING! I CAN SEE!
LOOK DOWN THERE!
IT'S BONE! AN' HE'S HURT!
OHMYGOSH.
OH, NO! THE LOCUSTS ARE ATTACKING HIM!
MOBY DICK
HEY!
MOBY DICK

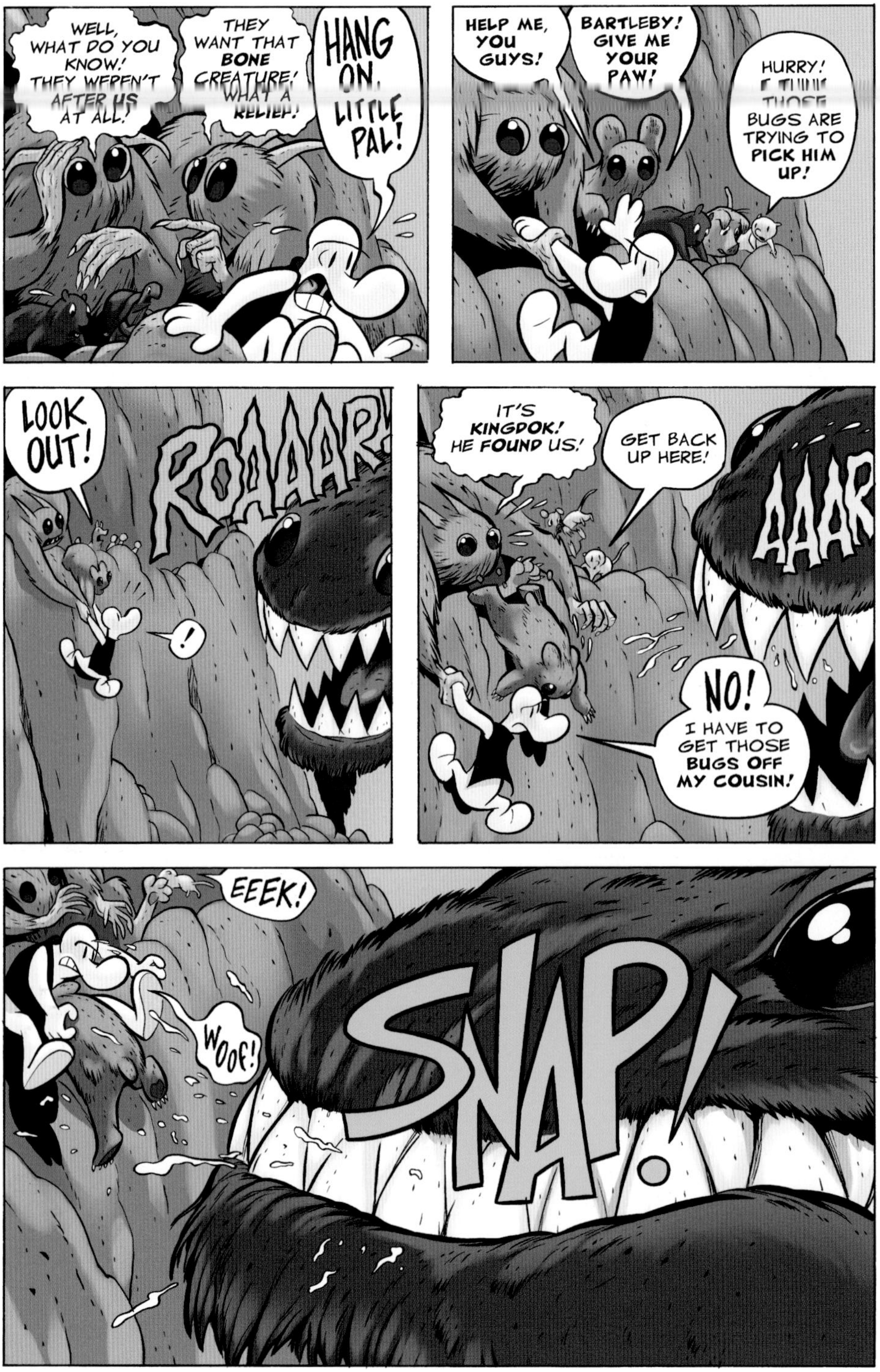
WELL, WHAT DO YOU KNOW! THEY WEREN'T AFTER US AT ALL!
THEY WANT THAT BONE CREATURE! WHAT A RELIEF!
HANG ON, LITTLE PAL!
HELP ME, YOU GUYS!
BARTLEBY! GIVE ME YOUR PAW!
HURRY! I THINK THOSE BUGS ARE TRYING TO PICK HIM UP!
LOOK OUT!
ROAAAR!
!
IT'S KINGDOK! HE FOUND US!
GET BACK UP HERE!
AAAR
NO! I HAVE TO GET THOSE BUGS OFF MY COUSIN!
EEEK!
WOOF!
SNAP!

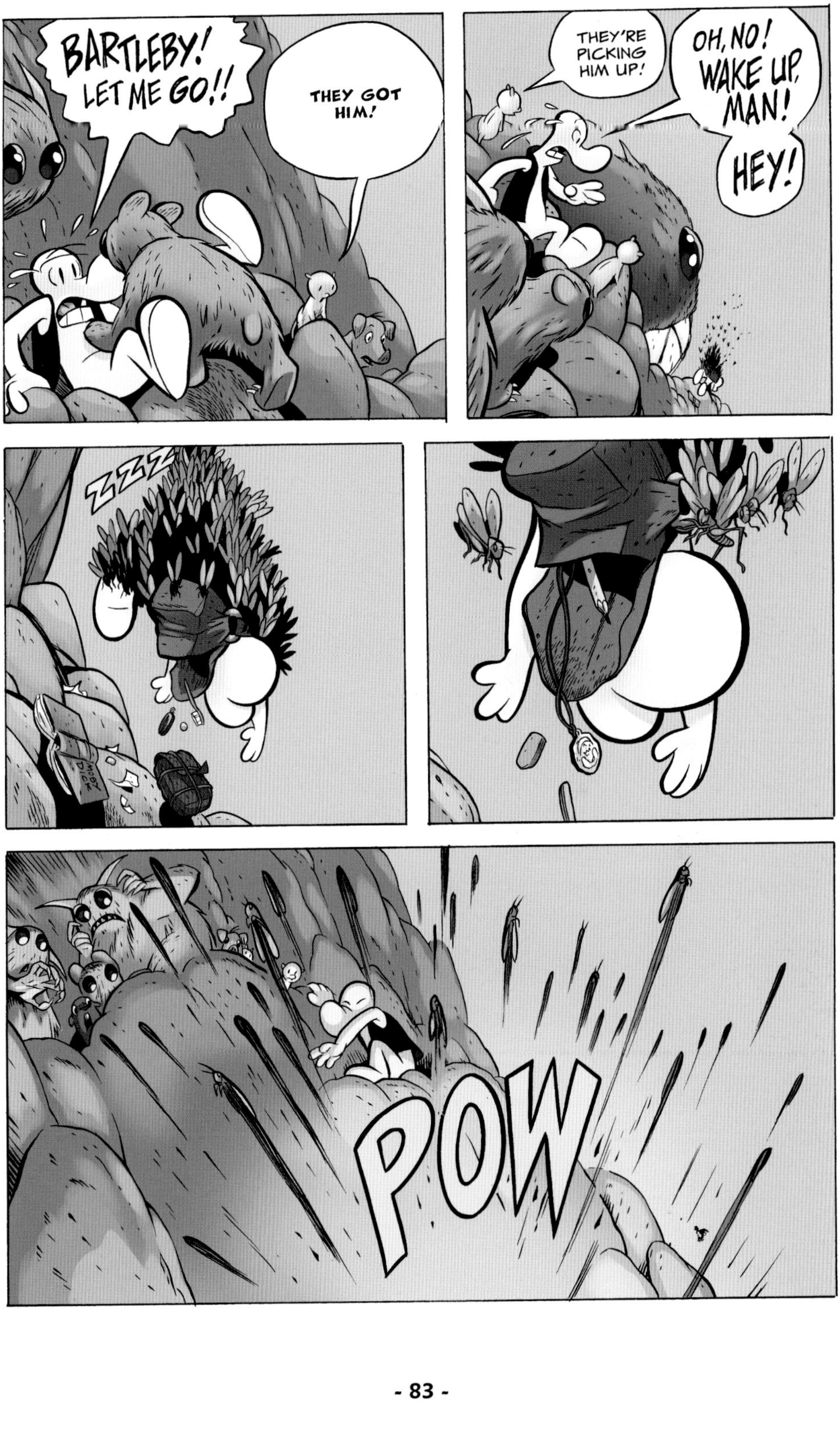
BARTLEBY! LET ME GO!!
THEY GOT HIM!
THEY'RE PICKING HIM UP!
OH, NO! WAKE UP, MAN!
HEY!
ZZZ
MOBY DICK
POW

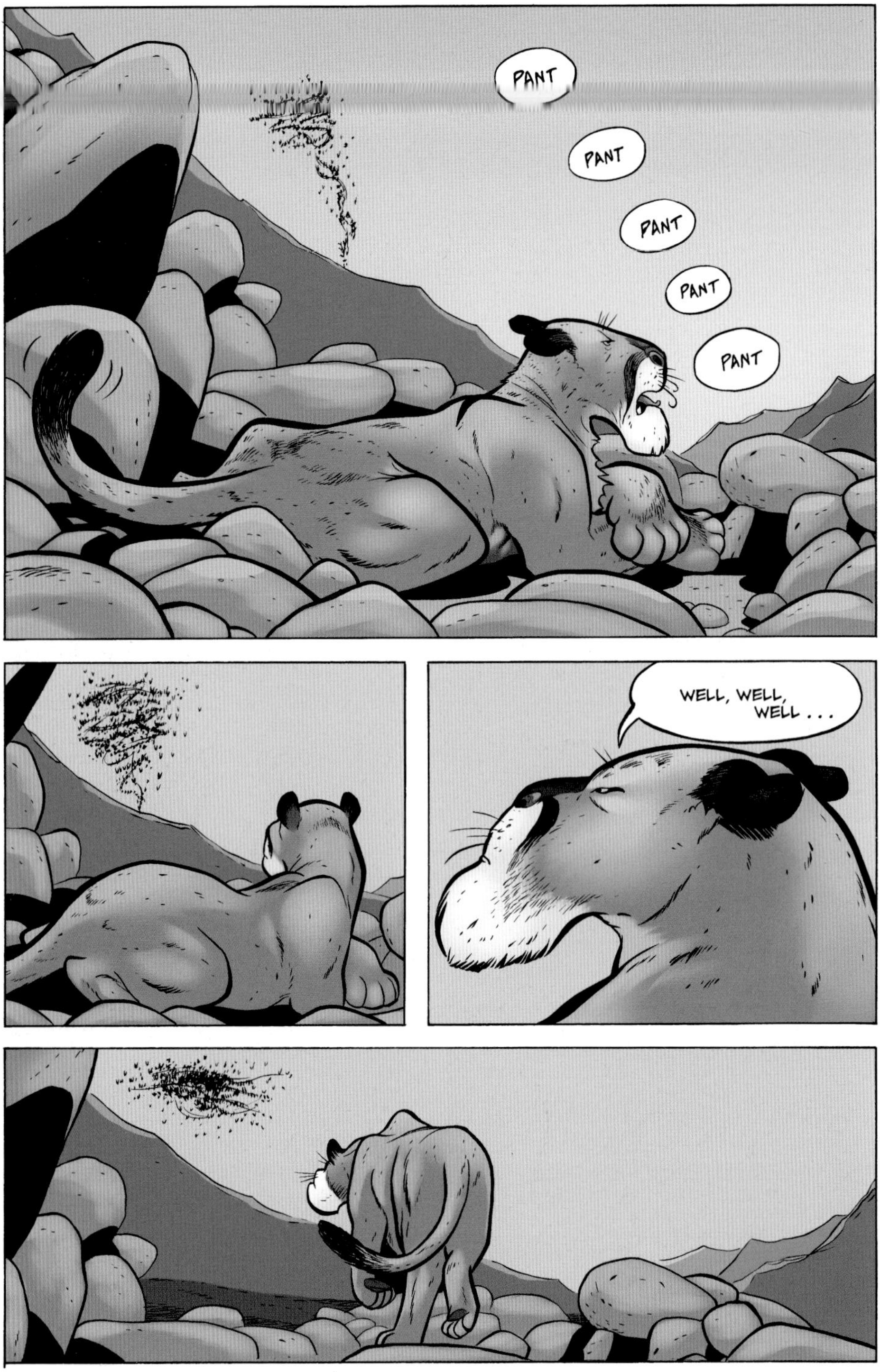
PANT
PANT
PANT
PANT
PANT
WELL, WELL, WELL . . .

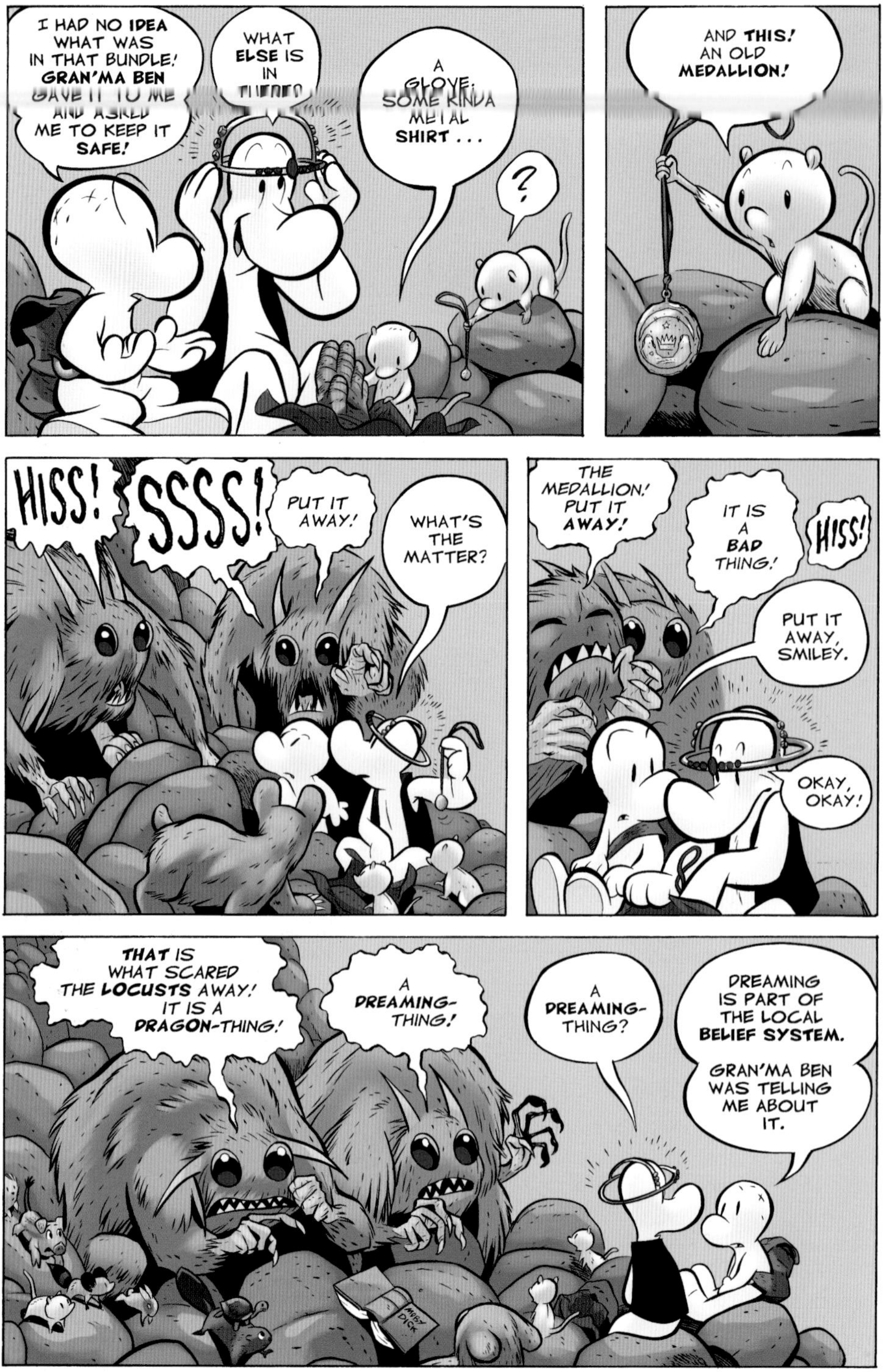
I HAD NO IDEA WHAT WAS IN THAT BUNDLE! GRAN'MA BEN GAVE IT TO ME AND ASKED ME TO KEEP IT SAFE!
WHAT ELSE IS IN THERE?
A GLOVE. SOME KINDA METAL SHIRT . . .
?
AND THIS! AN OLD MEDALLION!
HISS!
SSSS!
PUT IT AWAY!
WHAT'S THE MATTER?
THE MEDALLION! PUT IT AWAY!
IT IS A BAD THING!
HISS!
PUT IT AWAY, SMILEY.
OKAY, OKAY!
THAT IS WHAT SCARED THE LOCUSTS AWAY! IT IS A DRAGON-THING!
A DREAMING-THING!
A DREAMING-THING?
DREAMING IS PART OF THE LOCAL BELIEF SYSTEM.
GRAN'MA BEN WAS TELLING ME ABOUT IT.
MOBY DICK

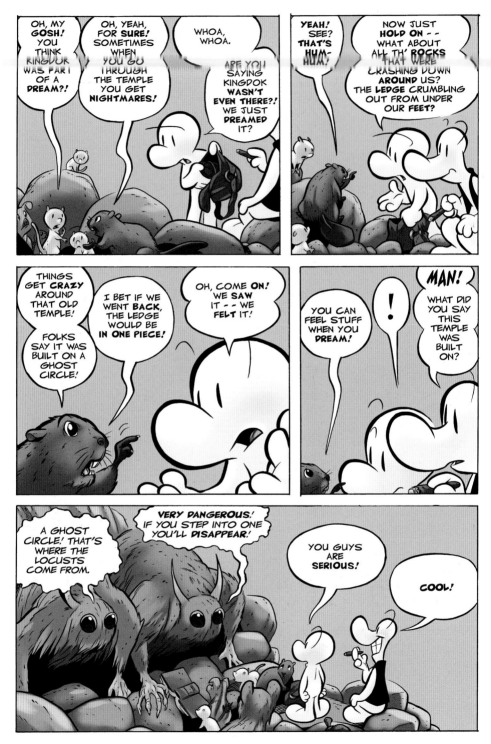

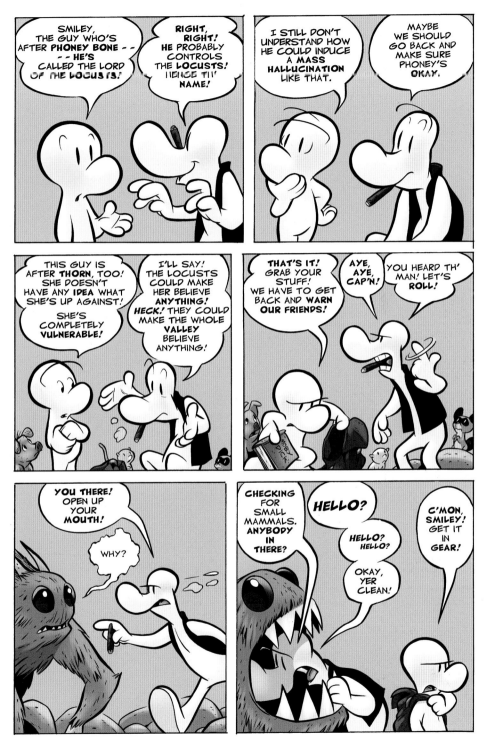

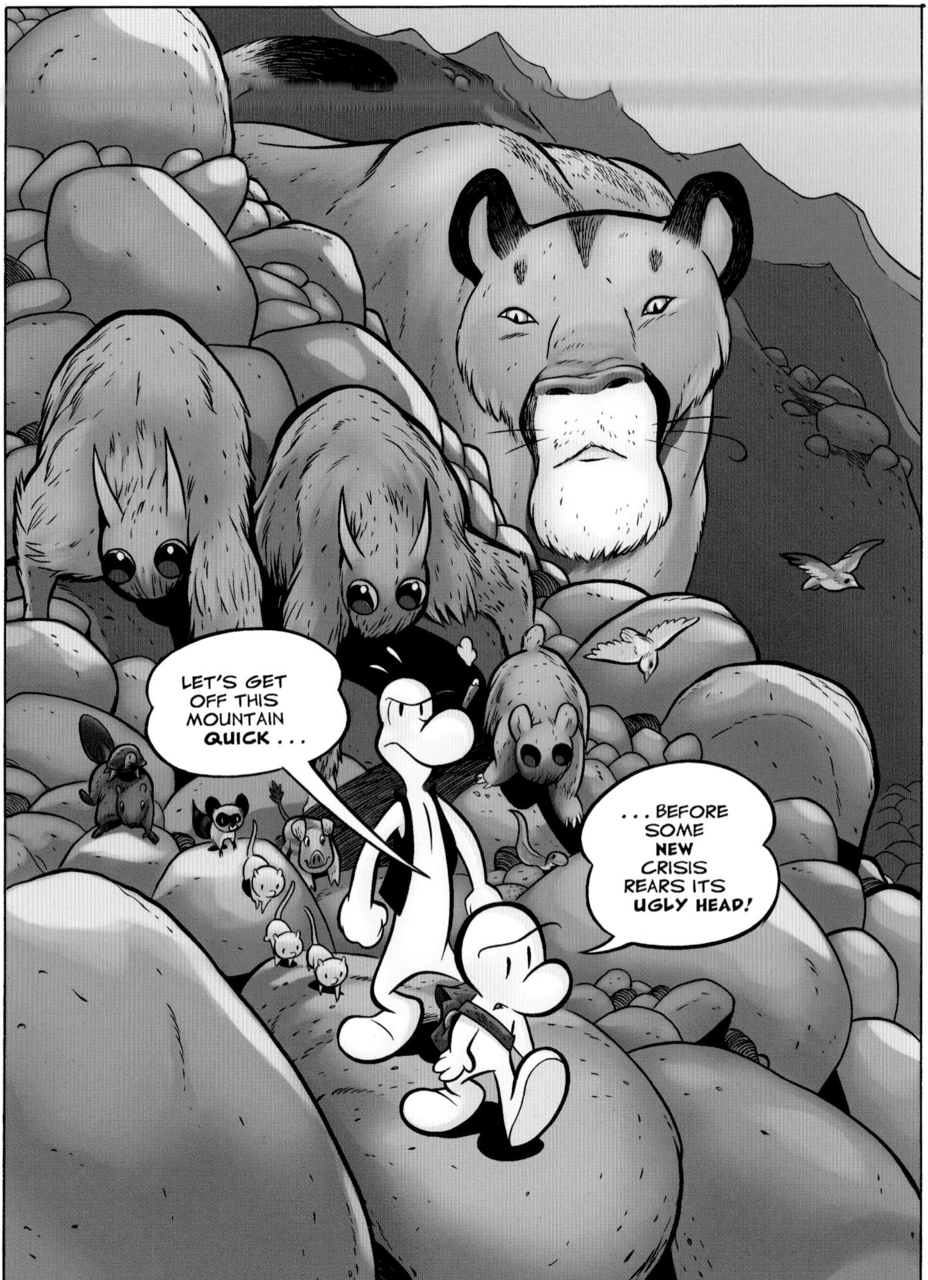
LET'S GET OFF THIS MOUNTAIN **QUICK** . . .
. . . BEFORE SOME **NEW** CRISIS REARS ITS **UGLY HEAD!**

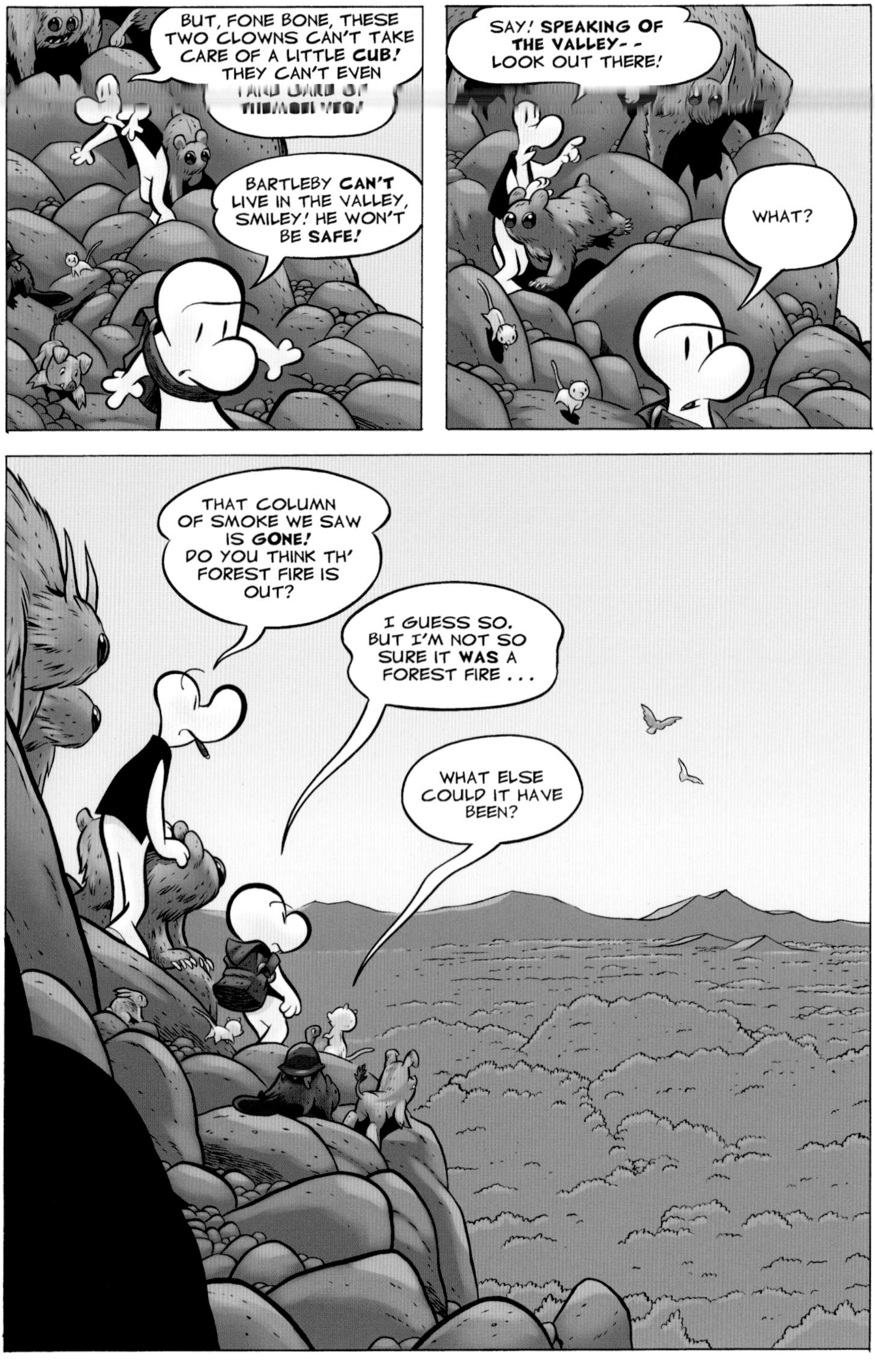
BUT, FONE BONE, THESE TWO CLOWNS CAN'T TAKE CARE OF A LITTLE CUB! THEY CAN'T EVEN
BARTLEBY CAN'T LIVE IN THE VALLEY, SMILEY! HE WON'T BE SAFE!
SAY! SPEAKING OF THE VALLEY- - LOOK OUT THERE!
WHAT?
THAT COLUMN OF SMOKE WE SAW IS GONE! DO YOU THINK TH' FOREST FIRE IS OUT?
I GUESS SO. BUT I'M NOT SO SURE IT WAS A FOREST FIRE . . .
WHAT ELSE COULD IT HAVE BEEN?

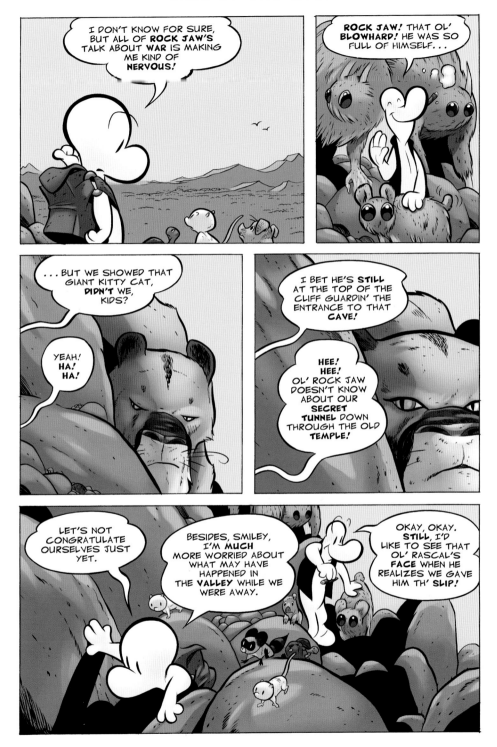

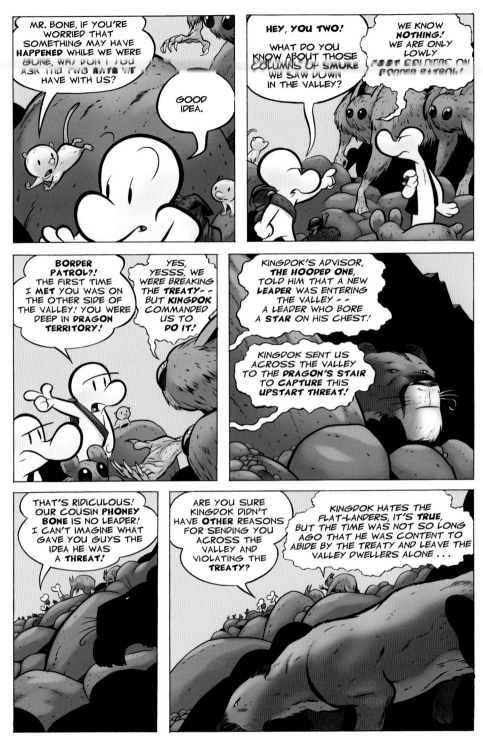

MR. BONE, IF YOU'RE WORRIED THAT SOMETHING MAY HAVE **HAPPENED** WHILE WE WERE GONE, WHY DON'T YOU ASK THE TWO RATS WE HAVE WITH US?

GOOD IDEA.

HEY, **YOU TWO!**

WHAT DO YOU KNOW ABOUT THOSE **COLUMNS OF SMOKE** WE SAW DOWN IN THE VALLEY?

WE KNOW **NOTHING!** WE ARE ONLY LOWLY **FOOT SOLDIERS ON BORDER PATROL!**

BORDER PATROL?! THE FIRST TIME I **MET** YOU WAS ON THE OTHER SIDE OF THE VALLEY! YOU WERE DEEP IN **DRAGON TERRITORY!**

YES, YESSS, WE WERE BREAKING THE **TREATY--** BUT **KINGDOK** COMMANDED US TO **DO IT!**

KINGDOK'S ADVISOR, **THE HOODED ONE,** TOLD HIM THAT A NEW **LEADER** WAS ENTERING THE VALLEY -- A LEADER WHO BORE A **STAR** ON HIS CHEST!

KINGDOK SENT US ACROSS THE VALLEY TO THE **DRAGON'S STAIR** TO **CAPTURE** THIS **UPSTART THREAT!**

THAT'S RIDICULOUS! OUR COUSIN **PHONEY BONE** IS NO LEADER! I CAN'T IMAGINE WHAT GAVE YOU GUYS THE IDEA HE WAS A **THREAT!**

ARE YOU SURE KINGDOK DIDN'T HAVE **OTHER** REASONS FOR SENDING YOU ACROSS THE VALLEY AND VIOLATING THE **TREATY?**

KINGDOK HATES THE FLAT-LANDERS, IT'S **TRUE,** BUT THE TIME WAS NOT SO LONG AGO THAT HE WAS CONTENT TO ABIDE BY THE TREATY AND LEAVE THE VALLEY DWELLERS ALONE . . .

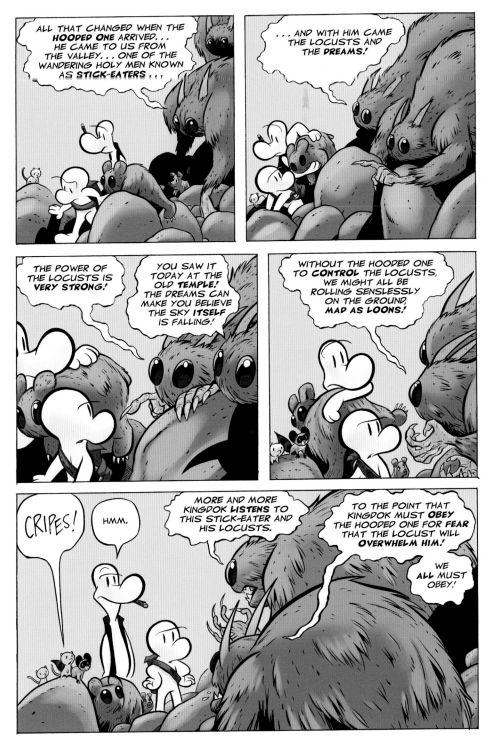

ROCK JAW

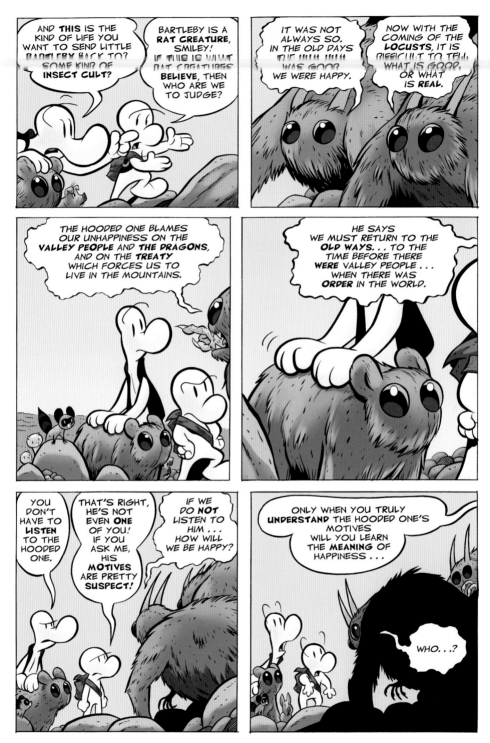

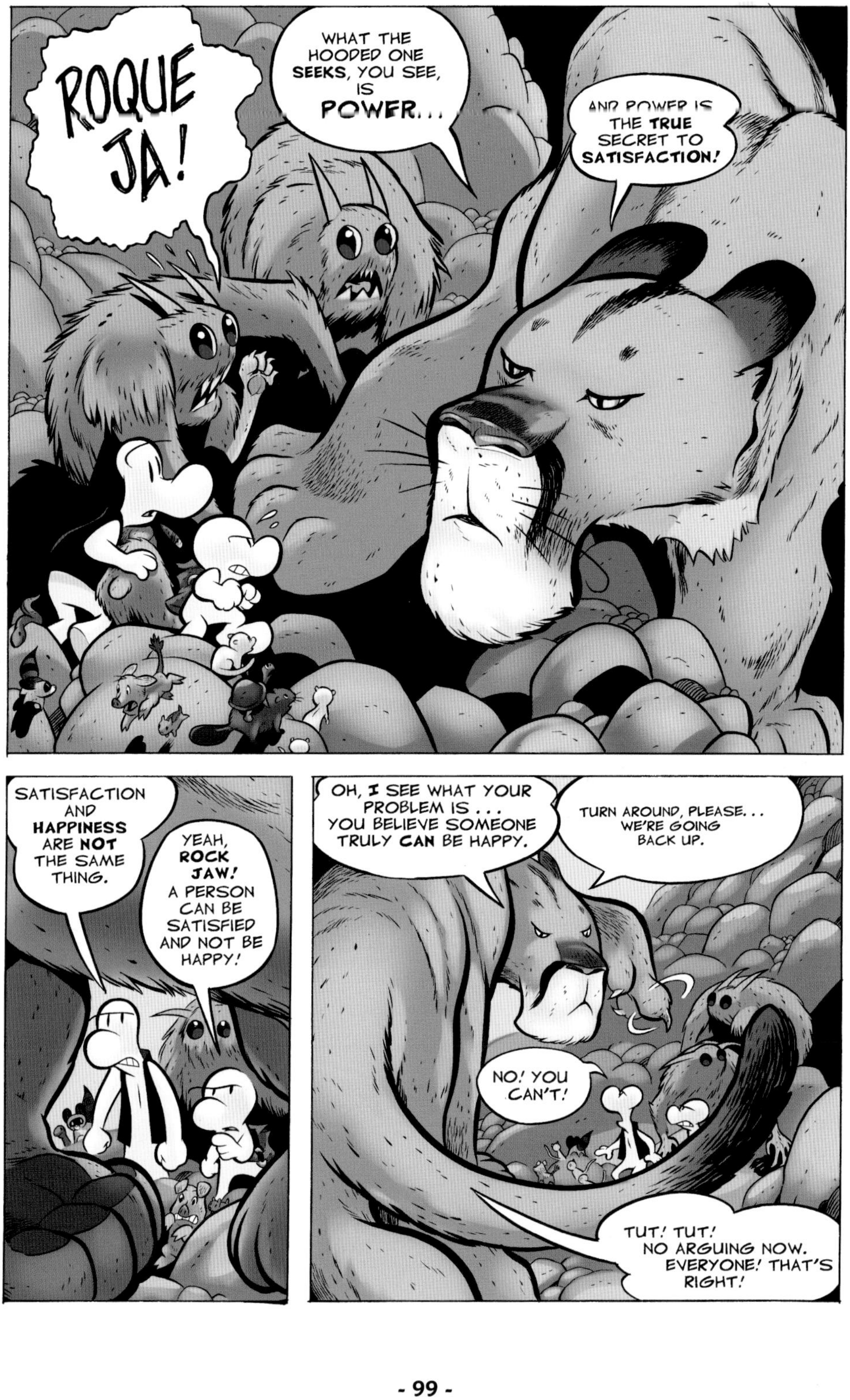
ROQUE JA!
WHAT THE HOODED ONE SEEKS, YOU SEE, IS POWER...
AND POWER IS THE TRUE SECRET TO SATISFACTION!
SATISFACTION AND HAPPINESS ARE NOT THE SAME THING.
YEAH, ROCK JAW! A PERSON CAN BE SATISFIED AND NOT BE HAPPY!
OH, I SEE WHAT YOUR PROBLEM IS . . . YOU BELIEVE SOMEONE TRULY CAN BE HAPPY.
TURN AROUND, PLEASE. . . WE'RE GOING BACK UP.
NO! YOU CAN'T!
TUT! TUT! NO ARGUING NOW. EVERYONE! THAT'S RIGHT!

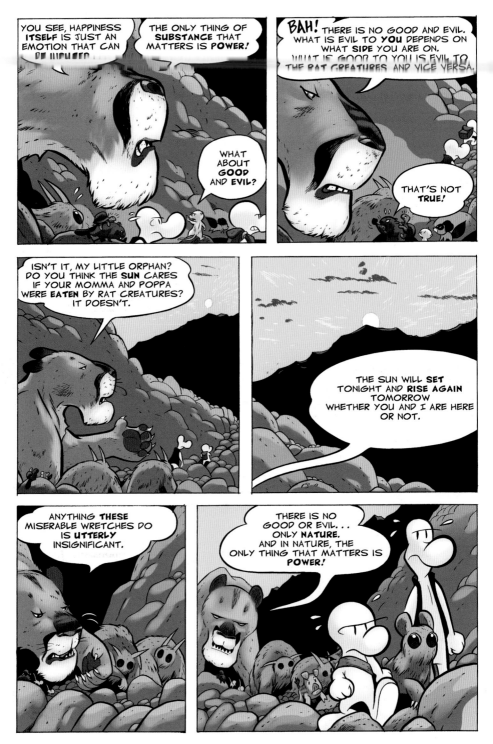

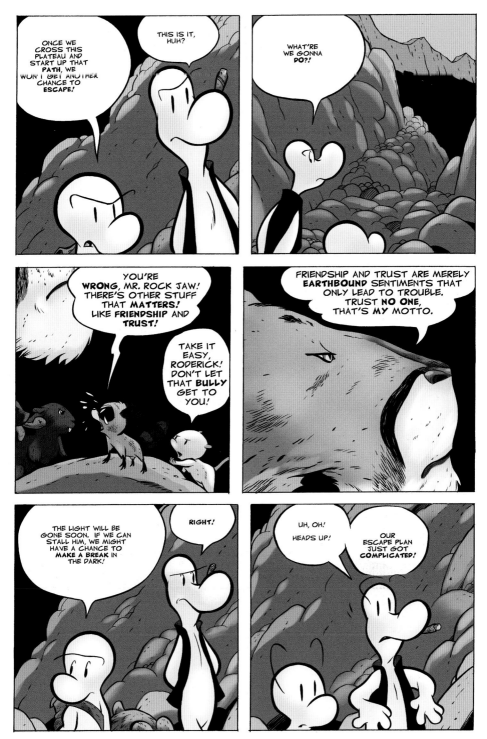

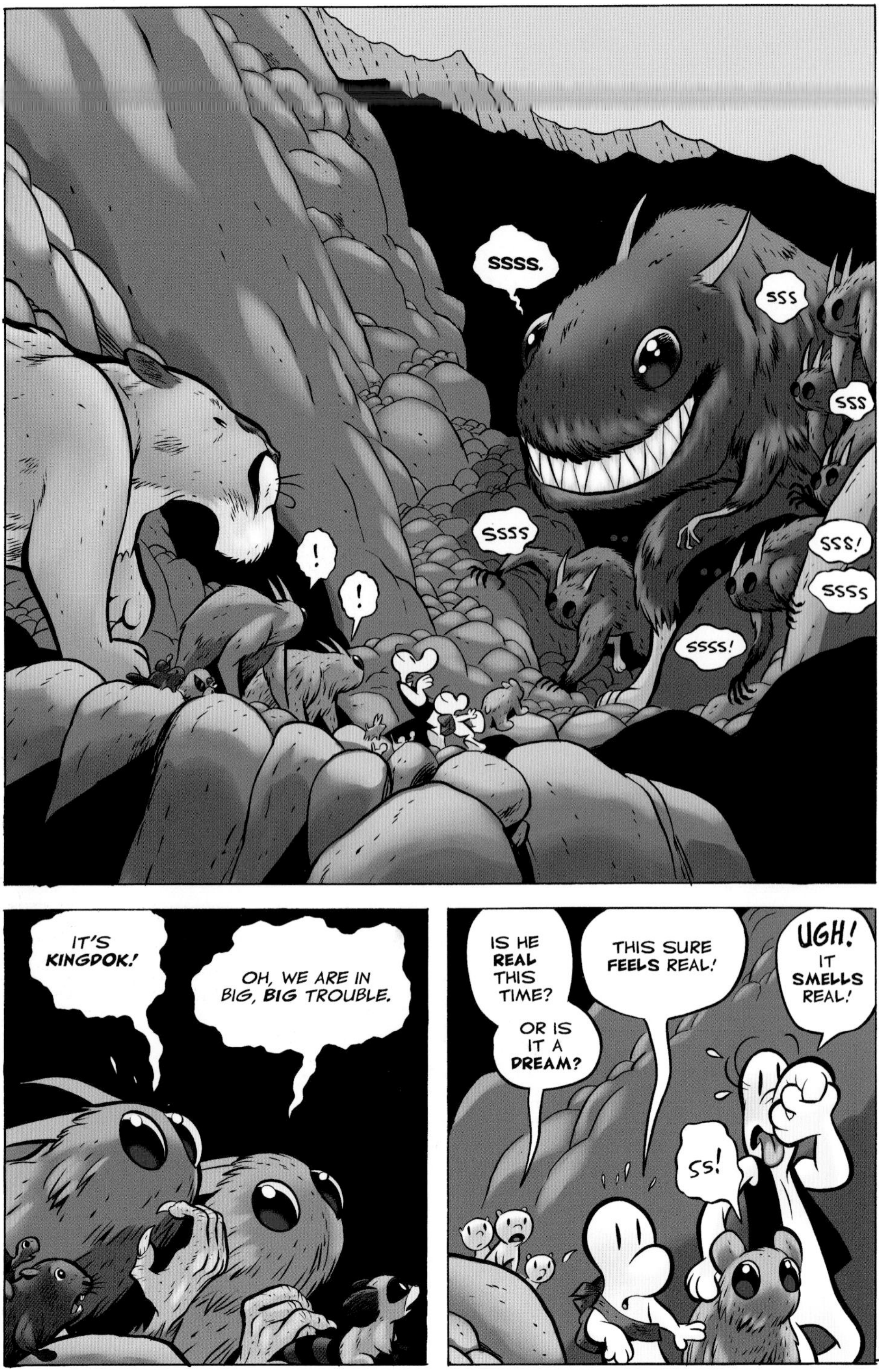
SSSS.
SSS
SSS
SSSS
!
!
SSS!
SSSS
SSSS!
IT'S KINGDOK!
OH, WE ARE IN BIG, BIG TROUBLE.
IS HE REAL THIS TIME?
OR IS IT A DREAM?
THIS SURE FEELS REAL!
UGH! IT SMELLS REAL!
SS!

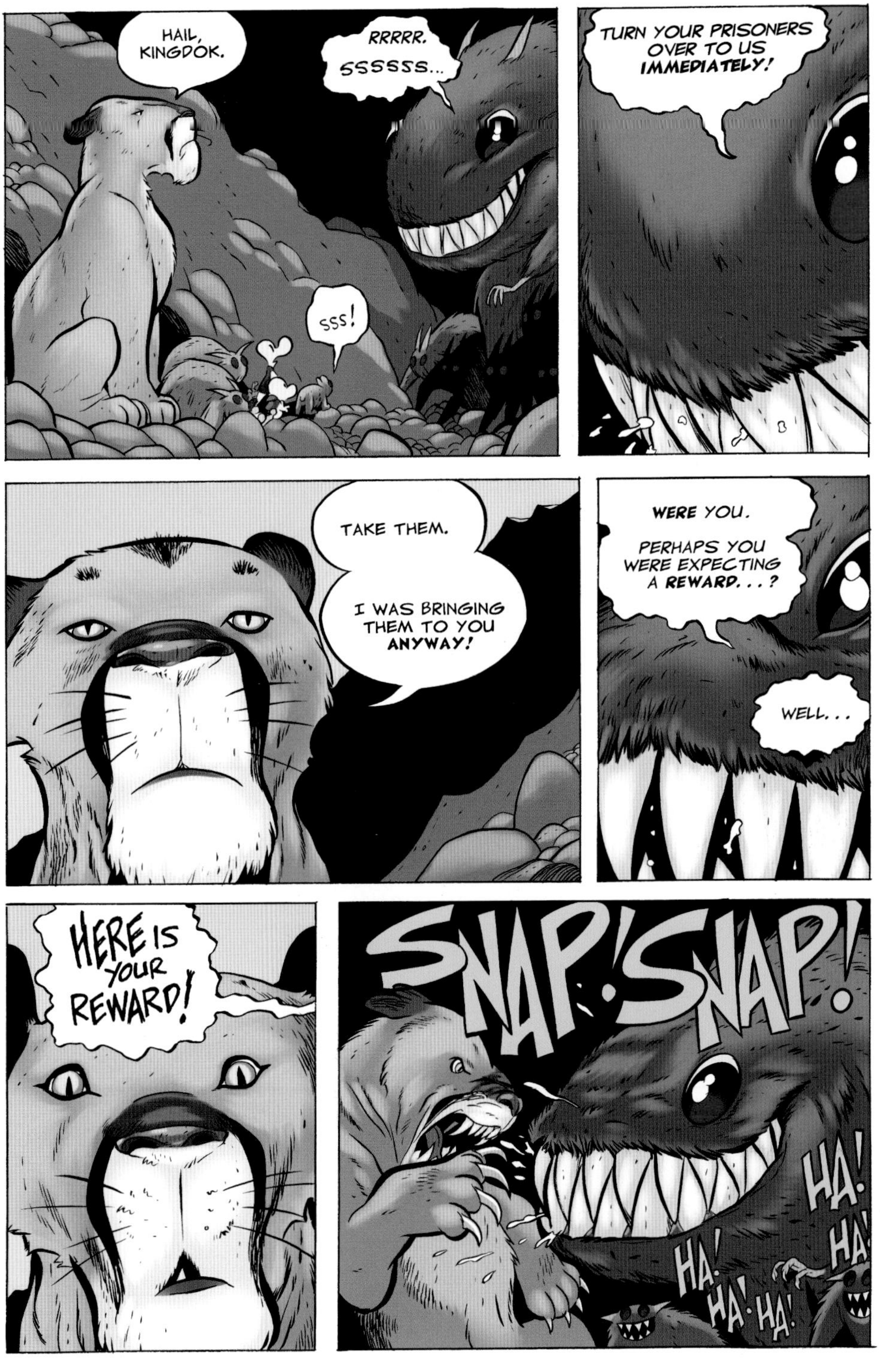
HAIL, KINGDOK.
RRRRR. SSSSSS...
SSS!
TURN YOUR PRISONERS OVER TO US IMMEDIATELY!
TAKE THEM.
I WAS BRINGING THEM TO YOU ANYWAY!
WERE YOU.
PERHAPS YOU WERE EXPECTING A REWARD...?
WELL...
HERE IS YOUR REWARD!
SNAP! SNAP!
HA! HA! HA! HA!
HA! HA!

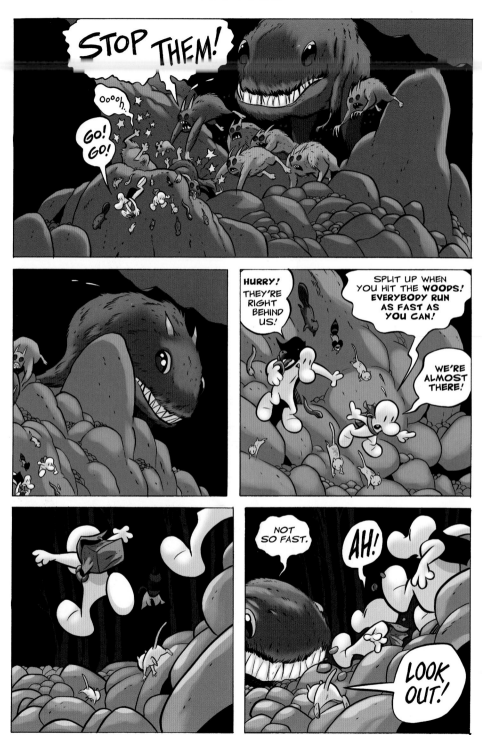

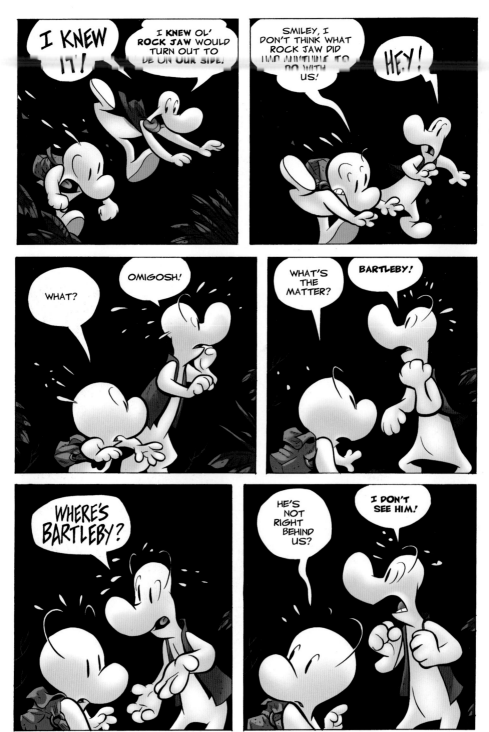

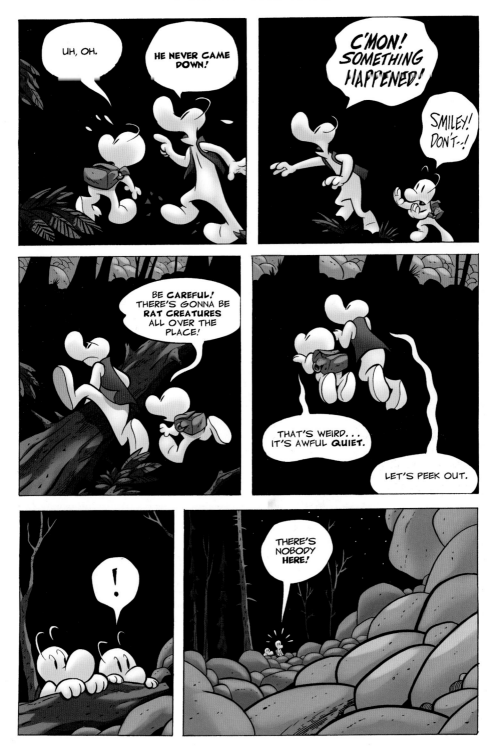

ROCK JAW

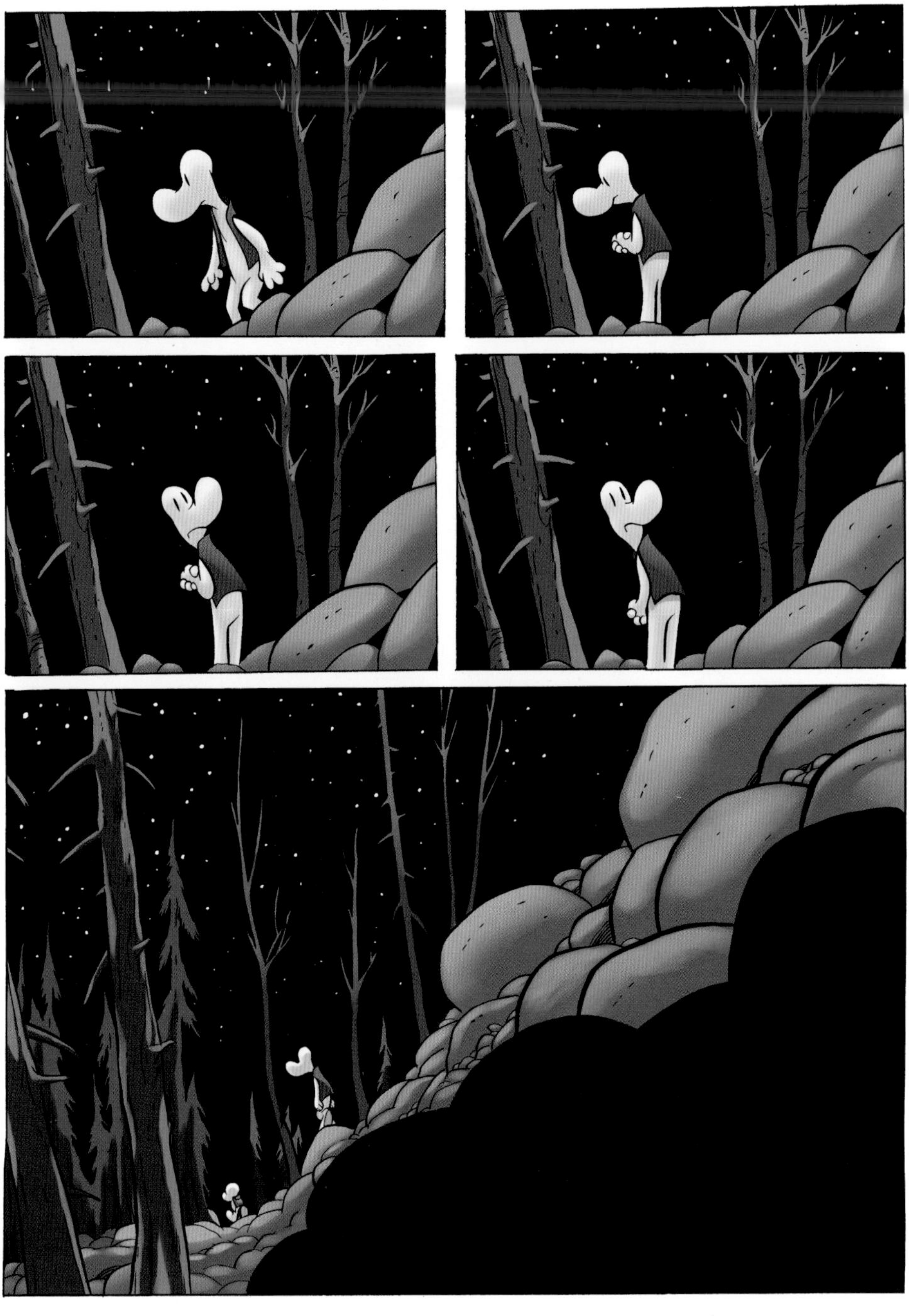

...TO BE CONTINUED.

About JEFF SMITH

JEFF SMITH was born and raised in the American Midwest and learned about cartooning from comic strips, comic books, and watching animated shorts on TV. After four years of drawing comic strips for The Ohio State University's student newspaper and co-founding Character Builders animation studio in 1986, Smith launched the comic book *BONE* in 1991. Between *BONE* and other comics projects, Smith spends much of his time on the international guest circuit promoting comics and the art of graphic novels.

More about *BONE*

An instant classic when it first appeared in the U.S. as an underground comic book in 1991, Bone has since garnered 38 international awards and sold a million copies in 15 languages. Now, Scholastic's GRAPHIX imprint is publishing full-color graphic novel editions of the nine-book *BONE* series. Look for the continuing adventures of the Bone cousins in *Old Man's Cave*.